The Cul-de-sac

THE CUL-DE-SAC

Christopher Null

TULE
PUBLISHING

Dedication

For Susanne

CHAPTER ONE

Klaus

THE RAIN WAS no help.

While one would think that a little water on the ground would soften things up after the long bake of yet another hot and dry California summer, once it hit the earth, the moisture had no impact whatsoever. The rocky terrain had to be dug out mostly by pickaxe rather than shovel, my tired arms chiseling out boulders as big as my head one by one and then tossing them aside into a crude mound. The rain—a wholly unexpected downpour for this time of year— only made the rocks slippery and more difficult than ever to deal with, especially in the dark.

A shallow grave wasn't an option. I'd learned that the hard way two years ago. Living on the outskirts of town has its advantages, but teeming wildlife is not one of them. Raccoons will eat anything, and coyotes can smell blood for miles. But the worst are the opossums. The monsters are strong, and their little hands can pick up rocks. Not the really big ones, but they can easily lift stones as big as a softball. They eat anything, but it's the sheer tenacity that really causes problems. They can undo a full burial mound in the middle of the night, and after a body is exposed to the elements, well, you've got a serious problem, not just from the raccoons, coyotes, opossums, rats, and other *ungeziefer*—er, vermin—but from the flies, wasps, and other bugs swarming around the thing.

I wasn't keen to relive the experience from the last time around, when on a Tuesday morning I found a carefully dug (though admittedly much too shallow) grave completely unearthed and the fresh corpse of the *hausfrau* within nearly ripped to shreds. There were bits of red dress scattered for thirty, forty meters, little fragments the raccoons must have finally decided weren't worth even attempting to eat. I had to cancel my work trip to Texas later that day—a whole other problem—and then spend all afternoon and the night that followed cleaning things up and digging a much deeper grave just to be sure the wildlife couldn't get to it. Fortunately, the cul-de-sac was dead quiet as usual, and no one asked any questions.

The experience was enough to turn me off of this business for more than a year. Until last night, anyway.

CHAPTER TWO
Alex

G OD, I LOVE the rain. California shuts down when there's even a light drizzle, and when it pours like it has been lately, this town becomes downright ghostly. Everyone's holed up and you can smell the smoke from the chimneys, even though it's not cold enough for a fire and I could swear I got an email that it was a "Spare the Air" day or whatever bullshit. Who could possibly care? I mean, who's giving out citations for having a fire on a rainy day like this, anyway? I've never heard of one.

When everyone else stays home that makes it easier for me to go places. Leaving the house has become...difficult, let's say, what with the seizures and having to constantly stop the drool from running out of the side of my mouth and down my face. That can be worse than the seizures, honestly. Normally, I like to combine my trips outside with visits to the dialysis center—where, at forty-eight years old, I'm still the youngest person in the place. Dialysis sucks, but it's better than the nausea and the bloating in my legs, and since I only have to go once every ten days or so, it's honestly not too bad. The really sick people—you know, the ones waiting for a transplant—have to go like three times a week or else they'll die. My kidney damage isn't going to kill me, the doc says. I'm just in it to keep the seizures and the other negative effects at bay. The dialysis doesn't do shit for the drooling though. For that I just carry a handkerchief with me and act like I'm a Southern gentleman who had a really big lunch, covering my mouth.

Anyway, after dialysis I usually feel great, so it's a good time to go to the market or get an oil change or do whatever errands I have to do that don't involve just buying something on Amazon and waiting for some minimum-wage flunky to throw a box at my doorstep. Now that I have the maid service and the gardeners, it's all pretty easy, but the house-keepers don't buy their own supplies and Amazon doesn't deliver bleach, so once in a while I have to drive all the way to Target or Costco and stock up on this stuff in bulk. Like I said, right after the dialysis, the risk of going into convulsions is as low as it's going to get, and that's pretty much the only time I can handle being out and about and in the land of Kirkland Signature products.

But now, with the rain, the stores are pretty much emp-ty. And I need garbage bags, laundry detergent, and Pine-Sol, according to the list the cleaning crew left. God, how the maids love their Pine-Sol. If it isn't clean, at least it smells like it's clean. I don't like to let them down, and my Spanish sucks, so I think I'll pick up one of those double-jug packs that are connected by the plastic handcuffs at the neck. That'll keep them *contento* for months. If I act like I'm even more sickly than I really am, maybe someone will even carry it to the car for me.

Maybe, I thought, I should pick up some firewood, too.

CHAPTER THREE
Peg

M Y GIVEN NAME Margaret was bad enough. Marge and Maggie and Madge were all even worse, and eventually I asked to be called Peggy. Well, with a name like Peggy, one doesn't exactly fly through the ranks of corporate America—not in the eighties, when I was trying to make it in advertising, living and working in San Francisco. People think of Peggy as either a child or a grandmother, and I couldn't handle either one. Peg was a bit more professional, and it fit my personality well enough. I can live with it, anyway.

But I can't help thinking that things would have been different if only my parents had been a little smarter about my name. A little more forward-looking. Outside the box, as we used to say. What if I'd been a Michelle? Or a Christine? Maybe even a Renee or a Jacqueline? Think about being introduced to Miss Jacqueline Stone at a formal dinner. *Miss Jacqueline Stone!* Why, it's almost romantic, isn't it? Instead, it's just *Hello! My Name is Peg Stone.* Ugh, I don't blame anyone for not wanting to talk to me. The name is just too off-putting to even look at on a name tag, not to mention having to say out loud with your mouth.

Jack didn't seem to mind the name. In fact, he got a kick out of it, calling me Peggle, Pegleg, or Peggy Sue, even though my middle name is actually Sharon. I didn't mind. I thought it was cute.

We'd met through work. He worked for the client, and I was the agency's manager on the account. We spent years working together on various campaigns and benignly flirting until he finally asked me out—for real—on a dinner date. It was a little strange because we'd already enjoyed many meals together in a professional capacity, and when we went on the date at least half the conversation was still about work. I was a little surprised that everything worked out as well as it did, and two years later I wasn't Peg Stone, I was Peg Jergensen. Jack was so tall, and I was so short. I thought we made the cutest couple.

By the time I met Jack I felt like there was more life behind me than ahead, and we both felt that we'd missed the window to have children. Who wanted to be the mom in her fifties on field trips and in "small groups" at your kid's elementary school? Besides, the various hormones and fertility treatments weren't nearly as mature then as they are today. If Jack and I had managed to have a child, he probably would have come out with an extra finger or something. Adoption didn't fit us, either. All the same, we moved to the suburbs to get away from the bustle of the city, which didn't agree with me.

And then he died. In the thick of the summer, we'd had an argument, and we agreed to take a walk so we could both cool down. It went the other way. The heat did him in, and he never came back home. He left a lot of loose ends with our finances—a new retirement account that hadn't been fully funded, a stupid investment property in escrow—and I ended up quitting work to take care of all of it. All of it made me a little crazy sometimes. But the good news is, work paid out a huge insurance policy, and I used the money to pay off the mortgage and invested the rest in conservative funds that would cover all of my monthly expenses and then some. I quit my job. What was the point of dealing with those turkeys anymore?

Normally as you get older, life speeds up. I found mine, however, slowing down, the abrupt emotional and physical hole left by Jack's departure inexorably growing larger, not smaller. Without the daily distraction of work and a relationship, I filled the time doing little projects around the house, watching television, trying to make the yard look nice (despite some neighbors who refused to play along), figuring out what to cook for dinner—either just one serving or two, with leftovers expected the following day. None of this amounted to very much, and after the initial rush of condolences, life became not just slow but also very quiet. I lost interest in the things we used to do as a couple: going to movies, dining out at the newest restaurants in the City.

When Jack was alive, we saw all the movies, sometimes going twice a week. When Oscar season rolled around, we'd argue about our favorites every night for months. Jack had a keen eye for editing and cinematography, and when the Academy didn't agree with his opinion, he'd throw his hands up in mock disgust. Now I don't really follow the awards anymore. It's just no fun without having a sounding board for my thoughts. Now I just talk mostly to myself.

We'd never really found our tribe after we moved out of San Francisco, and our neighbors on the cul-de-sac all seemed to keep to themselves, so we didn't have a lot of friends around town either. Check that: we didn't have *any* friends here. Everyone we knew lived in the City or the South Bay, and no one was trekking all the way out to the 'burbs just to visit the lonely old widow and her cat. I get it. What would we even talk about?

That was more than a decade ago. As time went by, it got worse. Neighbors probably thought our house was empty since no cars ever came or went except for my own, which was normally hidden away in the garage. Loneliness begat anxiety, and the two fed on each other. I did my shopping at Sunset Market down the road, saw the occasional movie, and went for a hike in the hills across the street once in a while, but aside from smiling at the cashiers and nodding to other trail-walkers, and the occasional chitchat with the quiet guy next door, I wasn't really interacting with people in a meaningful way. The cat died, and I let my hair turn gray, all the way. I started to get nervous about the prospect of leaving the house, but I didn't—I still don't—think of myself as a shut-in. I guess I don't usually think of myself at all, really.

What I do think about is the past, mostly, though it seems to slip a bit further away every day. Snippets of happy times in my childhood that are just single-frame images now, not lively video. A corner of a book peeled back to reveal just a few words on the page, just a hint of a fleeting memory of some moment rather than a bright, Kodachrome image. As my sixty-fifth birthday is just a month away, I'm officially a senior by every definition. I hate the term "senior moments," but since I don't think I'm developing dementia, I guess that's what's going on with me. I'm just getting old, starting to forget things, and getting upset a lot more easily about meaningless problems.

The doctors don't tell you that you'll not only forget the trivial stuff like the right word for this piece of antique furniture or the name of that actor in that show. You forget the important stuff, too. You start to forget everything, or at least lose track of it—what exactly happened and when. Who did what to whom. Why. A picture of a party I might run across would offer no clues about why I was there and what was being celebrated, and I had no one to ask to fill in the details. And no, don't get me started on Facebook. Not interested.

I know there are things I should have done differently in the past. And while usually this all makes me really angry, today I'm resolved to get off my butt and do something about it. *Forget doing something different in the past—let's do something different in the present, Peg.* Today is a new day. Anything is possible.

That's what they say, right?

CHAPTER FOUR

Eliza

"ARE YOU PACKED?" my mother asked casually, as if we were going on a weekend trip to Tahoe, not moving from the City to the stupid suburbs. Of course I wasn't packed. She only gave me the boxes three days ago, and I had stuff to do. The trucks wouldn't come until Saturday morning, and that meant I'd have all day tomorrow to put my stuff in the three types of boxes she was mandating: keep, donate, trash. Mom gave me a Sharpie to write the labels myself. "Be sure you put *Lizzie* on them so they don't get mixed up!" Ugh, *Lizzie*! She knows how much I hate that.

"Stop!" I yelled back at her from my bed.

"But you—" she started.

"Just stop!"

"You—"

I cut her off again. "I will deal with it. *Please leave!*"

Never one to let me have the last word, she called back, "Remember the truck's coming at eight on Saturday morning!"

Oh my God. Shut up. I could *spit*.

Hey, I didn't want to move out of San Francisco, and I sure didn't want to move to some dumb cul-de-sac on the edge of a town I couldn't even find on the map. It was somewhere up there, across the Golden Gate and out of the fog, hidden away in the trees where "we could finally have some open space," according to my parents, who bizarrely never seem to step away from their computers and phones unless they have to ride my ass about something I was supposed to do but didn't. It sucks to be an only child. I wish I had a little brother or sister if for no other reason than to give them someone else to harass besides me.

I guess the one good thing about moving to a new school is that there's a chance, just maybe, that there would be some kids who weren't completely lame.

They took me out to see it only once, and the cul-de-sac was completely stupid. "Look how safe it is! You can ride your bike in the street!" my mom had said, begging me to get on board with the place. Well, the cul-de-sac was on a steep hill, with the fat circle part at the top of the hill and the street that went toward the main part of town—what there was of it—at the bottom. Our new house was right on the corner at the bottom of the hill, which meant that riding my bike on the cul-de-sac would mean huffing it up a freakin' mountain, then riding the brakes all the way back down again so I wouldn't plow into traffic at the bottom. The other issue with her comment was that I don't even have a bike, because there's nowhere to ride it in San Francisco without getting killed.

"We'll get you a bike when we move!" she had insisted after I pointed this out.

"Whatever."

I didn't want to move, and I sure didn't want to ride a bike when I could be on the bus or the subway instead. Besides, the cul-de-sac was creepy. Too many trees and way too quiet. And based on my visit a month ago, everything under the green ceiling seemed dry and brown. Where were all the grassy yards you saw in the pictures?

"The schools are so much better," Mom would say. And I got that. My middle school in SF sucked and the high school didn't look any better. My friends at school? I wouldn't miss them. None of the girls I even remotely got along with lived anywhere near me, so we never hung out. Chilling for half an hour on the blacktop during lunch and talking about *Parks and Rec* and *Dance Moms* wasn't a real friendship. So, maybe I could start over in the suburbs and, you know, "find my tribe" in a new school.

I figured it wouldn't kill me to pack a couple of boxes so I didn't have to do it all tomorrow, so I took to emptying the bookcase in the corner of my room. My *Anne of Green Gables* collection? Keep. Legos? Donate. Old softball trophies from all those years, when I never even got a hit? Trash.

"Oh, I see you took my advice."

It was my mother, peeking through the door. I chose to ignore her and, as I finished putting the snow globe Grandma had given me into the "keep" box—yeah, I'm sentimental—I quickly threw myself back on the bed to relax with some Netflix and my phone.

"You need to tape these up," Mom said, a bit too aggressively considering how utterly basic her demand was. "What did you do with the tape I gave you?"

Jesus Christ, it's always something.

CHAPTER FIVE

Klaus

I THOUGHT FONDLY of the nurse. You're probably thinking of a young woman like you'd see in a movie, but that's not the right mental picture. She was in her early fifties, a "second act" career they call it, and after tiring of her life as an English teacher, she spent years going back to school to learn a trade in medicine. She had told me this was common, and that many of her fellow students were in the same position: sick of what they'd been doing for the last thirty years and ready for something new. I got it.

Of course she said she wanted to help people, too. And I suppose the best way to do that was by taking temperature readings, stitching wounds, and wiping *hintern*.

I saved the identification badge she always had pinned to her uniform. Scrubs, wasn't it? I would love to have had one of those little nurse's caps, but I guess those went out of favor in the seventies. Sure, the badge was risky, since it had her name and picture on it, but it was unlikely to be found in the safe with my other mementos. I especially liked it because it had a surprisingly good picture of her on it— better than real life—and I knew that would bring me joy down the road.

What was lingering in the safe? Cash, passport, some documents, and the collection.

The turquoise pendant belonged to the winery tasting room worker: the first. She'd poured me some swill and bent my ear in the way that women of a certain age tend to do, going on and on about what had brought her to California from, what was it, Missouri? Michigan? *Scheiss egal*—who cares? Buried deep in the woods, never discovered.

The small purse belonged to a fellow consultant, here on a job from out of town. She'd recently started a new engagement and found herself alone in San Francisco, due to fly back to New York on the red-eye that very night. People visiting from out of town always felt like good targets, and with her work engagement concluded she had let her hair down and was ready to blow off some steam. She just picked the wrong bar and talked to the wrong guy. At forty-two, she was the youngest of them all, and was the first to become a member of the collection out back, behind the house. When she was discovered missing, it made the papers for a few days. Everyone was baffled over what could have happened to her: "She just vanished."

The waitress was a unique burial at sea, dropped off the back of the boat I'd rented for the week, which I then scrubbed down with Clorox just in case anyone had seen her come aboard that night. I released her back into the world far offshore, and I nervously watched the news for weeks to make sure nobody washed up on the beach. Nothing ever happened, and as far as I know no one even filed a report that she was missing. I kept her tiny gold ring, surely an item of some significance that we never got around to discussing.

The homeless woman. *Ach*, I wasn't proud of that one. She was early on—eight, nine years ago? The second in line, anyway. It was a spur-of-the moment thing. She was standing at a stoplight that never seemed to turn green, waving a sign that read "anything helps." I gave her ten dollars and said I had some cleaning she could do at my house if she wanted to work for another fifty. She hopped in the back of the BMW, and that was that. Also buried in the yard. I kept her beat-up belt buckle. Burned the belt. It was disgusting, *widerlich*.

And the *hausfrau*. I called her that, but it wasn't totally accurate. She was newly divorced and living alone way out in Mendocino and just hadn't ever gotten a job after the husband left. She was just lying about, living off the alimony, and she struck me as lazy. I didn't feel too bad about her, but we did spend more time together than the others. Those were all over and done with inside of twenty-four hours. I knew more about her than any of the others in the collection, and I kept her silver necklace as a memento. I buried her in the yard a year ago—well, twice, because of the damn vermin. She was the last one before the nurse.

With the nurse's new ID badge, that was six. Four interred here, two elsewhere.

I'm sure that most people think that it is difficult to kill a stranger and get away with it, and that's probably a good thing. If everyone was doing this, it would be utter anarchy out there. You can't just have a world where one person can kill another person at random and for no reason. No one would ever leave their house. Society would collapse. Rules are important.

But someone like me, who's just taking one here and one there, nothing crazy, it's no big deal. It's like pulling a single leaf from one of the towering oak trees that overlook the quartet in the backyard. The tree isn't damaged. Another leaf grows in its place the following year, and life moves on.

Still, I feel *schlecht* about all of it. I knew these women had no one of significance in their lives—that's the secret to getting away with it—but still, I also knew it was not right that I should be the one to end it all for them. Knowing what's right and doing what's right, though, those are two different things.

Six was enough. I should stop at six. I would stop at six.

CHAPTER SIX

Alex

I T WASN'T GARBAGE day, but there was a massive truck outside making a hell of a racket all the same.

"What the living hell?" I actually yelled out loud, though there was no one and nothing around to hear it unless you counted my grandmother's extremely dated furniture, all of which had been carefully line-itemed in her will and remained exactly where she had left it when she died.

I didn't want to get off the couch, as I had already done so fifteen minutes prior in order to microwave a frozen burrito, but I shambled over to the window to peek out through the drapes so I could see what was going on. Street cleaning? Someone getting a new refrigerator? No. It was a full-on moving truck. The house next door, which I'm sure hadn't had its for sale sign up for more than a week, must have sold, and already the people were moving in. I knew that couldn't be possible, but then I realized that I couldn't exactly remember when the prior owners had moved away, nor was I able to quite recall their last name, though I knew for certain it started with an S.

A horde of laborers spilled from the truck and slowly got to work hauling boxes and furniture from the street to the house. God, they took their time. This was hourly labor at its finest, a lack of education or a history of crime paying them back for a life completely wasted with every step taken. Then again, it's probably a good workout. But if that's true, how come so many of these guys were fat?

Neighbors. The—hmmm, Simpsons? Stevensons?—the S people were empty nesters who had sent their last kid off to college years ago, and like all good old couples, they had obviously decided to move away to someplace smaller, warmer, cheaper, and with fewer stairs. I saw some balloons tied to their mailbox at one point a few months back and a couple of cars out front, but other than that small gathering to which I was not invited, there was no fanfare on the cul-de-sac surrounding their departure. I didn't even notice when they moved out. Must have been a small truck. It probably arrived early in the morning before I got up.

What would a new arrival bring? God, how much shit did these people have? And was that kids' furniture? A child on the cul-de-sac? What kind of parents would subject a kid to a street like this? Couldn't they see that if a kid rode his bike down the steep hill, he'd crash into a car at the bottom and die?

Besides, there were no other kids on the street for a child to play with. There hadn't been new blood on the cul-de-sac since, well, since my grandmother died and I moved in eight years ago. I was forty at the time, and probably the youngest person who lived on the street. When I moved in I didn't bring anything except some clothes, so I wouldn't be surprised if most of the neighbors didn't even know I lived here at all, except for Peg next door, who really seemed to want to be friends and kept dropping by with random baked goods.

I do remember that once the mustachioed guy—he lives at the end of the road, at the top of the hill, and farther up the long sloping driveway that finally takes you to his front door—had knocked on the door to give me a piece of mail misdelivered to his house. He peppered me with a bunch of questions for what seemed like hours but which was probably really under a minute because I'm sure he could tell I couldn't wait for him to leave. Smarmy and slick, definitely a blueblood type who moved here from New England or something. Worked in real estate, I think. Couldn't recall his name. Maybe I should write these things down.

CHAPTER SEVEN
Eliza

"WHEN ARE YOU going to start unpacking?" my mother asked, helpful as ever.

There was no answer that would satisfy her, so I told her what I thought would at least shut her up for a day.

"Tomorrow."

"Tomorrow I need you to help me unpack the kitchen," she said.

"It's fine. I'll do it after." I went back to watching videos on my bare mattress, which was lying directly on the floor next to the yet-to-be-assembled bed frame.

Perhaps realizing she had the opportunity to make another obvious comment, Mom asked, "Do you need help putting the frame together?"

I paused *Friends* and stared at her for a moment. Did she see a toolkit here? Even a screwdriver? Opportunity to be verbally sarcastic or simply roll my eyes—which to choose? Both were perhaps too obvious. "Yes," I said after a too-long pause—but only after going back to watching the show.

"I'll send your dad up with the drill," she said as she turned away.

Shit, she had me. I didn't think she'd want to do it right

now. Dad was surely busy in their bedroom or the living room or somewhere else, wasn't he? I felt panic, then resignation as she called out from down the hallway, "I'll bring up your sheets!"

"Mom!" I yelled to try to stop her, but it was too late. She knew to get out of earshot, or at least pretend to, if she wanted to avoid another argument—and get her way.

I was tired. Weren't they tired also? Why did everything have to happen *right now*?

Well, to be honest, Dad was able to put the bed frame together in, like, ten minutes, and Mom even put the sheets on the bed while I hid in the bathroom and finished watching the show. When I came out, they were gone. It was nice to have the bed put together, even if it was surrounded by moving boxes, and I knew I'd have a better night's sleep because of it. There's just something about sleeping low to the ground that feels dangerous and vulnerable. Like, if the mattress was on the ground, the monster that hides under the bed wouldn't have had anywhere to hang out, which means he could creep up onto the mattress with me instead.

Anyway, I didn't unpack any boxes that night, nor the next day, nor the day after that. And then school started.

CHAPTER EIGHT

Jean Claire

THERE'S NOWHERE TO hide in the suburbs. It's even worse in school.

Everybody knows who everybody is around here. There's only, like, two hundred kids in the class, so there's really no excuse to not know somebody except for the special ed kids they keep locked up in a whole other part of the school. There's only one middle school here, and there's only one high school. So all this talk of "making a fresh start" when you move up from one school to the other is pretty much bullshit. It's really all the same people, just in a different building.

Because everybody knows everybody, that's how you get a reputation. People know I get reasonably good grades— that's common knowledge. One kid even called me "Harvard" once. But maybe that was supposed to be a joke. Like, "OK, Harvard..." I couldn't tell.

Harvard was, of course, completely out of the question. I didn't have the grades or the extracurriculars to get in, and Mother would never pay for such a thing, anyway. I certainly wasn't interested in taking on any kind of debt, even a student loan. No way.

That's the other thing people say about me, that I was always coming up with ways to make money. I babysat. I walked dogs in the summer. I went thrifting and sold the gems on eBay for a profit. Anything (within reason) to make a buck, and every dollar I earned from my side hustles went straight into the bank account I'd gotten my big brother to help me set up before he escaped the suburbs for college. And that account was now growing nicely.

On day one of high school, we went through the usual routine of checking out our shitty, broke-ass laptop, getting a few textbooks, and doing menial assignments like writing a one-page essay entitled "What I want to get out of high school." Short answer: *Out of high school.* I filled the rest in with drivel that assumed the English teacher, Ms. Barbagianni, would want to hear. It didn't take more than ten minutes.

I spent the rest of the time taking stock of the people in the class, all of them familiar faces except for one. There was a new girl in school this year. She was in, like, three of my classes, and she looked like a bitch.

CHAPTER NINE

Peg

I ONLY CAUGHT a distant glimpse of the young teen, clearly walking home from her first day of school while I'd gone out to the curb to fetch the mail. She didn't look thrilled to be trudging along with a laptop in one arm and wearing a backpack that looked almost empty. Shouldn't it have been filled with textbooks on day one? Progress, I suppose.

The new family lived at the bottom of the cul-de-sac, so she didn't have much farther to walk, overloaded with books or not. My house, closer to the top of the hill, would have been a tougher slog, and it looked like she needed a break as it was. Her dirty-blond hair was a wreck, frizzed up like a woman who forgot to spray it down before a long day at the beach.

She looked sweaty. Not glistening, but a bit dirty and ragged. She was wearing a sweater that must have been oppressively hot in the muggy swampiness of the rain's postscript, and she was hunched over just a bit, dragged down by the weight of the backpack and, I'm sure, the daily horror of being a teenager. She disappeared into the house on the corner, which must have been what all the ruckus was about a few days ago: moving trucks.

A child on the cul-de-sac? What a delight! Maybe this was the sign I needed that things were going to start perking up for me. A little youth was all we needed to breathe some fresh life into the cul-de-sac.

The girl's parents must have put a lot of time and fore-thought into choosing just the right place to raise their daughter. A fine high school she could walk to just a mile and a quarter away. Virtually no traffic aside from the mail van and the occasional delivery. Quiet and peaceful and safe. I'd never once heard of any real crimes taking place anywhere near us, though kids sometimes sprayed graffiti on the side of the supermarket between here and the school. That was to be expected. As long as this new girl didn't fall in with the wrong crowd or make any trouble on the street, she was going to do great. I was sure of it.

God knows, everything was different today. I would have had to use a wagon to carry my textbooks home, and of course we didn't have computers back in the seventies. I'm old enough to remember having to do homework on a slide rule, a gizmo this poor girl wouldn't have a clue what to do with. Come to think of it, neither would I anymore.

What was she interested in? What kind of classes was she taking? I guess I could look up the school online and see what they offered. Surely, it was all courses in building robots and speaking Chinese nowadays, right? I liked that the schools were teaching kids practical information, some-thing they could use to get a job in the real world. What a world away we are from home ec and metal shop. Surely she was destined to become a scientist or a professor or something…something important, I could tell. She needed a little cleaning up and a better hairstyle, but she was young. Thirteen? Fourteen? There would be time for all that.

I realized I was standing at the mailbox, holding a stack of junk, looking down the hill at the house on the corner for far too long. The girl had disappeared minutes ago, and here I was standing around like a loopy-loo, as my mother used to say, lost in my daydreams and oblivious to the world around me. Oh well, the beauty of the cul-de-sac is that surely no one noticed. I could have stood here for an hour and never encountered a soul.

Until now, maybe. A child on the cul-de-sac! How exciting to have new people—young people—on the tiny street. But who was I kidding? Probably this young family would want nothing to do with an old woman like me. I quickly calmed myself through the breathing exercises I'd been taught and, as they said, "mindful thinking." *There is nothing to be nervous about, Peg. This is good. A little change never killed anyone.*

It was finally time to get out of the house a bit more.

CHAPTER TEN

Alex

"YOU ON THE list?"

The voice came from around the partition. I couldn't see him, but I could tell he was an old man. Must've been incredibly lonely to have to strike up a conversation from the dialysis chair with someone he'd never met and couldn't even see. I paused the video game on my phone and set it in my lap, then took off my headphones.

"Pardon?" I asked. I figured an old-timer would prefer a good old-fashioned *pardon* to a curt *what*.

"You on the list? The transplant list?" he said.

"Nah," I said. "Transplant wouldn't do me any good. I'm just here to clean my blood. The dialysis keeps things working well enough."

"What's that? What's wrong with you?" he asked.

"Heavy metal poisoning. For me, being here is kinda like changing the oil in your car."

"Heavy metals? What, you grow up in a shipyard or something?"

"No, lead. Lead poisoning. Long story." I hoped he would leave it at that, and he did.

Old-timer was quiet for a while before he piped up again

after what must have been an agonizing few minutes racking his brain for something to say.

"I got kidney failure," was his eventual response.

"You don't say."

"Yeah," he said. "Killed my daddy, too. Probably gonna kill me. No one my age gets a kidney transplant."

"How old are you?"

"Seventy, last month."

I'd read the brochures and knew the statistics and, like he said, at his age he didn't have a great shot at getting a donation from a dead kid or something. Probably didn't have a loved one who could participate in one of those multiway kidney transplants with him either. Or maybe he was afraid to ask. He sounded older than seventy, anyway.

"Probably gonna kill me."

"Yep," I said. I guess he was looking for affirmation. "We all gotta go sometime."

It was surprisingly easy to talk to the old man behind the partition. He couldn't see me, drooling into a handkerchief, my hair patchy thanks to a combination of my malady and my DIY haircuts. My shirt was too big and my pants were too short and, oh shit, I looked down at my phone and noticed I had accidentally unpaused my game and died while I was talking to the old dude next door. I let out a sigh. I'd already played the game before all the way through, but I couldn't remember much about it, so it felt new this time.

"I've got at least three more hours in the chair," he eventually said. "Why don't you tell me that story of yours and help pass the time?"

"Hmm, I'd rather not. Maybe you can tell me your story instead."

"Fair enough, son." And then he launched into it. "I'm a San Francisco native, grew up in a Victorian in the Sunset District…"

He started droning on and on about Playland and the slow decay of the Sutro Baths, and it finally dawned on me that if I couldn't see him, he couldn't see me either. I put my headphones back on and grunted out an "mmm-hmmm" every few minutes to keep him happy. Then I picked up my phone and tapped the icon for the game and—what else?—started over.

CHAPTER ELEVEN
Klaus

THE TRIP TO Virginia had come up suddenly and taken longer than I'd expected, but the servers were installed, the software was tuned, and the client was happy. My flight back home to California was at seven a.m. the next day, connecting through JFK, which left me with just one evening to kill in Richmond.

I did what I always did: turned to the internet to search for the best bar within five blocks of my hotel, preferably one with a good beer selection. There were plenty of choices, but I decided on a sort of English pub, transplanted to the Colonies, with soccer on TV, a pool table upstairs, and Guinness on tap. I settled in at a table by the fireplace, enjoyed a plate of sausages and potatoes, and drank deeply from my pint of locally made Vienna-style lager. It wasn't a German *helles* or a *dunkel*, but it was close enough, and it reminded me of home. I hadn't been back to Munich in close to a decade, and drinking the beer made me wonder if it was time to plan a trip. Perhaps chain it to another work trip to the East Coast, which was pretty much halfway there anyway.

The bartender was cute, but it was the two older women

sitting together at the bar who caught my eye. Locals, definitely, both a bit overweight but hiding it well underneath sweaters that were baggy and, considering it was nearly ninety degrees outside, not entirely seasonally appropriate.

I felt that itch. I would have been happy with either one, but I preferred the blonde. She seemed sadder and didn't talk as much. It's better when they're quiet. Perhaps the brunette was taking her out to celebrate good news at work or reporting back from a vacation with her family. I noticed the chatty brunette had a wedding ring on. The blonde did not.

Of course, it would never work in a setup like this. There were two of them, and the scene was much too public, the bar too crowded. A German in Richmond would raise eyebrows. I'd spoken to the bartender about my homeland when I'd ordered the beer and the sausages. Even if the brunette left and I slid in to take her spot next to the blonde, what then? Too many witnesses and too much risk, even though I always pay in cash. If the police got nosy, someone would piece it together eventually. My client's offices were too close.

If I were going to make a move, it would have to be outside, away from prying eyes. A pity that people didn't smoke anymore. How natural it would have been to run into her in the huddle out by the street. It would have been a trivial matter to ask if there was another bar nearby, one with more exciting cocktails, and would she care to join me, a stranger in town just looking for some conversation, for a quick nightcap? It had worked before. Naturally, I had not attempted to fly here with any of my precious chloroform—

not easy to come by now, even on the dark web—and it wasn't like I could have some delivered to the pub. Cyclopropane and sevoflurane wouldn't be available, either, unless I bribed someone to steal it from a hospital for me.

If I were to do it, it would have to be the old-fashioned way. Given the limitations of working so far from home, that would probably mean a thick plastic bag over the head and holding her down for a minute or two until she passed out. There would be struggling, so we'd need to be close to an alley or some kind of dark area where we wouldn't be seen. The bag would muffle the screaming, however.

My car would have to be nearby so I could get her in the trunk or—less suspiciously—the back seat. I'm reasonably sure that someone had seen me drag the consultant into the car that night in San Francisco, but as I was shoving her into the back seat, the would-be witness probably assumed she was simply drunk, not dead. That woman was tiny, though. I'm not sure I could hoist the blonde at the bar into any part of the car with any amount of grace.

I realized the potatoes on my plate had grown cold as I daydreamed about a plan that was never going to happen. It would be exciting and challenging to take my first outside of California, but it would require preparations I simply hadn't had the time or forethought to complete. Perhaps I should extend the trip another day, try to get the job done tomorrow night. *Ach*, an even worse idea. I was being foolish and careless.

Besides, I had to remind myself, I'd agreed that I would be done with six. Six was a good number, and I had nothing else to prove to anyone. Seven was not some magic number that would make everything better, any more than number six had. *Schon gut.*

Eventually, the two women left together. There would have been no way to pull it off anyway, so why was I beating myself up?

I finished the beer, paid the bill by leaving cash on the table—out of habit—and walked back to my hotel, where I packed and slept restlessly for just a few hours. I was up by four-thirty in the morning to get to the airport, only to find my connecting flight from New York delayed for hours. We landed at SFO, and I fetched my car and drove back home, through the City, the sad ride down 19th Avenue, across the Golden Gate, and into the suburbs. By then, it was well past sundown. The entire day *verschwendet.* Wasted.

As I made the final turn, that hard left that took you into the secluded cul-de-sac most people would unknowingly drive past, I immediately noticed the squat little house on the corner. The older couple that had lived there had moved out some months ago, and now it looked like every light was on in the place, as if the new residents were afraid of the dark. They didn't have curtains yet, and I slowed the BMW to a crawl to see if I could get a look at who was inside. There was certainly plenty of activity inside. Stacks of boxes, furniture in disarray, and several people in constant motion, carrying useless *krimskrams* inside. It certainly looked frantic. Hadn't these people organized their belongings beforehand, or had it all just been packed in random boxes?

I counted at least two people inside, a man and woman

in their forties, I'd guess, but I was certain that this was more than just a couple moving in. To be sure, it was a family moving into the cul-de-sac, and that would mean some number of children.

And that was terrible news, because that would come with activity. Visiting family members. Babies being pushed in strollers. Birthday parties. And everyone on the lookout for danger to their precious *kinder*.

CHAPTER TWELVE
Alex

THE DOPE FROM Amazon had left my package next to the mailbox, all the way down by the street. The lazy jerk. Most delivery types knew it was tough for me to get around, so they did me a solid and brought packages to the door. It was a few dozen steps for them—nothing—but it was a massive amount of work for me.

Oh well, probably best to check the mailbox anyway, I thought, slipping on the shoes I kept next to the door and shuffling down the path, cane in hand.

"Alex! Alex!" a voice called out from my right as soon as I was two steps out the door. It could only mean one thing.

Peg came bounding out of her house and rushed toward me, clutching something circular in her hands. What would it be this time?

I kept walking toward the mailbox as she jogged over in her blue blouse and yellow capri pants, the ensemble all smeared with flour. "I was making apple pie, you know, because it's the season," she said, beaming. "I accidentally made an extra one, and I figured you would want it."

I looked at the pie through one eye. She'd tried to make one of those fancy interlocking lattice crusts, but the end result looked like a chain-link fence a rabid dog had chewed its way through.

"Maybe not my best work," she said, seeing my consternation. "But I'm sure it's going to taste delicious."

"Thanks, Peg," I said as warmly as possible. "Maybe you can put it on the kitchen counter for me? Door's open."

"You got it."

She rushed inside while I picked up my package and fetched the mail, a week's worth of what looked like junk. Peg never emerged, which meant she must be waiting for me inside for another one of her impromptu chats. I resigned myself to the next fifteen minutes, though I suppose Peg was wholly harmless and, ultimately, a good enough diversion for the moment.

Inside I found her sitting on the couch, idly staring at the vast collection of owl-centric objects that lined the walls behind the TV. I couldn't blame her, as some of the items were truly bizarre, collected by my aunt over decades of traveling and thrift-store shopping. I was at times guilty of wondering about the origins of a few of the more perverse sculptures myself.

"Isn't it exciting?" she asked, once I'd joined her on the couch.

"Isn't what exciting?"

"The new neighbors. We're going to have fresh blood on the street for the first time since I don't know when."

"I don't know what there is to be excited about," I said. "I'm sure these people will be just as useless around here as the family they bought the house from."

"They even have a teenage daughter," she said.

"What, you're going to have the girl over so you can do each other's hair?"

Peg smirked and rolled her eyes. "No," she said. "It's just nice to have some youth around us. The cul-de-sac is so quiet and boring, it's like a retirement community. Nothing ever happens here."

"Yeah, that's why I like it," I said.

"God, Alex. You're no fun. Never have been."

"I know. Not sure why you like hanging out with me. I've got nothing to offer you at all."

"Well, until now you were the only thing that qualified as a neighbor around here. I don't know if I've ever seen anyone else in the flesh who lives on the street."

"What about the mustache guy?"

"Oh, Darren something, right?"

"No idea," I said.

"Yes, he did knock on my door once years ago. I've only ever seen him driving up or down the street since then. He doesn't even wave."

I shrugged.

"Do you think the new girl goes to the local high school?" Peg asked.

"If she's a teenager, where else is she going to go?" I replied. Peg was always good for at least a few stupid questions.

"She could be homeschooled. She could go to a private school somewhere. I don't know. I was just wondering. Maybe she's a cheerleader."

"A cheerleader? That's your angle?"

"Why not? I was a cheerleader," she insisted, frowning a bit.

"OK, whatever. I'm just saying girls now play a lot of real sports, too, you know."

"Of course I know that," Peg said. "I'm not an idiot."

"Peg, no one thinks you're an idiot! Jesus!" She could be frustrating at times.

She stared at me, smirking for a bit. I'm sure she knew, deep down, that I kind of thought she was, maybe, a little bit of an idiot.

"Why do I keep coming over here, anyway?" she asked.

"I ask myself that all the time," I said. "It's probably because you've got nowhere else to go."

Peg shrugged. She knew I wasn't wrong.

CHAPTER THIRTEEN

Eliza

I COULD TELL Mrs. Barbagianni was going to be one of those teachers. She was already huffing and puffing around the classroom, rolling her eyes and rubbing the bridge of her nose all the time. I'd heard that two people had already been suspended—and this was only the second day of the school year.

She started class with the announcements. "Today," she intoned as loud as her squeaky voice could go, "is the start of fundraising for the school year. That means all of you get to go ask your parents, neighbors, and friends to buy holiday wrapping paper and other delightful goodies to support all the wonderful activities we do at school." I picked up on the sarcasm right away. The guy next to me with his face flat on the desk and a hoodie pulled up to cover his head, probably not so much.

"And the best news," she said, "is that you all get a chance to win something, too." Mrs. Barbagianni handed a stack of paperwork to the person in the front row of each column of desks, instructing us to "take one and pass it back," as if we were helpless children who'd never been in a classroom before.

"I'll just read you the rest from the official messaging document," she said, picking up a paper from her desk. I could tell she went off-script here and there. It went like this:

OK, kids, we have a long-running tradition here, and since you freshmen are all new to the school this year, this will be your first time to be a part of it.

Every year, the PTA and the administration work together to raise money to support vital school programs. This year, our goal is to raise $100,000 in order to fund new computers for every classroom. If we reach our goal, each class will receive up to two new Macintosh computers, which will be available for class projects, research, after-school use, or additional student needs.

As usual, we will be enlisting your—the students'—help by selling holiday wrapping paper, gift bags, and stocking stuffers, all of which your friends and family can browse via the catalogs I've just handed out. There are dozens of products available, and everything is priced between ten and fifteen dollars, so nothing will break the bank.

If every student sells just five products, we'll easily reach our $100,000 goal. But this year, we're asking everyone to stretch a bit and try to sell ten products minimum. Any student who does reach the ten-product minimum will be entered into a drawing, and the winner of the drawing gets to spend a full minute in the Money Machine! Have you guys seen the Money Machine? It's like a phone booth with a fan in the bottom and it blows cash all around you. Whatever you can grab in sixty seconds you get to keep! It's a lot of fun. I see some blank looks out there. Do you guys not know what a phone booth is?

Anyway, the point is, you are not just raising money for your school, you can raise money for yourself, too. And all you have to do is get out there and sell ten items. So talk to your parents, your relatives, your neighbors. Your parents can also take the catalog to work and help you sell there. I've heard of kids who got a hundred orders in a single day because their mom or dad was the first one to bring in a fundraising catalog to the office. That's why we like to get this going so early in the year, so we can beat the other schools to the punch.

Any questions? Order forms are due within two weeks, so don't let this sit in your backpack forever. Put the catalog on the dinner table when you get home, and get out there and do some selling this weekend! If we all pitch in, we can reach our goal and have those computers in the classrooms before Christmas.

A hand went up in the back of the room. A scraggy-looking kid wearing pajama bottoms. Trevor was his name, I think.

"Yes?"

"You said we're all pitching in, Ms. Barbagianni?" he asked.

"That's right."

"Well, does that mean you're selling wrapping paper, too?"

Mrs. Barbagianni didn't answer, narrowing her eyes at him.

"Any other questions?" she asked.

THE WALK HOME from school wasn't difficult, but it was on the long side, over a mile, the last part of it a woodsy, uninhabited stretch of road that I bet got pretty spooky at night. But nearer the school, the road was flat, straight, and crowded with suburban homes on either side. A bit farther along was Sunset Market, situated in a small strip mall where a lot of kids went to grab lunch.

Suddenly, there was a voice behind me, and it sounded familiar, with a bit of an accent I couldn't immediate place. "You're new, right?"

"Huh?" I said, turning.

"You're in Barbie G's class with me. English."

I recognized her. Jane something? Shorter than me by a lot, with hair that was long, straight, and brown—but with a single pink streak running down the side. Black yoga pants and a Vineyard Vines long-sleeve, tucked in in front.

"Barbie G?" I asked.

"Barbagianni. People call her that. Actually, I think we have three classes together. Biology. Also P.E."

"Oh yeah, hey," I finally said.

"Did you move here recently?"

"Yeah, like a week ago," I said, stopping for her to catch up.

"Really? *Why?*" she demanded, as if that was the worst idea ever.

"I dunno," I said. "Something about how we can play in the street and not get stabbed or something."

"I guess you moved here from the City."

"Yeah. My parents say it's 'a cesspool' and that 'it's no place to raise a kid anymore.' I told them I'm not a kid but whatever. What's your name again?"

"Jean, Jean Claire," she said.

"You got the two names going on, huh?"

"My mom's from the South," she said. "The deep South." She'd heard it all before, I'm sure.

"Well, I'm Eliza. One name."

"Yeah, I know. Where's your house?"

I pointed in the direction we were walking. "I don't know all the street names yet, but you go like half a mile this way, then turn left at the grocery store, then keep going for a while on the way to the hiking trails until you get into the area where it's just trees. There's a cul-de-sac, and that's where we live, right on the corner."

"Huh, never been out that way," she said, shrugging.

"Don't you live over here too?" I asked.

"Uh, no. I live the other way from school. But the grocery store is this way, and a bunch of kids stop by the store for snacks and drinks after school and hang out, so..." She shrugged.

"Yeah, I've seen the crowds already."

By then we'd started walking again, but at an awfully slow, lazy pace. Growing up in the City, I'd been trained to walk with purpose in order to keep trouble at bay. Eyes straight ahead. No electronics in hand and no earbuds, so you can maintain awareness of your surroundings. It had worked. I'd never been robbed or attacked or anything, though I spent every day walking to school and more recently had started riding the subway and bus by myself. It scared my mother shitless, though. She couldn't take it anymore, I guess.

Jean Claire looked down at my hand, which was clutching the fundraising catalog Mrs. Barbagianni had passed out earlier in the day. "You going to sell wrapping paper?" she asked.

"Oh, I dunno."

"My brother graduated last year. He always sold it because he wanted to get into the Money Machine, but he never got picked," she said. I couldn't tell if she was proud of him or if she was making fun of him. "I did hear this one kid got like three hundred bucks a couple of years ago, though. Mostly the machine is full of ones, but they have some twenties, fifties, and a single hundred-dollar bill in there too. They make a big show of it when they put it in. They said he got the hundred plus one of the fifties. The secret was that he wore sweats and he shoved all the money down his pants so it couldn't blow out of his hands."

I snort-laughed. "Well, that's cool."

"Yeah, totally." Jean Claire laughed awkwardly. "I'm definitely going to sell enough to qualify for the Money

Machine, whatever it takes. And, you know, we could sell together if you want."

"Like door-to-door?" I asked.

"Yeah, we just have to sell twenty items total, and we make a deal that if either of us gets in the Money Machine, we split the cash evenly. That's twice the chance that one of us can get in there. It's a lower payout, but a lot more than nothing. Big upside if you ask me."

"Sounds like you've thought this through."

Jean Claire blushed. I guess she really needed the money or something. "Well," she said, "my brother says selling with a friend is more fun anyway. We can sell on your street or mine or both, whatever."

"Sure, why not?" I said. "I guess it wouldn't hurt to see what freaks are living on my block."

"Ha! I know, right," Jean Claire said. "Bunch of pervs, I bet."

We had finally made it to the grocery store—Sunset Market—and Jean Claire stopped as we walked through the parking lot.

"You going in for anything?" she asked.

"Nah, I'm not hungry."

"Yeah, me neither. Sometimes there are good sales in the candy aisle, though. Anyway, text me your address. I'll come over tomorrow afternoon, and we'll go meet the freaks." I gave her my phone and she punched in her digits. Maybe living out here in the sticks wasn't going to be quite as bad as I thought.

"Sounds good, I'll send it. See you tomorrow, I guess."

"Yah, bye!"

I turned to walk away and Jean Claire called out, "Hey, Eliza!"

"Huh?" I said, turning.

"I'm so happy you're not a bitch!"

CHAPTER FOURTEEN

Lew

D INNER WAS READY. Frozen lasagna, which Judy mercifully could not fuck up. At least it would be better than the greasy Chinese takeout from last night. And the McDonald's we had the night before. For our first Saturday in the new house, it was a "home-cooked meal," or as close to it as we usually ever had.

The dining room and kitchen were still stacked with moving boxes. As the three of us sat down, I asked Judy, "How long is it going to take to get this all unpacked?" I said it in my nicest possible voice but, I mean, what else did she have to do all day?

"As long as it takes, Lew," she said. "I'm going as fast as I can. And as you can see, I had to make dinner." She gestured at the foil tray on the table. To protect the wood, she had placed it on top of a decade-old phone book the previous owners had left behind.

I smirked at her effort. "Really?" I asked.

"Yes, and I even made a salad."

She had emptied a bag of salad onto three paper plates, then squeezed out the little bag of dressing that came in the kit, globbing roughly a third onto each plate. She hadn't even tried to stir it around a little. I worked on that myself and nodded, saying nothing further about the matter. I was sure Lizzie didn't want to hear it—again.

I turned to my daughter. "Nice that we have more space here, right Lizzie?" I asked.

"Uh, sure," she said, almost looking me in the eye.

"I mean, we moved here so you would have some room to spread your wings."

"My wings?" she said. "Great. Well, good news on that front. We have to sell wrapping paper and stuff to people, to raise money for school."

"Oh, that's great, honey!" Judy said, ever the supporter. "What can we buy?"

Lizzie gave her a bit of a side-eye before going on. "Whatever you want, I guess. If we sell enough stuff, we get entered into a drawing for a big prize. I'm going to sell with this girl from school tomorrow, go door-to-door on our street."

"Door-to-door? Is that safe?" Judy asked.

"Is it safe? Isn't that why we moved here? Because it's so safe?" she said. "I mean, that and the whole thing about my wings?"

I piped in, "I think it's great, Lizzo. You've already made a friend?"

A moderate grimace, probably at the Lizzo crack. "Sure, I guess," she said.

"Selling door-to-door really builds character," I said, putting on my best smile. "I think you're going to learn a lot about yourself along the way." This was great news. Lizzie had never had the chance to do anything like this back in the City. Maybe this was the first sign that things were going to perk up for her—for all of us.

"Well, there are like seven houses on this street, and one of them is ours and another one is burned down," she said, "so I don't know how much you think I'm going to learn. Besides, I just want to sell twenty items with Jean Claire so we can go in the Money Machine."

"The Money Machine? What's that?" Judy asked.

"It's supposed to be an old-timey telephone booth like the ones on TV, the kind that you stand in. It's full of money, and a fan blows it all around while you're inside. You get to keep what you can grab in a minute."

"This is a prize for selling the most?" Judy asked.

"They pick someone at random if you sell enough items."

"So we give you money for wrapping paper and the school gives you some of the money back through this Money Machine?" I asked, just for clarity.

Lizzie shrugged. "I guess."

"Sounds about right," I said, trying not to roll my eyes.

Somehow, Lizzie had nearly finished her plate over the course of this short conversation, one in which she had done half the talking. The quicker she ate, the quicker she could get back to her phone.

"I'm glad you're selling with a friend," I said. "Smarter that way. I think you'll learn as much from having to cooperate with someone else as you will from having to interact with strangers. Great life lesson, Lizzie, great life lesson."

I remembered that the Giants game was on, so I retrieved my phone from my pocket to quickly check the score. It hadn't been our year so far, but we'd had a string of wins this August, so maybe things would turn around enough to get us into the wild-card slot for the playoffs. Long shot, but still. I tapped around to see the stats for the game, and then I had another quick peek at my email.

"Hey, Judy, Giants are winning," I said. She didn't respond. Only when I looked up and started to repeat myself did I realize I was the only one left at the table.

CHAPTER FIFTEEN
Jean Claire

"IF I HAD to walk this far to get to and from school every day, I think I'd die," I said.

Eliza was standing at the door of her house, still in her pajamas from the look of it. "I know, right? I told you it was a long walk," she said.

"Uh, no, you didn't," I said. If she had said it was going to be this far, I would have gotten a ride, or I would have just bagged on the whole thing. Anyway, I was here now, and if Eliza would get dressed, then we could get going. Maybe her mom could take me home later.

"Well, you're here now. Let's go before my parents come out to talk to us. I'll get my shoes," she said.

"You're going out like that?"

"Yeah, why?"

"Because you look like you just got up, and no one's going to buy anything if they think you're a homeless person. At least brush your hair."

Eliza already had on a pair of filthy Keds sneakers, but she sighed and kicked them off again. "Come upstairs and I'll change," she said.

As we walked upstairs, I could tell she wasn't lying about

having just moved to town. Every corner of every room and every hallway was crammed with cardboard boxes. It looked like people were getting ready to leave, not moving in. "Are you guys going to unpack or what?" I asked.

"We're working on it."

I couldn't tell much about Eliza from her room. Her bed and its frame had been reconstructed and a sloppy pile of sheets occupied the mattress, but otherwise there was nothing but boxes everywhere. I could see the outline of a desk and a chair along one wall, but cardboard surrounded it completely. I sat on a corner of the bed while Eliza disappeared into the closet—big enough to walk into but only barely—and I could see her fishing around in the box she was obviously using either as a suitcase or a dirty laundry bin or both. She pulled out a wadded-up pair of blue jeans and a clean*ish* T-shirt, then disappeared into the bathroom down the hall.

Eliza didn't much seem like the other girls at school, and maybe that was a good thing. Like, we had enough in common but also enough that was different. And she didn't seem at all like a stuck-up princess like everyone else. Maybe she would be someone who could really understand what I had to deal with at home—and why I wanted to get out of there.

When she reemerged, she was reasonably put together, her hair pulled back into a tight ponytail, her face washed, and her teeth presumably brushed. Good enough for selling overpriced wrapping paper to strangers, I guess.

Her outfit smoothed out, Eliza beamed and gathered up

her sales sheet, catalog, and a pen. "Where to first, then?" I asked.

"The house across the street."

CHAPTER SIXTEEN

Lupe

"¿*QUE?*" I never opened a conversation like this with English, no matter who was at the door. These two *chicas* looked like they could be trouble. I was sure they were selling something.

"Uh, hi," said the skinny, shorter one, dressed in yoga pants and Ugg boots. The pink streak in her hair annoyed me. "We live across the street, and we're raising money for our school."

"Well, *I* live across the street," said the other one. Taller but a little sloppy. Her shirt needed ironing. She jabbed a thumb at the short one. "She's just my friend."

I played dumb, just stood there and stared at them. It got awkward, quickly.

"So," Sloppy said, "would you be interested in buying some wrapping paper for the upcoming holidays?"

"There's also gift bags and stocking stuffers," Skinny said. She thrust a catalog toward me, and I took it from her without comment. I flipped through the paperwork. *Dios mio*, this stuff was garbage, and expensive. The wrapping paper rolls were so thin they looked like they would be good for three or four presents at most. The gift bags weren't shiny, and they weren't even printed with Christmas decor. They were just plain bags colored a dirty red and green, with small handles. The stocking stuffers were junk I couldn't imagine putting in a *calceta*. What kind of school did these girls go to?

I closed the booklet. "I no live here. Just work here," I finally said, intentionally butchering my English.

"Sorry," Sloppy said. "Is your boss home?"

I nodded. "He home, but he blind."

A voice boomed out from behind me. "Lupe! Who's at the door!" It was Mr. Percy, of course. Up out of his chair and shuffling his way down the hall toward the front door.

I turned to him. "Mr. Percy, it is neighbor girls from across the street. They sell paper for school."

Mr. Percy finally made it to the entrance, standing a few feet behind me, where he could keep one hand on the doorframe to the sitting room that no one ever sat in. He was out of breath from the exertion, huffing and heaving from walking twenty whole feet, which is what happens when you sit on your *trasero* all day, listening to the radio while I bring you food. I turned back to the children outside and watched both of their eyes—and mouths—slowly open. The scene of this old, Black, wheezing *gordo* was not something familiar to those in this neighborhood or any of the others like it in this upscale county. And few people ever saw Mr. Percy. If he needed something, I would go get it while he just sat in his chair. The only time he ever left the house was for doctor's appointments, and that was an all-day situation every time.

"Paper for school?" Mr. Percy asked. "What the hell is paper for school?"

"It's Christmas wrapping paper," said Skinny. "To put presents in."

"I don't need no wrapping paper because I don't give no presents to nobody," he said, with more anger than required. I'm pretty sure he would have spit on the ground if only he had been outside.

"Oh, well, OK," Skinny said. She turned back to me. "Maybe you would like to buy some wrapping paper yourself, then?" Mr. Percy began shuffling back to the living room.

I felt bad for the girls and thought about it. But twelve dollars for a roll of paper that would cost three dollars at the drugstore? How could I tell them no politely? The easy way, of course. Pretend I didn't understand and that I was broke—the latter of which wasn't untrue.

"Oh sorry, no *dinero*." I shook my head mournfully, as if I might cry at the thought of another Christmas with no gifts.

"Lupe!" yelled the old man. "Hungry!"

Saved by the bell. I handed the catalog back to Sloppy. "I go now," I said and slowly closed the door. They hadn't stepped inside, so it wasn't that hard to send them on their way.

"Nachos!" Mr. Percy yelled. I watched the girls leave, going back across and up the street to the next house, deeper into the cul-de-sac. Then it was off to the kitchen to fetch the Velveeta, which is how he likes his nachos.

CHAPTER SEVENTEEN

Alex

WHEN THE DOORBELL rang, I was deep into my third hour of online poker, my TV blaring HBO in the background. The more noise, the more activity, the faster it was to muddle through the daily horror of life.

I considered not answering it, but I was losing badly, already down a hundred bucks on the day. Maybe this was a sign, divine intervention telling me that I should call it quits for now.

I got up and stumbled to the door—slowly and a little dizzy from getting up too fast, but otherwise intact—and after pulling aside the curtain, I saw through the window that it was not divine intervention. Rather it was two teenage girls, and it was too late to turn around. They had already seen me, and one was waving hello. Sigh.

I opened the door wide, in part because I realized I needed to lean against something to stabilize myself for a moment. The blonde one stuck her hand out by way of introduction. "I'm Eliza, I just moved in next door," she said.

I considered her hand for a moment, wiped my own on my shirt to get it a bit less sweaty, and gave it a shake. She must have taken a confidence class or something, because her grip felt really strong for such a young girl.

"Alex, lived here for years. Been wondering when I'd see one of you, live and in color."

"Yep, here I am." She went on, "So my school is having a fundraiser, and we're selling wrapping paper. Can you support us?"

"You the sister?" I asked the brunette, who bizarrely had a vein of pink running down one side of her hair.

"No, I'm the friend. We're just selling together."

"Got it," I said. "So what's in it for you?"

"What do you mean?" Eliza asked.

"You get a prize or something if you sell the most cup-cakes, right?"

"Sort of, yeah. And it's wrapping paper, not cupcakes," she said.

She was getting increasingly flustered by my insolence, but whatever. "It's a figure of speech. So what's the prize?" I asked. This, I knew, was supposed to be about *supporting the school*, not *bribing the students*. But she played ball with me.

"You get to go in the Money Machine and grab all the cash you can in a minute."

Fair enough. Teach the kids cutthroat capitalism in addi-tion to salesmanship, why not? She was waving the catalog in my face by this point. "I guess I can take a look, but I need to sit down."

I became aware of the all-too-familiar feeling of a small ball of spittle growing in the corner of my mouth. Attempt-ing to avoid embarrassment, I snatched the catalog and turned, subtly wiping my face against my shoulder in the process. I walked back to the couch, leaving the kids behind. Clearly, they had been carefully informed not to enter anyone's home that they didn't know. Sure enough, as I flipped the catalog to the back, there it was in black and white, one of the Rules for Door-to-Door Fundraising. It was rule #2: "Never enter a stranger's house." Rule #1 was "Sell with a parent." I laughed inwardly.

I hollered back as I walked. "Come in if you want!"

There was some muttering between the two. Should they come in; should they wait outside? But I think they just knew I wasn't a threat, so in they came, shutting the door behind them.

I plopped back on the couch where I had been lying and muted the TV. It was a *Game of Thrones* replay, which was risky because of the boobs situation, but I figured the odds were in my favor that we'd be safe while they were in the house. How long could this possibly take?

I perused the catalog and quickly deemed that the stuff inside was a bunch of garbage. "Wow, this looks like a bunch of garbage," I said.

"It's just wrapping paper," Eliza said. "How bad can it be?"

"It's so small," I said. "And a lot of it is ugly."

"Well, pick something that's not ugly. Look," she said while pointing at the open page, "the one with the snow-flakes is pretty."

It wasn't bad, but the reality was, I had not wrapped a present for anyone in close to a decade. With my shaky hands, I was reasonably sure I wouldn't be able to wrap a present, anyway. Scissors? Forget it. On the rare occasions when I needed to send a token present to someone in my extended family—like Josh's wedding three years ago—I just emailed an Amazon gift card. No one had ever complained as far as I could remember. No one said thank you either, but whatever.

I was torn. Should I send her packing? Or buy something to make her feel better and be a proverbial good neighbor? The girls stood there in silence, and I could see them slowly scanning the room, taking it all in. What a sight it must have been to see a lone, middle-aged man in a den of floral pink and olive green, gold tassels on the upholstery and drapes, not to mention the many sculptural owls staring out from the built-in shelving that was now partially obscured by a large-screen TV I'd plunked on a card table. I swear I saw one roll her eyes at the other.

I thought about kicking them out right there but, you know, I would have done the same thing as them to get a chance at some free cash. Well, to be honest, at her age I probably would have thrown away the catalog and said nothing to my parents about it. As a casual anarchist teenager, I didn't sell anything for charity. Although that Money Machine did sound like a good incentive.

"What do you think?" she asked, interrupting my daydream.

"Oh. Right." I tried to pull it together. "OK, give me the snowflake one and throw in the little bear in the stocking." I didn't ever get a Christmas tree, for obvious reasons, but I didn't mind being a little festive when the temperature dropped down. Change of scenery.

The two girls exchanged an excited glance. It was their first sale, I could tell, in part because the order sheet inside the catalog was totally blank.

"Great!" she cried, snatching the catalog back and pulling out a pen. "Snowflake paper and bear-in-stocking...key chain. It's not an ornament, but I guess you can use it however you want. The paper's $12 and the bear is $13.50 so that's..." She trailed off.

"That would be $25.50," I said after a few seconds of waiting. "For real, you can't do 12 plus 13?"

"It's 12 plus 13.50," she retorted.

I started to argue the obvious, but she blurted out over me, "I'm just not good in math, OK?"

"Fine, whatever. Is there tax?"

Her eyes popped open wide like a deer caught in the headlights, as she clearly had no idea if tax had to be collected. She flipped the catalog over and began scouring the fine print.

"We have an 8.5 percent tax rate here, so it's another...$2.17," I said, after working out the math in my head.

Both girls slowly looked up from the paper at me. "Anyone able to add that up?" I asked.

The friend pulled out her phone and tapped away at the calculator app. Seeing I was right, she asked, "How did you *do* that?"

I shrugged. "I've always been good at math, but there are a lot of tricks you can take with problems like that. You kind of just back your way into the answer. I had a book on math secrets and shortcuts when I was a kid, and I guess it's just one of those things that has stuck with me."

"I can't *even*," Eliza said. It's rare to see a teenage child look genuinely impressed, but the girl seemed truly dazzled, her mouth gaping open.

"You can even," I said. "So, is there tax or not?"

She went back to scrutinizing the paperwork and shrugged. "Looks like not."

"OK, so how do I pay for this?"

"A check is preferred."

Oh brother, a check was definitely not preferred by me, and I could tell that today's shakes were going to make writing longhand pretty much impossible.

"If you need a check, you're going to have to fill it out. I can sign it," I said.

"Uh, I don't know how."

"Well, it isn't that hard. If you get my checkbook I'll give you the check for—what?" I asked, quizzing her.

"For $25.50."

"Right. It's on the kitchen counter, right over there," I said, pointing. I pretty much only ever used it for paying the property taxes on the house.

I'm sure the mess in the kitchen was something else—the weekly maid service didn't come until tomorrow, and I liked to give them a challenge—but she came back quickly enough. With screwy hair like hers, she didn't have much of a leg to stand on. I could tell she was biting her tongue. The girl was a bit of a punk, but I saw a lot of myself in her.

Maybe having her as a neighbor wouldn't be so bad. It's not like she was moving in here with me, after all.

I walked Eliza through filling out the check. Explaining how to write out the numbers in words instead of numerals led to another semi-argument and one voided check, but eventually she got it. When she handed me the pen to sign, I leaned over the coffee table—glass, brass border—to try to write my name down on the signature line. It was slow going, the shaky, jiggling script looking almost cartoonish. I got a rough "A" out and the rest of it was just a scribble. Still, it took at least ten seconds, and again I could hear the girls' thoughts: *What the hell is wrong with this guy?*

I handed her the checkbook and told her to rip it out—carefully—and she did.

"Wow, Mr.—"

"It's just Alex," I interrupted.

"OK. Thanks so much for this," Eliza said.

"You're right, by the way. You are our first sale," the other one said.

"We're supposed to have all the stuff in about six weeks, in plenty of time for Christmas, and I'll deliver it directly." Eliza put the check in her pocket and smoothed out the catalog to present to her next victim.

"Super. Can't wait," I said. "You can show yourselves out, I assume."

"Yeah," Eliza said. "I guess I'll see you around the neighborhood then."

"Sure thing," I said. "Sure thing."

CHAPTER EIGHTEEN

Peg

THE MOMENT I'D been waiting for had finally arrived, and my expectations were wholly surpassed. The visitors were every bit as delightful as I had hoped. The new neighbor girl, Eliza, had a certain bohemian quality that reminded me of my youth. And her friend, Jean Claire, was just so charming and spunky. That devilish streak in her hair—she would be capable of mischief.

And here they had given me a catalog of goodies to peruse, with Christmas right around the corner. OK, it was a few corners away, but still coming up. Wonderful wrapping paper, bags, and so many tchotchkes that would look just perfect decorating the house.

It was so hard to choose! "Maybe I can call out the items I want, and you can mark them down on the paper for me?" I asked.

"Uh, sure!" Eliza seemed confused but excited. Not as much as me, but still excited.

"Do you want some tea first?" I asked. "Do you girls drink tea?"

They both demurred. Starbucks junkies, surely.

"OK," I said, flipping back to the beginning of the catalog. "I'll take these wrapping papers." I read off the item number and prices. "The multipack of gift bags and, let's see…the squirrel snow globe ornament, the lighted reindeer statuette, and the wreath-shaped napkin rings. And I do like this cute Christmas sweater ornament. Let's get that too."

"The ugly Christmas sweater one?" Eliza asked.

I checked the fine print and was a little surprised. It looked cute to me. "Yes, the *ugly* sweater." Jean Claire was adding up the prices as we went with the calculator on her iPhone, which was smart. "What's the total?" I asked.

"It's $124.50," Jean Claire said. "Ten items, right, Eliza?"

She confirmed it. "Wonderful, do you need a check?" I asked.

They did. I got my checkbook from my purse—they probably wouldn't appreciate my Simple Springtime check design, but it was important to me—and wrote the check out as instructed on the back of the catalog.

"Wow, this is great, Mrs. Jurgensen," Eliza said, eying the name on the check. "I don't think my parents will even buy this much stuff."

"Yeah, thanks for supporting the school," Jean Claire said.

"Please, call me Peg," I said. "Anyway, I don't *really* need this much wrapping paper, but I do like to help out. It's all so beautiful."

"We'll deliver it personally in a few weeks when it comes in," Eliza said. "Peg," she added, perhaps a bit too slowly.

"That sounds wonderful," I said. "You know where to find me."

CHAPTER NINETEEN
Eliza

"THIS IS *AMAZE*," I said as we left Peg's place and continued up the hill, now entering the big-bulb turnaround of the cul-de-sac. "We've already sold twelve items and we haven't even talked to our parents."

"Getting to twenty is going to be so easy," Jean Claire said. "We'll be done in like fifteen minutes."

Next door to Peg's was the spooky house that had burned down. Well, maybe not burned *down* but burned, anyway. The roof was mostly gone, and the upstairs of the house was badly charred and crumbling. The windows downstairs were now boarded up, with numerous official notices stapled all over the front. The whole thing looked like it was sagging in the middle, but maybe that was just an illusion. The grass and weeds were growing tall around the place, making it look very much like the apocalypse had started right here in the middle of suburbia.

We stopped to stare. "What do you think happened?" Jean Claire asked.

"Dunno," I said. "Probably smoking in bed."

"Yeah, probably."

The brick house at the very tip of the cul-de-sac was an

old-timey-looking place and the biggest house on the block. To get there meant climbing up a steep driveway, which was at the end of the already-steep road. If you walked here all the way from our house at the bottom of the hill in one go, you'd probably be too exhausted to talk. We trudged up the driveway, panting. The manicured hillside on either side of the narrow drive was very pretty, and a stark contrast to the wild, out-of-control yard surrounding the burnt house. I could definitely see living in a place like this, if you never had to walk anywhere, at least.

I rang the bell of the brick home—one of those *ding dong, ding dong, ding ding ding dong* bells—and waited. The door eventually opened, just a crack. I could see the face on the other side was a man, probably about my dad's age, with a mustache, which always made me laugh. I started giggling a little, and Jean Claire gave me the side-eye.

Mustache opened the door all the way, obviously not concerned that we were there to rob him. "Yes?" he asked.

I had my routine down. "Hi, I'm Eliza, your new neighbor down the street. We're selling Christmas wrapping paper and other items for our school, and I was hoping you would take a look at the catalog."

He shrugged and took it without saying a word. As he flipped through the catalog, I could hear noises coming from upstairs. Like a drag...*thump*. Drag...*thump*.

"Do you have kids?" I asked.

Mustache looked up from the catalog and paused. "Dogs," he said.

"Oh." Drag...*thump*.

After that he hurriedly picked out two items—both sets of gift bags, no paper—and paid in cash. It wasn't until he filled out the order form that I saw his name: Darren Charles.

"OK, work to do," he said, shooing us from the entry hall and out of the house.

"Great, well, thank you," I said. "We'll be delivering the items in a few weeks."

He didn't catch the end of that. He'd already shut the door.

CHAPTER TWENTY

Klaus

I SAW THE whole thing from my occasional observation point in the window-filled turret at the very top of the house. First they walked across the street from the new house, then diagonally back to her next-door neighbor's house, then to the smaller house tucked away up the hill and in the trees. They stopped to consider the house that had burned down some years ago, before my time, then on to the big house on the hill, the one where the strange man with the thick mustache was always coming and going. Darren Charles. I'd met him once, and he was the one I kept my eye on. In fact, he was the only one on the street I ever saw at all. From what I could glimpse of his driveway, he was either going to and from work, or going to and from Costco, coming back with boxes and boxes full of food every weekend. I would have assumed he had a large family, but I had yet to see another person come in or out in some ten years living here. So either he was hiding an army in his attic or he was preparing for *Weltuntergang*. The end of the world, as they say.

They left the Charles house and continued around the cul-de-sac to the inevitable: my house. I knew they would make it here soon enough, and I was preparing myself for the doorbell to ring. It would have been better if one of them had come by herself, but I supposed a naïve twosome would be workable. For now.

"You don't look like sisters," I said, after opening the door to their ringing. "I assume you are the new neighbors down the street, yes?"

"Oh, we aren't sisters," the taller one said. "She's just my friend from school. I'm Eliza. I'm the new neighbor."

I chose not to put my hand out for a shake. Too forward. Hold back.

"Ah, the friend. And what brings you to my home today?"

"We're raising money for our school. Selling holiday wrapping paper and gifts."

"You're our last stop," said the shorter one, the friend.

"It's very surprising to get a visitor," I said. "The cul-de-sac has few people living on it, and none seem to venture out on foot."

"We're starting to realize that," Eliza said.

"And the hill is no joke," the friend said.

"Indeed, it isn't. Very steep!" I laughed a little. So observant, the little one. "Well, let's have a look at what you're selling."

I flipped through the catalog she offered, and Eliza was only too happy to narrate my reading of it. "That one's the best seller so far," she said, pointing to a roll of wrapping paper adorned with fluffy white *schneeflocken*. "We've sold a lot of wrapping paper, really. The lady across the street bought like five rolls of it. But there's a lot of other—"

"Lady across the street?" I asked.

"Yeah, right there," she said, pointing.

I peered out the window at the house, which was well-maintained, but I couldn't specifically recall anyone going in or out of it.

"Yeah, a nice old lady," Eliza said. "I mean, a really nice woman. Not an old lady." She paused, awkwardly. "She's really nice."

"I see," I said.

I continued flipping quickly through the catalog, but none of it was very interesting. "*Ach*, well, perhaps I can buy a roll of paper from you if it's for your school, yes?"

"Yes," she said. "Which one would you like?"

I flipped back toward the middle of the catalog. One of the papers had caught my eye, a medium green color with olive-colored evergreens and metallic gold lines creating a pattern atop it. I found the contrast of the soothing green and sparkling gold to be quite exciting to the eye—and *nostalgisch*. "That one."

"Really?" she said, making a face. "OK."

"What, you don't like?" I asked.

"No, the customer is always right," she said. "That's what my dad says."

"Well, he is a very wise man. How do I pay you?"

"It's twelve dollars, so either a check or cash is fine." I realized I had been presented with a sudden yet perfect opportunity. Destiny, or *schicksal*—perhaps. "I'm sure I can find twelve dollars in cash," I said. We were still standing in the threshold, so I pushed things just a bit further. "Why don't you come inside while I go find my wallet?"

Eliza and the friend looked at each other. I knew what they were thinking: don't go into a stranger's house, of course. Probably another thing her father said.

"Umm," she stalled.

"It could take me a while to find it," I said, smiling. The smile was the first rule in gaining trust. I stepped back from the door, farther into the house, leaving the portal wide open and making it clear I would not slam it behind them, turning my back and slowly walking away to subconsciously let them know that I trusted them as well. We were all friends here, all good neighbors.

After a long hesitation, she finally called out, "We can wait here; it's fine."

"Very well," I called over my shoulder. "I'll be right back."

The game wasn't up, of course, and I took my time getting my wallet. I knew right where it was: on the coffee table in the living room, just a dozen steps away, right around the corner and out of sight of the girls. But I lingered in the living room, standing by a bookcase for several minutes, wondering if they would eventually venture inside to look for me, call out, or simply leave, abandoning the sale. I ran a finger over the spines, thinking about what it would be like to wrap my hands around their warm, skinny necks, one at a time, maybe do one while the other one watched? The books were dusty. I would need to get the *putzfrau* in soon to clean up.

The girls did nothing. They just stood there, and when I finally gave up and came around the corner, they were both just staring at their phones. They were in no rush. We all had plenty of time.

"*Ach*, sorry," I said. "Twelve dollars, here you go."

"Great, thanks." She had filled out a form while I was gone and already marked my line as paid. "We'll be delivering the orders in a few weeks. Obviously, I know your address, but what's the name for the order?" she asked.

"Klaus," I said. "Klaus Fischer."

CHAPTER TWENTY-ONE
Peg

M Y YOUNG VISITORS had left hours ago, but I was still over the moon with excitement. I could tell that Eliza and I were going to have so much in common, and there was surely so much I could teach her. I couldn't wait to see her again, but I realized I didn't have any way to get in touch with her. I would have to wait for her to come back to deliver the wrapping paper I'd bought earlier in the day. I wouldn't dare drop by her house unannounced.

I was feeling so good about things that I figured I could celebrate a little, and the best way to do that would be to make a special meal for myself, something I hadn't eaten in a long time. Fettucine carbonara had always been a favorite when I was younger, but Jack didn't like eggs, so I never made it while he was alive. I couldn't really remember quite how it went, so I trotted out my trusty *Better Homes & Gardens New Cook Book*, ring-bound of course, and found the right page, the paper stained and water-damaged and no longer able to lie flat even after years of being smushed on the shelf.

Ah, now it was all coming back. Onion cooked in butter, then bacon and prosciutto, chopped up. I could get pancetta if I wanted to be decadent. Then some wine, a mix of whipping cream and milk, and an egg yolk, which makes it gooey and delicious. Some Parmesan cheese to finish. Pour it all atop fresh pasta and serve hot. I could have a simple green salad on the side for the vitamins and the fiber.

It was a fat bomb, for sure, even with the salad. But I'd done a half hour of TV yoga earlier and—you know, what if I walked to the grocery store to pick up the ingredients instead of driving? Seemed like I would come out even on the calories, right? But the dinner hour was approaching, so if I was walking, I'd better head out now. I tied on the tennis shoes I wore on my increasingly infrequent hikes—they weren't even dirty—slung my purse over my shoulder, and headed out the door.

The walk to the store was quiet, and I walked extra slow as I reached the bottom of the cul-de-sac to try to get a look through the windows of Eliza's house, maybe catch a glimpse of her and her family. I didn't see anyone, though all the lights were on. Perhaps they were out shopping as well. Maybe I'd run into them at the store. Best to hurry.

Around the corner and down the long, meandering connecting road I walked, trying to enjoy the warm air of late summer and, as Dr. Starr had once told me years ago, practicing my mindful breathing if I started to feel anxious. Breathe in, count to four. Breathe out, count to four. Repeat. It worked better when you were sitting still or lying down, but it was fine at a measured walking pace, too. Besides, I wasn't feeling stressed at the moment. I told myself I was happy, and that the evening would be even better than the day had been.

Sunset Market was not crowded. It never was, really, and I quickly found the ingredients I needed. I'd been shopping here for fifteen years and knew the layout better than the employees, although to this day no one ever greeted me by name. Just that smile of friendly recognition and a courteous "how ya doin' today?" before ringing up my items and asking if I needed a bag. I always brought my own, as I kept a super-portable one in my purse.

Was it too early for dinner? I was feeling hungry after the walk to the store and back, and though it wasn't quite six o'clock, I figured I could get started. I liked to get everything set out on the counter before I started cooking—like they do it on TV—and I had a lot of little prep bowls I bought on Amazon just for this purpose. With just myself to cook for, there was plenty of room in the dishwasher for all the extra stuff.

I chopped the bacon (no pancetta, sadly), portioned out the cream, and separated the egg. I washed the salad greens, measured out the already-grated Parmesan cheese, and had just turned on the fire beneath a pot of water on the stove when I took one last look through the recipe to make sure I had everything covered. And there it was: parsley. It was just a tablespoon of snipped parsley leaves for garnish, but what an important garnish it was! Carbonara was just a sea of yellow noodles with some brown bacon chunks in it. The parsley really did add something that made the dish look so much more appealing, so much fresher. Could I skip it?

If I drove, I could be back with the parsley in ten

minutes, maybe fifteen if there was someone in line at checkout, which I doubted. I didn't *need* it, but this was a special dinner, and I just knew I would regret it forever if I didn't take the time to make it right.

So I grabbed my purse, took out my keys, and fired up the Volvo in the garage for the first time in days. It took me all of three minutes to get back to Sunset and park. I walked inside and headed straight for produce.

CHAPTER TWENTY-TWO

Klaus

THERE WAS SOMETHING familiar about her, an older but fit woman who was too short to reach some greenery on the top shelf. She was struggling to get the last bunch of parsley, pushed way to the back of the bin, and—as was the norm at Sunset Market—there were no employees around to ask for help.

"Can I get that for you?" I asked from behind her, placing my small basket of groceries on the floor.

She jumped and quickly withdrew her hand, stepping back and almost crashing into me.

"I'm sorry, I didn't mean to startle you, but perhaps you could use a hand?" I said as she turned around. She was quite pretty, but her wide-eyed expression made her look a little wild, *verrückt*. I had seen her before; I was sure of it.

"Oh," she stammered. "No, I'm sorry." She laughed nervously, though I didn't understand what was funny or what she had to be sorry about. "I didn't see you."

"It's fine," I said. "Here." At 1.9 meters tall, it was simple for me to reach the parsley and hand it over to her. "Do you have a bag for it?"

"Oh, no. Sorry," she said, again. She quickly tore off a

cellophane bag and struggled to open it. The parsley dripped water onto the ground while I waited patiently. As she got it open, she said it again. "Sorry."

"You keep apologizing, but I assure you there is no need," I said, smiling.

She giggled a bit. "Oh, sorry!" she said. I wasn't sure if it was ironic, but I doubted it. I dropped the parsley into the bag for her. I could see she had no wedding ring, but she was wearing other jewelry, so I assumed that meant she was unmarried. That would be very rare for this area, but not unheard of.

"I'm sorry—there, now I said it—but I am sure I know you from somewhere," I said.

"Oh, I don't think so. I'm good with faces," she said, "and you don't look familiar."

"Well I assume you live nearby, correct? Perhaps we both go to the same gym." I didn't go to a gym, but I was fishing.

"No, I work out at home."

"Do you ever go to Dante's?" Our local dive bar.

"Oh, no." Of course she didn't.

"Well, it must be something else. I live around the corner, up near the hiking trails on the mountain, so maybe I've seen you out there," I said, giving up.

"Oh, well so do I. There's a small cul-de-sac up that way—"

"This can't be!" I said, interrupting. "We must be neighbors. I think then that you live across the street from me, next to the house that's fire-damaged."

"Yes!" she said. Her eyes lit up and she relaxed her posture. "And you must live in the big house with the turret on top, and with the wide stretch of wooded hillside next to it. Is that your property?"

"It is," I said.

"I love that house. I can't see it well from my window due to all the trees, but I enjoy looking at it whenever I leave home."

"Yes, I'm sure I've seen you, coming or going. Is it just you then?"

"Yeah, just me. All by my lonesome."

Interesting. I said, "You won't believe this, but I was just talking about you. Or rather, two girls were at my house talking about you to me, earlier today."

"Eliza and Jean Claire! Aren't they charming?"

"Very much so," I said.

"Isn't it wonderful to have a new neighbor on the street? And I guess you're a new neighbor, too, since we've never met. Two new neighbors in one day." She looked away almost dreamily as she spoke.

"Klaus Fischer," I said, extending my hand.

"Peg Jurgensen," she replied, shifting the parsley to her left hand to shake mine. Both of our hands were a bit wet and cold, which was remarkably unerotic.

"How long have you lived on the cul-de-sac?" I asked.

"Oh, fifteen years or so. More, I guess."

"Unbelievable! How could we not have met until today? I've lived here for a decade."

"Honestly, I don't get out much. Kind of a homebody. I was just in the middle of cooking dinner, actually, but I forgot the parsley, you see."

"What are you cooking?" I asked.

"Fettucine carbonara, an old favorite."

"That requires parsley, does it?"

"A little."

"I see."

I considered Peg Jurgensen during a momentary pause in the conversation. She was a skittish one, and I knew there was a story to be told about why, but this wasn't the time for it. Yet she had not pulled away, and despite her being in the middle of preparing a meal, had not excused herself. She was smiling, a bit, so why not press my luck? "Well, perhaps we could get together at some point in the near future. I could share one of *my* old favorites with you."

"OK, maybe." She was hesitant, but it wasn't a rejection. In fact, she was blushing. I quickly looked around, out of habit, to see if anyone was watching. The store wasn't empty, but no one paid attention to two people of our ages having a quiet discussion in produce. I was confident we weren't being actively observed, anyway.

"Give me your phone number and I'll get in touch with you. Perhaps a coffee? I would say you could stop by any time, but I travel often for my work."

"What do you do?" she asked.

"Computer consultant. I set up and fine-tune systems for big companies all over the country. I'm sure you would find it fascinating for me to talk about." I laughed broadly. Sometimes women didn't realize I was joking when I said that.

She laughed a little, relaxing just enough. "Do you have a pen?" she asked.

"Just tell it to me."

She recited her number quickly. "You don't need to write it down?"

"No, I'll remember." I would write it down as soon as she was out of sight, but I thought it was a nice trick to act like I could easily remember it.

"OK then," she said, skeptical but perhaps also relieved that I would not actually call her.

"Until next time, then," I said. "Enjoy your carbonara." I put my arm out to shake hands again, and she accepted it. Both of our hands were finally dry. The encircling of our fingers felt much warmer than I had expected.

CHAPTER TWENTY-THREE

Peg

WHY, WHY, WHY *did you do that?* I asked myself on the drive home. Such a fool!

Yes, Klaus seemed nice enough. That German accent was a little strange, but I guessed it was something I could probably get used to as long as he wasn't going to do something like make me drink schnapps. Heck, maybe he could teach me the language. I may be sixty-four years old, but I could still learn some new tricks. *Swallow your fear, Peg. Embrace the future.*

But there was a bigger concern. I didn't know how old Klaus was, but his graying hair and the light lines on his face made me guess he was in his early fifties. He was certainly handsome, his swept-back hairdo giving him quite a distinguished look. He had been dressed casually but not in the slovenly shorts and flip-flops you usually saw draping the pudgy bodies of the older men in the neighborhood. Once the men around here turned forty, it was like their wardrobes miraculously disintegrated, leaving behind nothing in their drawers aside from ratty T-shirts, sweatpants, and San Francisco 49ers merchandise.

Peg, you could surely do worse.

But did I want to do anything at all? Surely, his invitation meant more than a platonic dinner. What would be the point, at my age, of starting a relationship with someone new? Romance—what would that even be like in 2019? Making out on the sofa? He would expect to have sex at some point, probably soon. Did I need to have protection? Would he want to see paperwork to prove that I don't have any STDs?

And what about this dinner, anyway? German food— schnitzel or sauerbraten, probably. What was sauerbraten, anyway? I would have to consult the *Better Homes & Gardens New Cook Book* when I got home. The name alone didn't sound very appetizing.

Calm down, Peg. It's just a dinner. It may not even be that. He had been very vague about the invitation. In fact, it hadn't been an invitation at all, just some mention of—what was it? Sharing some "old favorites" with me. No date had been set. He had probably forgotten my phone number already.

I was pulling into the driveway. I was so distracted, I had almost left the parsley at the grocery store but remembered to grab the bag at the last second. I parked in the garage, shut the door, and put Klaus out of my mind for a moment. I had dinner to finish, and the water for my pasta was now boiling, as I'd left the burner on underneath it. Terribly dangerous, but a time-saver now that I was home and could whip everything together.

I dropped the hard noodles into the water and slid the chopped bacon in the pan so it could fry up. As I washed my hands in the sink, my gaze drifted to the entry hall. Was Klaus coming home yet? Drying my hands on a towel, I quickly walked over to the window in front of the house, peering out to see if I could catch him entering his driveway, but the street was empty.

CHAPTER TWENTY-FOUR

Klaus

NOW THIS WAS unexpected. But was it necessarily a bad thing? Twice in one day, a blessing had been presented to me. If I were not to take advantage of this incredible opportunity, it would be like spitting in the face of God.

I stopped to remind myself that the *hausfrau* had not gone smoothly, and I had since made an agreement with myself: stop at six. Six was a good number, and it was much better than five. Ending on five would have been a grave mistake. Still, I was not in a competition. There was no reason to tempt fate.

But, this was new information, wasn't it? And it deserved new analysis. The nurse, number six, *had* gone smoothly. Perhaps that was the real sign I should be paying attention to—a calling that had been urging me to return to duty.

And really, seven was a very good number. Eight was also a good number. Which was the *best* number, though? Seven may be lucky, but it sounded rather pedestrian these days because of its reputation. The number eight was good luck for the Chinese. And, of course, it was larger.

It was best to take things one at a time, of course. Going for eight wasn't off the table, but there was certainly no rush to get there. First, there was seven to consider.

That said, I did not like to dawdle. The longer you spent with them before you took them meant nothing except a lot of additional risk. Someone could see you. You could leave behind evidence. She could snap a picture of you and send it to a friend when you had your back turned. Too much familiarity was very dangerous. If I was going to do this, I really needed to focus on what was right in front of me: the very real and unexpected prospect of number seven.

But perhaps this was madness. Perhaps I should see if a romance might happen with the Jurgensen woman. It had been years since I'd been in an actual relationship—and Dora was still with us, last I heard. Perhaps Peg was someone who could help me take my mind off my thirst. Maybe she was even a good cook, despite her apparent forgetfulness.

She had appeared very lonely at the grocery store. No wedding ring. The secret to success was to take someone with no significant attachments. It would be foolish not to at least, as they say, test the waters. See what the possibilities were. Feel her out a bit.

I would call in a few days. Who knew what might happen?

CHAPTER TWENTY-FIVE

Lew

I WAS LATE again to dinner, but not by more than a few minutes. Judy wouldn't say anything about that as long as I complimented whatever she had made for dinner. "Mmmmm!" I would need to exclaim after my first bite. "Even better than last time!" I had practiced in the car.

Getting used to the commute would take some time, but I'd get there. My former fifteen-minute subway ride was now at least an hour each way as I trekked into and out of San Francisco. Getting home by six-thirty for dinner wasn't easy, and even a small fender bender could throw another half hour on top of the commute. Lizzie didn't care—she was well past the age of coming to greet me at the door when I got home—but it was tough on me to get home and be so completely exhausted. I'm sure I would get used to that, too.

The cul-de-sac was intended to be a fresh start, to get Lizzie into a better school and fresher air, and most of all, to bring us closer together as a family, like it used to be, when Lizzie was a baby. But with my commute now stretching regularly into darkness, I was away from home longer than ever. I moved to the City in the first place because it meant I wouldn't have to drive so much, but now I was a slave to the car.

The weekends meant a reprieve from it all. Even I had to admit the change of scenery was at least refreshing, with the squealing bus brakes and late-night screaming matches replaced by the near-constant chirping of all manner of birds and the midnight howls of creatures I had yet to identify. I knew I'd have to put in double the effort on Saturday if I really wanted to reconnect with Lizzie.

Finally I made it home, and I tore into the garage and up the steps to find Judy waiting at the table, places set. She hadn't called Lizzie to dinner yet, so I hollered up the stairs for her to come down, which she did begrudgingly after a brief delay. Dinner was some kind of chicken and rice casserole made with cream of mushroom soup. Green beans on the side with store-bought rolls.

I washed my hands to kill some time and took a peek at my phone before sitting down with Lizzie. I never liked having to wait for her. Judy said nothing. She just sat upright in her usual seat, in an absent-minded daze.

I broke the silence. "So, how was school?"

"Fine," Lizzie said.

"Nothing special today?" Judy asked.

"We turned in the order forms for the wrapping paper—that's about it," Lizzie said.

"Well, how'd you do?" Judy asked, probing for something, anything.

"Fine." A long pause. "I guess Jean Claire and I sold the most in the class."

Judy's eyes lit up like she'd won the lottery. "Oh my

God, that's awesome. So you get to go in, what is it, the Money Monster?"

"The Money Machine," I chimed in. See, I listened.

"The Money Machine," Lizzie repeated as if I weren't there. "And I don't know yet. They pick from all the top sellers at random."

"How's your schoolwork going?" I asked, striving for relevance between bites of food. I glanced down at my plate and suddenly remembered my lines. "Mmmmm! So good, Jude! So good."

She smiled back at me. Sincerely, I think.

"Fine," Lizzie said. There was silence for a while as we ate. Then, reluctantly: "I am having some issues with algebra."

A problem, and one I could maybe solve! "Really, what are you working on?"

"Well, I understand how to solve the x equals whatever equations, but when there's x and y, I just don't get it."

"It's tricky," I said. "Do you want me to help you with your homework?"

"It's not like that, Dad. I just don't get it. My teacher sucks."

Judy chimed in, always angling to be of help. "Maybe we could look for a tutor?"

I braced for the inevitable vitriol, but Lizzie surprised me by not rolling her eyes. She took a bite and turned her attention to Judy's end of the table. "Actually," she said, "I may have an idea about that."

CHAPTER TWENTY-SIX

Eliza

"NOW TELL ME again why you think this man would be interested in tutoring you?" Mom asked, as we slowly walked up the hill, deeper into the cul-de-sac. She was struggling with the steepness of the road, even though it was only a few dozen steps from our house. Out of shape.

"I don't know," I said. "I just have a feeling that he would want to do it."

"But he's not a teacher?"

"I don't think so. He doesn't look like a teacher."

"What does a teacher look like?"

"I dunno," I said. "Like a nerd."

"Well, I'm not sure how I feel about this, Liz—Eliza." She used my preferred name so as not to anger me further, I'm sure. "What if he's a—a pedophile?"

"Stop it, Mom! He's not a freakin' pedophile. He can barely walk."

"He could try to drug you—"

"Just stop!" I walked ahead of her to the house next door and rang the bell, not even waiting for Mom to catch up. She arrived before he answered, the slightest bit out of breath.

As it had before, the door slowly opened wide, and our new neighbor Alex took up a kind of haggard position that pushed one shoulder hard into the doorframe, awkwardly propping his ultra-skinny body up. His dark brown but slightly graying hair was a bit of a mess, overdue for a cut, and he looked like he hadn't shaved in at least two days.

"Ah, it's you again!" Alex said. "Who's this?"

My mom butted in and put her hand out. "I'm Judy van Damal. We're your new neighbors next door."

"Ah, hello." Alex shook her hand loosely. "I've already met your daughter and her friend. How many more of you are there?"

"Just my husband, Lew. I'm sure you'll meet him over the fence in the backyard, maybe when you're both out mowing the grass."

Alex turned and looked back at nothing in particular. "Mowing the grass, right."

What was my mother even talking about? The man could barely walk. What was she thinking that he could mow the grass. I suppressed a snicker and crossed my fingers in the hopes that he wouldn't invite her inside. Alex said nothing further, waiting for Mom to get to the point.

"Well, Lizzie here has something to ask you," Mom said.

"OK, go ahead," Alex said.

I stood up straight and planted my legs shoulder-width apart, the "power stance" my dad had taught me to help speak with confidence. "Well, you're so good with math, I was wondering if you would help me with my algebra. Like, as a tutor."

Alex looked terribly, terribly confused, and he said nothing.

"Lizzie just needs someone who can help her get a better grounding in the class," Mom said. "I don't have the brain for math, and Lew, well, he doesn't have the patience to be a good teacher."

"I see," Alex said. "I'm really not a teacher either, though."

"Oh, what do you do?" my mother probed.

Alex thought for a second. "I'm retired. Actually, I'm independently wealthy. Well, independently self-sufficient at least. Basically, I don't do anything at all."

"Oh, we would pay you, of course," Mom blurted out. I guess she thought he was fishing.

"Well, I don't really need the money."

My mom looked past Alex and into the darkened home. The glow of a television was visible in the distance, as was what looked like a pile of unfolded laundry—perhaps washed, perhaps not. "Maybe Lizzie could help you out around the house then."

"Mom!" I seethed at her. "Maybe you can go home, and I can talk to Alex some more about this myself." I'd brought my math workbook—*Algebra: Structure and Method*—so I could show him some of the things I was having trouble with, just in case he said yes.

"Is that all right with you?" Mom asked Alex.

"Uh, sure," he said, still clearly baffled about this abrupt turn of events in his life.

"Great, well, I wrote all of our contact information on

this paper," she said, handing over a small note card, "in case you ever need to get in touch with us. Or, of course, just drop by any time!" She laughed nervously. Mom really wasn't cut out for small talk, I guess.

Alex and I stood there and watched her walk away— much quicker this time, since she was going downhill— though I suspect she hid behind the hedges down at our house, attempting to eavesdrop. Too far away to hear anything, though.

Finally, Alex turned his attention to me. "I don't like surprise visitors," he said. "You should call first."

"I don't have your number."

"You didn't write it on that form?"

"No, you didn't give it to me, and it wasn't on the check."

"What was that for, again?"

"Wrapping paper, remember? And you bought a teddy bear."

"Did I? All right."

"So," I said, "what's it gonna be? Can you help me with this math?" I thrust the workbook at him, which he took in one hand. I guess it was heavier than he realized, as he nearly dropped it.

"Listen—what was your name again?"

"Eliza."

"Right. Eliza, I'll be honest and say that I just don't think I'm going to be a great teacher for you. I'm just not going to be helpful to you in that way."

"You're so good with numbers, though."

"Well, I don't know about that, but you know that doing math and teaching math—those are two different things."

"You'll never know until you try," I appealed.

"Well, maybe you're the one who's just not trying hard enough," he shot back.

"I don't know why you're being so mean to me," I said. "The lady next door is really nice."

"Maybe she should tutor you in math."

I just stared at him for a moment, his sickly frame drooping ever so slightly. "What's wrong with you, anyway?"

Alex paused. "That's a long story, and I don't know you well enough to tell it. But I have memory loss and trouble with spatial awareness, which makes me dizzy. I have an overproduction of saliva, and sometimes I have seizures, which I promise you don't want to see."

"How did that happen?"

"That's part of the long story."

I stood quietly, waiting for him to break the silence. Alex hefted the algebra book up to his chest and flipped through it for a surprising length of time.

"Well," he finally said, "all of this does look pretty simple. If you can't do this stuff, you're not going to make it through the rest of high school." He closed the book and handed it back, then finally said, "I guess I could teach you some tricks to make it easier."

"Great, how about this weekend?"

"Fine. Saturday at two," he said. "Bring pencils and paper. And the workbook."

"OK, thanks. What do I tell my mom about paying you? If we don't pay you something, she'll think you're a pedo."

Alex laughed—like a real laugh, not a fake laugh like Mom had. He thought for a second. "Tell her to pay whatever she wants."

"OK, see you Saturday," I said. I thought I heard Mom scurrying away from the hedge, back up the driveway to our house, but I wasn't sure.

Alex called out as I walked away, "Cash only! No goddamn checks!"

CHAPTER TWENTY-SEVEN
Klaus

"WELL, HOW WAS your dinner?" I asked.

I was surprised that she had answered. These days, it is all too simple to merely let a call go to voice mail, never to be returned. No one ever answers the phone, so I'd already prepared myself to leave a message.

"Oh, Klaus! I wasn't expecting you!" Peg sounded genuinely surprised. I realized she didn't have my information in her handset, so only my phone number came up. Yet she had answered it anyway, blind. Hoping, perhaps, that a phone call meant good news.

"How did you know it was me?" I asked, laughing.

Peg laughed as well. "Your accent is very distinctive," she said. "I don't think I could forget it."

"Well, I will take that as a compliment."

"You should!"

"So...the dinner?"

"Oh, it was good. But richer than I remembered it. I don't know that I can handle that much egg and cheese in my diet anymore. I still have leftovers."

"Everything is fine in moderation, am I correct?"

"Correct," she said. "Words to live by."

There was more chitchat, but I barely remember it. What I had eaten. Whether I had any family. What sauerbraten was. She said that she was a widow with no children. I had to explain again what I did for a living and why I was often away from home.

It sounded like Peg's life was very empty but that perhaps she was working to change that. "Do you travel?" I asked.

"Not really. I tried going on a cruise a few years ago but got sick the first night. I spent most of the trip in my room, watching TV."

"Sounds like bad luck."

"Maybe so. I guess I'm just cursed!" She laughed. But maybe she wasn't wrong.

"Well, you certainly deserve to see more than what you can spy from your window or in the aisles of Sunset Market."

"I'm not opposed to it," she said. "I just wouldn't know where to go. Not by myself anyway."

"True, traveling alone can be complicated and sometimes lonely, but it can be very rewarding. But I do agree, I always prefer to travel with a companion. Unless it's for work. It is easier and faster to get things done by myself than to have to discuss the situation with a colleague."

"It sounds like you're quite self-sufficient."

"I like to think so," I said. "You have to be in today's world."

"That's so true," she said, wistfully.

"Listen," I continued. "I'm calling because I would like to invite you over for drinks and a light snack if you would be amenable. I have a delightful Riesling I'd love to share with someone."

"Oh, well..." she started, clearly preparing to make an excuse.

I interrupted. "I was going to suggest fondue, but after your comments, perhaps that's not the best choice for the occasion, and the *leberknoedel* is probably out of the question."

"*Leber...?*"

"*Leberknoedel.* It's a dumpling made from beef liver, and it's quite delicious. My mother used to cook it for me as a child, when I still lived in Germany."

"Ah," she said, audibly recoiling at the concept.

I tried another angle. "Smoked salmon, perhaps? Seafood and Riesling are always delightful together."

Another pause, and I continued. "Perhaps Wednesday? I have a short trip coming up to Los Angeles, but I'll be back after lunch. Cocktail hour? Five o'clock? Strictly casual."

Finally, I had worn her down. "Well, OK. That sounds lovely. Can I bring anything?"

"Absolutely not," I said. "Just your pretty little head."

Peg laughed.

CHAPTER TWENTY-EIGHT
Jean Claire

"I LIKE YOUR accent wall," Eliza said, looking at the single, bright purple wall that stood out as a colorful contrast in my otherwise pink room. "Maybe I should paint one in my room."

"You'd need to unpack first, don't you think?" I said, not really looking up from the old episode of *New Girl* streaming on my phone. I had one earbud in, one out, so I could pay attention to at least some of what Eliza was saying. It was enough to get the gist, anyway.

"What are you, my mom?" she replied in mock anger. "Besides, it's easier to paint if the room isn't full of stuff. I'd just have to move it all out anyway."

"So when's that gonna happen?"

"Well, I guess I have to pick out colors first. How do you do that, anyway?"

"You go to the paint store," I said. "They have swatches."

"Swatches. I guess I need swatches." Eliza kicked her legs on the bed where we were flopped side by side, avoiding the day's homework. I could tell she was considering it. "Maybe my dad can take me this weekend after tutoring."

Tutoring? "What tutoring?" I asked.

"My neighbor is going to tutor me in algebra starting this Saturday," she said.

I stopped the video and took out my other earbud. This required my full attention. "What neighbor?"

"The guy next door, Alex."

I literally could not believe my ears. "The creepy guy who could barely walk?" I said. "*What* are you even *talking* about?"

"He's not that much of a creeper. Besides, he's obviously a math genius. And he said he would help me."

"What, you asked him yourself?"

"With my mom."

"And Mr. Shakyhands is going to teach you algebra? What, was he a math teacher or something?"

"No."

"What was his job, then?"

"Uh, I'm not sure," Eliza said. God, this girl was thick in the head.

"You're crazy. My mom would never let me get tutored by a pedo."

"Omigod, he's not a pedo. You saw him for yourself. He's, like, an old man."

I shrugged. "Your neighbors are pretty weird, you know," I said.

"Yeah," Eliza said. "I know. Everyone is weird these days."

I was well-attuned to the sound of Mother coming up the stairs in her clogs, and the conversation that was about to take place I could have recited exactly.

First she would knock, *maybe*, two light taps, then the door would open before I could answer. The door would swing open wide all the way, but she would not enter, standing behind the threshold as if an invisible force prevented her from setting foot inside. Today she was wearing the ankle-length, navy-blue dress that was part of her small, regular wardrobe rotation. It did her figure and her stringy, black hair no favors.

"How much longer will your friend be here?" Mother asked, which was pretty rude considering Eliza was right next to me.

"I think she's leaving soon," I said.

"Good, because it will be dinnertime soon, and then it will be time for worship."

"I know," I said, trying not to gag.

Mother stared at me for a moment before turning and leaving in silence.

Eliza knew by now that this was her cue to start packing up, which was easy because she'd never even taken her computer out of her backpack, and to begin the long walk home. It would have to be on foot. I hadn't had to directly warn Eliza. Somehow she, and everyone else, already knew without being told: Mother was not someone you asked for a ride.

CHAPTER TWENTY-NINE
Alex

"DO YOU WANT to walk me through the pictures again?"

Peg was over. No food this time, which was unusual. But I was happy she'd brought the mail in as well as the newspaper someone had mistakenly thrown into my driveway.

I'd walked her through the photo album before, but it had been a few months, maybe longer. So why not? Usually I did it by myself, which was less horrifying and embarrassing.

The photo album had been the neurologist's idea. The idea was pretty obvious: flip through these twenty or so photographs once a week and try to remember what or who was pictured in them, what the situation was, how you felt at the time. They were mostly snapshots from the 1970s and 1980s, a seemingly random collection of photos taken by my parents, family friends, or myself. The concept was to regularly reinforce my memory, strengthening connections between the synapses, the way someone practicing a foreign language or memorizing lines for a play would do, through rote repetition. Over time, the thought was that I would be able to pick out exactly who was who, and why they had been important to me at some point in the past, and my brain would sort of reprogram itself.

I wouldn't say it was working very well. While some of the faces were clear—I could easily pick out my mother and father—many others remained mysterious every time I went back to them, week after week. Flipping over the plastic transparencies, each containing just one picture, would reveal the back of the photo, where a caption—sometimes short, sometimes lengthy—would outline the particular goings-on in the snapshot. They were like the world's most pathetic flash cards, the text all written in longhand by my mother in the months while I was recuperating in the hospital (and then the psych ward) after my incident. May she rest in peace.

Why did I bother with the photos? I had always told myself it was simply for the brain exercise, to help with day-to-day life, but deep down I knew I wanted to keep my more distant, happier memories alive. I was happy that most of my past had slowly faded away, but there were some things I knew I shouldn't let go.

The photos were a greatest hits collection of those high-point moments—or, at least, my mother's interpretation of them. I didn't really know any better, so I was happy to defer to her wisdom on the matter, and I had to take her word for it that the scenes in the photographs had played out in reality the way she had described them in text.

On the first photo, there was me, opening a gift that contained one of those super-soaker squirt guns—my eleventh birthday, according to the writing on the back. Friends and neighbors surrounded me, and Mom had listed all their names on the reverse, noting they were "clockwise, from top left." This photo was one of the busiest in the collection, but my attention was always drawn to my younger self, scrawny but shirtless in the center of the frame, obviously taking a break from time spent in a swimming pool. My eyes were closed in the picture, but my mouth was wide open in an authentic, amazing smile. I'm sure I took that squirt gun straight into the pool after the present opening was done and had a blast with it, though I can't remember it at all.

Me and a neighbor girl, about the same time as the first photo, caught mid-dance, each with one foot in the air. Everyone seemed happy, though this was something I think we were required to learn for school. Her name began with an M. I flipped the page. Ah, "Missy." Partial credit.

Me, older, on the stage at the school play.

A more recent shot of my cousin Josh and his parents, my aunt and uncle...Bob? Burt? Standing in a field that looked like a rice paddy or some fetid Texas swamp. I'd been told that Josh and I were very close in our youth, though we couldn't be more different today, at least from what I've seen online.

A picture of my mom and dad in the early seventies at an Emerson, Lake & Palmer concert.

Two guys throwing a football, early eighties. Second cousins.

Me under the Christmas tree, very young, with a new bike, a bow still on the handlebars. The bike had a black plastic disc zip-tied to the front, and while I don't remember anything else about it, I could always remember the number emblazoned on its front: 32.

My dad watching a television program with someone of importance on the screen. He is smoking a cigarette. On the reverse: "Dad with Gerald Ford, 1974."

A picture of a house, taken from the street. Obviously, the place where I grew up, though I can't remember anything about those years.

A photo of me with, inexplicably, two of the Dallas Cowboys Cheerleaders, my head coming up to their boobs. The back only reads: "Trip to Dallas."

Various shots of my friends in the 1980s, always laughing. Probably pictures that I took all in one go with a disposable camera. Our clothes are all too big, and everyone has acne. Their names are carefully inscribed on the backs of the pictures, though there aren't any dates or other details attached.

A photo taken at an anonymous, endless beach, everyone in shadow under big hats. "S. Padre Island," reads the reverse.

Me in a *Buck Rogers* T-shirt, sadly looking out a window, slicked with rain.

The whole family at Disneyland or Disney World. Which is which? I recognized the mouse ears. Mom is the only one smiling. It looks incredibly hot.

Pictures of my grandparents, one shot of each couple. Carefully identified by their full names—not "Gramps" or whatever—along with their dates of birth and death, and the addresses of their respective cemeteries. In case I wanted to go visit.

A photo of my high school graduation, wearing a black cap and gown. Looks like a huge bummer.

Me in an Ohio State sweatshirt, much too big, moving into what is clearly my freshman dorm room. I look miserable. I can remember the feeling more than the mechanics of the day. For some reason, this photo also reminds me of my time after college, living in Chicago in the late 1990s and 2000s. An awful lot of drinking.

A picture of a baby. Me, as an infant. "Alex's First Photo" in careful calligraphy.

Finally, the most recent photograph and the only one from this century. Peg teared up when she saw it, probably as she'd done the first time around. The photo was me, in a hospital bed, completely knocked out, with a tube running up my nose.

The aftermath of my suicide attempt.

CHAPTER THIRTY
Eliza

W E WERE ONLY ten minutes into it, but already the session wasn't going well, and I could tell that Alex was deeply regretting his decision to tutor me.

"I'm deeply regretting my decision to tutor you." He sighed, rubbing his forehead.

Alex slumped back into the couch and looked toward the television out of habit. He'd turned it off when I arrived— you know, for focus—but clearly he wished he was watching some show instead of trying to teach me algebra.

"How can you not understand this?" he asked. "What is a negative of a negative?"

"Hmmmmm," I stalled.

"A minus of a minus," he said. "Two minuses."

"A plus?" I said, with minimal confidence.

"Right, a plus. You can remember it because when you take the two minuses and put them together, they make a plus sign."

"Wouldn't that be like an equals sign?"

He was starting to look angry again. "I'm not being literal. I'm just trying to give you a trick that can help you think about it in an easier way. Making math easy is all about learning the tricks. Take the two minus signs and turn them into a plus, in your head." He made a cross with his fingers to demonstrate the idea.

"OK."

"OK," he said. "So let's do this one again."

The problem was $-3(2x - 12) = 0$. *Solve for x.* I worked through it out loud. "So, minus 6x...and 12 times 3 is 36..."

"Go on."

"It's *plus* 36?"

"Right."

"So minus 6x plus 36 is zero."

"So how are you going to solve that?"

"I move one to the other side."

"Right. Move the minus 6x, and remember it turns positive when you move it to the other side of the equals."

"So it's 36 equals 6x," I said, with growing assuredness that I had a basic understanding of what I was doing.

"And x equals?"

I did the math in my head, without a calculator. "Six."

Alex smiled and sort of jumped up a little. "Six, you got it!"

He wiped his mouth with a paper napkin he'd fished out of his pocket, then put it away. He slumped back in the chair, looking exhausted. "OK," he said. "I think that's about enough for today."

I looked at the clock on my phone. "What? I've only been here fifteen minutes. It's supposed to be an hour!"

"We never talked about that," he said.

"I've only done one problem. Look at all this homework

I have to do by Monday." It was a full handout of problems like the one we just finished, with lots of parentheses, minus signs, and *x*s that would need to be solved for. "My mom will freak out if I come home and I show her we only did one problem."

"Maybe you can work on a few by yourself. I'm just gonna close my eyes for a minute or two."

I worked on a handful of problems in silence, then nudged Alex out of his fake nap. "Look at these."

He held the paper in one hand until it began to shake too much, then put it down in his lap and leaned over a bit to read it.

"Well, you got one right."

"Which one?"

"You tell me," he said. "Do them again until you figure it out."

It went like this for a while. He would sometimes give me tips, sometimes not, and mostly he just looked upset.

"My brain hurts," I said, as we got toward the end of the hour.

"My brain hurts too," Alex said. "Everything hurts. I need a real nap now."

"Maybe I'll get better over the week," I said. He was a bad teacher, but he was better than Ms. Bell, who seemed to understand less about math than I did. After an hour of practice, I was at least getting a handle on the "two negatives makes a positive" situation. The last three problems I tried I'd gotten correct without needing his help, and the homework sheet was almost completely filled out.

"Maybe," he muttered.

"If I have problems during the week, I'll just text you," I said.

"Please don't," he replied dryly.

"Can I call then?"

He sighed again. He was always sighing. "If you have to."

I took out the $30 in cash that Mom had given me and put it on the table, packed up my stuff into my backpack, and stood up to leave.

"I'm sure it'll be easier next time," I said. "See you next Saturday."

I think he was crying a little, but I'm not sure.

CHAPTER THIRTY-ONE

Peg

"I'M SO GLAD you came."

Klaus told me this twice during our—what was it, a date or a meeting? A meet-up? I don't know the lingo. I didn't take what he said as coming from a place of desperation. He seemed genuinely happy and also a bit surprised that I had come to his home. I guess I was surprised, too.

Upon arrival, Klaus gave me a tour of the house. It was quite tidy and modestly decorated, but one feature of the décor was impossible to believe: every room was crammed with books. Yes, they were all arranged neatly on shelves, but there were so many of them. Even the hallways were, tastefully, lined with books.

"Did you read all of these books?" I asked. "I'm sure you get asked that all the time."

"Most of them," Klaus said. "Some I still plan on reading in the future."

"It looks like they aren't all in English," I noted.

"No, many are in German. I'm still quite fluent," he said. "I try to read in French and Spanish some of the time, but it's very difficult. I often have to use a dictionary."

"Lots of Nietzsche, I bet!" I tried to make a joke, because, well, Nietzsche was the only German writer I could name.

Klaus looked taken aback. "Nietzsche? I'm sure I have some of his more noteworthy works here, but it's not a canon I celebrate."

"Oh?" I asked. I knew nothing at all about Nietzsche.

"Nietzsche was looking for attention. He would make *grossartig* claims in one book, then forget all about them in the next. He also wrote of the *Übermensch*—the Superman— a more highly evolved type of person not bound by the rules of good and evil. It's all very egotistical."

"Wow, I had no idea."

"Nietzsche famously claimed that God is dead. It is this *Übermensch* that killed him."

"Oh my, that's deep."

"And I assure you that God is not dead. He is alive and among us."

Perhaps an oddly worded sentiment, but I nodded.

"I prefer the philosophy of Camus and the existentialists."

"Hmmm?"

"That life is absurd and meaningless, and that if there were a meaning, it would be impossible to know what it was."

I nodded my head and considered Klaus in silence for a moment. Dressed in a button-down dress shirt, his cuffs undone but the sleeves hanging loose, he looked like he had either just gotten home or was preparing to go out. I wondered if he had other plans later, after we had finished the salmon.

"I don't know if life has no meaning," I finally said, spontaneously laughing a little. "But I suppose I can understand the sentiment."

"Neither do I," he replied. "But I don't think there is any value in searching for one." He laughed a bit. "Even Camus rejected the label of existentialism. He simply saw how foolish it was to always be seeking the meaning of life and never being able to find one. Yet it is human nature to do so."

"I guess," I said. The conversation was making me a little uncomfortable. I realized I could use that glass of wine he'd promised. Klaus read my mind.

"But this is rude of me. We should open the Riesling and enjoy it while it's cold," he said. "It is so much more human to discuss philosophy with a glass of wine in one's hand."

We moved to the kitchen. Spacious but a bit dated, it was clear he had done no remodeling since he bought the house. I would have heard the construction from across the street, I'm sure. Klaus poured the wine, then produced smoked salmon from the refrigerator, also as promised. He laid out crackers, a jar of fancy mustard, and some little pickles on the side. I didn't think the pickles went well with the wine, so I mainly just ate the fish and crackers, which were quite delightful. The wine was also yummy—not too sour, not too sweet. I watched as the wine bottle quickly grew wet with condensation. Was it warm in here?

"How long have you lived here again?" I asked, taking a healthy sip of the ice-cold wine.

"Oh, ten years. I think. Maybe more? And you? Fifteen years, I believe you said."

"Yes. Moved here with my husband Jack in 2004. He died not long after that."

"*Ach*, I'm so sorry."

"Don't be," I said. "It's in the past, and Jack is always with me. Would you like to see him?"

Klaus didn't flinch the way some people do when I say that. "Certainly."

I reached into my purse, which was still slung over my shoulder, and retrieved from the interior pocket the small locket I kept there. The gold case was worn down from being handled and no longer shined brightly, and the decorative etching was now invisible. I opened the case to reveal a tiny picture of Jack's face, taken what must have been twenty years ago. I wondered what he would have looked like today had things gone differently that day. Certainly still handsome, anyway.

I showed the photo to Klaus. "That's him. That's Jack."

He took the case, looked at the photo somberly, and handed it back to me. "It must hurt very much to lose someone close to you," he said.

"Of course it does," I said. "There's just so much guilt that you have to carry when someone dies."

"Ah," he said. "I understand completely."

"Still, it doesn't have to be the end of your life as well."

Klaus smiled and nodded. "Certainly not. And you seem to have successfully moved on with your life to a place that must be very fulfilling."

"Well I don't know about that," I said, drinking again from my glass. "Honestly, it's not very fulfilling at all."

"Really?" said Klaus, leaning in toward me. "Tell me more."

CHAPTER THIRTY-TWO

Eliza

"I THINK I got it," I said.

"OK, explain the trick to me," Alex said, plopped on his usual spot on the couch, the seat compressed and sunken deeply from sitting in the same place forever.

"X percent of Y is the same as Y percent of X."

"Go on."

"So if it's hard to figure out 26 percent of 50, I can spin it around and do 50 percent of 26 instead."

"Right, which is?"

"Thirteen."

"You got it." Alex was almost smiling. Almost, but not quite.

"I just can't believe it's true. I mean, how is it possible that 26 per—"

"Don't worry about it!" Alex snapped. "You don't need to know why it works, just that it does work. What's 8 percent of 25?"

I thought about it for a couple of seconds. "Two."

"Right. Now let's work on the practice problems." He handed my workbook back to me and waved a shaky finger in the general vicinity of the assigned homework.

I was feeling good from mastering the percentage problem, and not in the mood to do more math for the time being, so I changed the subject to something I'd been wondering about throughout a couple of weeks of these tutoring sessions. I put the book down for a moment. Alex was staring at a video game on his phone, oblivious to me.

"So why do you live in this house, anyway? Way out here in the middle of nowhere?"

Alex shrugged. "Because it's free, I guess."

"How'd you get a free house?"

"My grandmother died. She left it to me. My parents are both gone, and I only have a couple of cousins. They didn't need the place."

"Where'd you live before?"

"Chicago, mostly."

"And what kind of job did you have? Not teacher, anyway."

"Computers."

"Just computers?" I asked.

"Data analysis. You wouldn't understand," he said. As if on cue, he withdrew a small napkin—it looked like an old fast-food napkin—from his pocket and dabbed at the corner of his mouth, where things were getting a bit moist.

"Maybe I want to do data analysis when I graduate."

Alex smirked, then put the napkin back in his pocket. "I don't think you'd like it. What do you really want to do?"

"I dunno," I said.

"Yeah, I don't blame you. You'll figure it out later."

"That's what everybody says."

"Well, they're right."

I looked around the place. God, it was so dated. The dead grandma explained the décor, at least. "So when you moved here, you just figured you'd leave it the way your grandmother had it? Like, out of respect or something?"

He glared at me. "I'm not much for interior design," he said.

"Oh really?" I approached the wall of shelves behind the big television in the living room, which was turned off for our tutoring session for once. "This isn't your collection of decorative owls?"

"Uh, no," he said. "I mean, I guess it is now."

"So you're into owls now?"

Alex rolled his eyes. "No, I'm not into owls. I just don't have anything else to put there."

"How about the pillows?" I asked, pointing to these old, brown, owl-embroidered throws scattered around the couch.

Alex sighed. "I just don't care, really."

"Well, that's a bad attitude," I said.

"Really?" he asked, eyeing me carefully. "I'm not seeing a lot of effort put into this," he said, waving his arm up and down. True, there was a ketchup stain on my hoodie, but that was only because I hadn't done laundry lately.

I let it slide. "So you don't have to work anymore, right? This all looks pretty bourgie to me. I could do this. Lie here all day, watch TV, and play games."

"Believe me, kid," he said. Sometimes he called me "kid." "I'd rather be doing something productive."

"Why?"

"Because this shit gets boring after a few years. You may think your routine of going to school or your job every day sucks, but it's way better than doing nothing."

"Yeah," I moaned. "And high school is going to be the best time of my life, right?"

Alex looked me in the eye. "I sure didn't say that. High school was murder for me."

"Is that why you're so messed up?"

"For starters."

I was getting frustrated with the runaround. "How come you won't be straight with me?"

Alex put his phone down completely and finally looked me in the eye. "Because you're too immature to discuss any of this stuff with."

"I'm mature," I insisted.

"Fine," he said, glaring at me. "I tried to kill myself, and this is how I ended up. Happy now?" He took out his napkin again and dabbed at his chin.

I didn't know what to think or how to feel. I wasn't happy; that's for sure. But I was more curious than ever. "So, like, you're sad that it didn't work?"

"Basically. And don't ask me why."

"Why what?"

"Why I tried to kill myself. I'm sure that was going to be your next question. It's always the next question."

"And you don't want to talk about it, right?"

"Right." Alex looked away, staring out the window while I took in all this new information. Now I was more curious than ever. What had gone so wrong in his life that he thought he had to commit suicide? Why would you want to kill anyone, especially yourself? I was determined to find out more, but at the same time, I just felt so sorry for this lonely, broken guy.

"Earth to Eliza," Alex said, jolting me out of my daze. "Let's finish up those problems. We're about out of time."

I returned to the homework and used the tricks Alex had taught me to go through them, one by one, really concentrating this time. When he checked them over afterward, it turned out I got them all correct—a first.

"Good job," he said, smiling just a little.

CHAPTER THIRTY-THREE

Klaus

P EG WAS BEGINNING to grow on me. She was unusual, unlike any other woman I'd met in recent memory. She spoke her mind freely, even if she didn't seem to exactly know what she was talking about most of the time. Seemingly without a filter. She laughed, and she laughed a lot, even if what was being said was not funny. That was refreshing— even if she was faking it.

It was an unseasonably chilly day in late September, and it marked Peg's fourth visit to the house over the course of a few weeks. We had never done anything or gone anywhere except meet here, Peg scurrying across the street to ring the bell, and she seemed fine with that arrangement. To prefer it, even. Originally our dates had taken place in the late afternoon; now they were stretching well into the evening. Tonight I had prepared a dinner of steaks with mustard sauce, broccolini, and *spaetzle*, a personal favorite I always made from scratch. I served it with a Barolo wine, which I could tell that Peg didn't really like.

"It's a bit heavy for me," she said. That wasn't an uncommon opinion. Most women I'd met didn't like red wine at all, much less a monstrous *riesen* of a wine like Barolo.

"Should I open something else?" I asked.

"No," she said. "I'll be fine with this."

She sipped at the wine gently, which didn't do anything for my agenda, unfortunately. The more they drink, the more careless they became. It wasn't rocket science.

I had thought by this point that Peg would be over and done with, buried next to the others on the wooded hillside, nothing more than a fond memory just like all of them. But here she was, living and breathing and eating my steak and not drinking my wine. I refilled my glass. Why was I dragging this out? I enjoyed her company, but wouldn't I enjoy taking her much more? The longer I waited, the more risk I introduced. Surely her DNA, her fingerprints, and *Gott* knows what else was all over the house by now. A thorough cleaning was probably in order.

I made a point to ask myself if I should reconsider. Perhaps Peg was indeed better for me alive. I now had a dinner companion on regular occasions. Someone to share a glass of wine with. Perhaps the tentative hand-holding sessions in the kitchen would lead to something more in the near future. Maybe even a trip to the bedroom. What would I find beneath the skirt and blouse? Peg was cautious, but I was in no hurry. If I did make the choice to take her, she would be gone forever. And then I would be back to drinking wine alone and speaking to no one, with nothing but another trinket to remember her by.

But perhaps this was all foolish. The logical brain says I should have taken her the first night, when she had picked at the salmon. It would have been a simple matter to offer that we wander through the backyard, pick mushrooms or something, then strike when her back was turned, and I could have completed the burial before nightfall. Now it was dark, and soon the wildfires would be starting. They had been burning in Sonoma and the neighboring counties north of here every fall, and once they started, no one would want to be lingering outside anymore. And nothing sounded worse than trying to bury a body while wearing a face mask.

At least she was short. The grave didn't have to be so big, especially if I buried her on her side, with her knees drawn up against her chest. I'd discovered this trick a few years back, and it was a real time and space saver.

It slowly dawned on me during my dreamy *tagtraum* that Peg was speaking. She had said quite a bit, actually, and I knew that it would be incredibly rude to ask her to repeat herself. I fell back on an old trick that had gotten me out of similar trouble in the past and said, quite slowly, "I don't know."

It is a response that can be used for almost any situation when you haven't been paying attention, and I was confident it would work with this one, too.

"You don't know why you decided to live in this out-of-the-way cul-de-sac?" she asked.

"Not really," I said, recovering. "I needed a place with room for all my books."

"It's just that this is so far from the City, so far from anything. Why does a young man choose to live in a place that's so remote, especially when you could live anywhere?"

I thought for a moment before answering. "I suppose I've

always been drawn to things that are off the beaten path, things that are quiet, things that are lonely. For me, the cul-de-sac is, quite literally, the end of the line."

"But you have so much energy. Don't you get bored living here?"

"Never, Peg. How do they say it? I make my own fun."

"Well, I'm having fun," she said.

"As am I."

And I was having fun, just of a different sort. The taking should wait. We'd come this far, so there was no harm in waiting further. I would impose no specific deadline on myself and raised my glass in a toast.

"To us," I said.

Peg smiled and then clinked glasses with me. I took a sip of the wine, as was the custom when a toast has been made, but she put her glass back down on the counter.

A definite breach of etiquette.

CHAPTER THIRTY-FOUR

Eliza

"OK," BARBIE G said from the front of the class on an otherwise sleepy Monday morning. "Today's the big day! We have all your holiday sales orders, ready to deliver," she said. "So at the end of the period, grab the bag with your name on it and get these treasures dropped off to the folks who bought them."

A collection of paper grocery bags, many with wrapping paper tubes sticking out the top, were lined up to the side of her desk. Each had a name scrawled on the front in Sharpie. I could easily see the one marked "Eliza/Jean Claire," as it was the biggest.

"However, I do have some bad news," Barbie G continued. "It's the Money Machine. Apparently, the fan is broken, so we won't be able to have the drawing of top sellers today, and we'll have to reschedule the big event for later in the year."

A chorus of groans and boos lit up immediately and so fiercely that you would have thought she was kicking a puppy. Jean Claire made a face and slumped back in her seat, disappointed. Even if she didn't get picked to go in the Money Machine, I think she would have been excited just to see all that money flying around.

"Barbie G, that sucks!" yelled Trevor from behind his hoodie.

"Trevor, I've told you before. It's *Mrs. Barbagianni* in this class. And you didn't sell any items," Barbie G said. "It wasn't going to be you, anyway."

"Yeah, but now we don't get to get out of class for the assembly."

"We'll still have the assembly. It just won't be today."

"Still," he said, sniffing. "Sucks."

"Well, have some patience. I'm sure they'll get it fixed soon."

✕

AT THE END of the day, Jean Claire and I split up our orders. She would deliver the stuff we'd sold near her house, I would deliver the stuff to the residents of the cul-de-sac. I trudged home with the rolls of paper and other stuff awkwardly poking out of the paper sack I'd been given, planning to deliver the items as quickly as possible that afternoon.

I didn't wait after getting home, dropping my backpack inside the front door, and trying to make myself a bit more presentable by pulling my hair back into a ponytail and smoothing out my shirt. I marched out on foot, heading up the street. I skipped Alex's house, since I was going there soon enough for tutoring—and I knew he'd yell at me for making him get off the couch for something so unimportant. Peg's house was next, and since the bulk of the stuff in the bag was hers, it was "the logical place to start," as my dad would say.

I rang the bell, but no one was home, which seemed strange for a Monday afternoon. Out shopping, probably. I didn't want to leave the items on the doorstep and figured I'd try her again later. I continued up and around the end of the cul-de-sac, past the burned house and on to the massive mansion at the end of the block. I was huffing and puffing after climbing up the steep driveway. I rang the bell. Again, no answer. Frustrating!

I stepped back from the entryway and took a broad look at the place. All the curtains were drawn, and all the lights appeared to be off except for one on the second floor. I could see flickering behind the white drapery and in the cracks between the pieces of hanging fabric. The room was dark, but the TV was on. Either someone was careless and left it running or someone was in there and didn't want to come to the door.

I wasn't going to give up that easily. I banged on the door with my fist.

"Hello!" I shouted toward the TV window. "I have your bags!" I realized only after yelling the phrase how silly it had sounded. Surely Mr. Charles had forgotten the order altogether and would have no clue what I was talking about. I figured it was less likely that anyone was going to come to the door at this point, and the last thing I wanted to do was climb up that hill again, so I just dropped the bags on the porch, tore off a piece of the paper bag, and wrote "*Thanks! – Eliza*" on it with the pen in my back pocket. He'd remember what is was eventually.

I really had only one more delivery I could make on the cul-de-sac: the creepy German guy who had tried to lure Jean Claire and me into his living room. He only had the one roll of paper, the ugly green and gold one, and I figured I would probably be dropping it and running like I had at the Charles house. Best to see if anyone was home before doing that, though. I climbed the steps and rang the bell. Shortly after, I heard footsteps inside.

CHAPTER THIRTY-FIVE

Klaus

PEG WAS OVER once again, but this was an uncharacteristic and spontaneous afternoon visit. She had baked brownies. I didn't think they were very good, but I appreciated the gesture. I would have to be sure to destroy the plate when I was finished, lest something tie her back to me. I had poured us large glasses of white Burgundy to help them go down a bit easier, and the wine was helping.

The conversation had turned to travel. Peg was warming herself up to the idea of taking a trip, and maybe we could take one together, she'd wondered aloud. But where would we go? Skiing in Canada? New York City for Christmas shopping?

"I've been to New York, but never in the winter—and not in a long while," she said. "Maybe I should buy a guide book to see what's new."

"Please do not buy a guide book," I said. That would be juicy evidence, I was sure. "No need to waste your money. I know the city well. It sounds like a wonderful idea. Let me look into it for us." I made another mental note that I was going to have to get into her house sooner or later to look for evidence she'd already created. Clear her computer's search history, destroy any diaries or other notes that mentioned me.

"Do you have a computer, Peg?" I asked. Why not get to the point right away?

"Of course," she said. "But I don't use it much except for paying bills."

I doubted that, but I held my tongue. "*Ich verstehe*—er, I understand," I said. "I'll plan an itinerary for us."

Peg seemed pleased, and I was about to take another small nibble off the brownie when the doorbell rang.

I was startled by the abrupt chime, spilling some wine on my sleeve and almost dropping the confection. No one ringing the bell at this hour would have any legitimate reason to call on me. I had no deliveries scheduled, so it was either a solicitor—which was almost unheard of this far away from anything else—or some kind of utility worker asking if they could shut off the water for an hour to do work on the line. Neither would be welcome right now. No witnesses.

"Aren't you going to answer the door?" Peg asked. I'd been standing there, still, lost in my thoughts, for much too long, and now I faced a dilemma: answer the door and risk exposing my relationship or ignore the door and look suspicious in front of Peg.

"Of course," I said. I put the dry, crumbling brownie down on the napkin I was using as a plate and strode with purpose to the door. I wanted to make sure Peg wouldn't follow, and since there were two rooms between our usual spot in the kitchen and the entry hall, I was confident she wouldn't be seen from outside the house. On my way to the door, I casually bumped up the volume on the stereo system in the living room, which would serve to drown out any incidental chatter or other noise from the kitchen.

Nonetheless, I cracked the door only a few inches out of an abundance of caution. It was the neighbor girl again. She looked sweaty.

"Hey, I'm glad you're home," she said. "I have the wrapping paper you ordered."

"*Was ist das*?" I asked, out of habit.

"Wrapping paper. You bought it a few weeks ago. I was here for the fundraiser, remember?"

"*Ach*, of course. Yes."

I could see the nosy girl trying to peek into the house. Obviously, she heard the music and her curiosity was piqued. Perhaps I had turned it up too high. The girl handed the paper over, a long tube of green and gold. Yes, I remembered the pattern.

Suddenly, I heard from behind me, "Who is it, Klaus?" It was Peg, calling from the living room, having clearly left the kitchen against my expectations and completely against the plan. I don't think the girl heard her—after all, I had barely heard her—but she certainly heard something and kept trying to see past me.

I couldn't risk Peg coming around the corner, which could be happening any second. "*Danke!*" I almost yelled at her, then quickly shut the door. I wouldn't say it was a slamming of the door, but it was definitely abrupt, and it almost caught the girl in the nose. She stood there for quite some time, but fortunately the glass surrounding the front door was frosted so there was no way for her to see inside.

And there was Peg, hands on her hips. "Well, I was start-ing to miss you," she said. She walked forward, took my left hand in her right, and gave me a small kiss on the cheek.

"Ha, me too." I smiled.

"What's this?" she asked, noticing the wrapping paper.

"Ah. The girl from down the street. She was making her deliveries."

Peg's eyes lit up. "Oh, how fun! That must mean she has my order as well. Maybe I can catch her before she gets too far."

Peg motioned toward the door, but I was in the way and we were still holding hands. I gripped tighter. "Oh, no, she didn't have anything else with her," I lied. "I'm sure she'll be by your house soon." I smiled broadly to distract her. "Besides," I said, "I'm hungry for another brownie."

I rushed her back to the kitchen, never letting go of the hand. My God, it was so warm. Just the slightest bit damp because she was sweating a little. Nervous, as usual. I set the roll of paper down on the kitchen counter and brought her close to me, using my free hand to stroke her neck. It was also warm like her hand, warmer even. So soft, but with a gentle corduroy texture, the skin wrinkled by time and the elements. She was self-conscious and blushed, grabbing my hand to pull it away.

She looked down for a while, embarrassed about some-thing, then looked up and stared me in the eye. She asked, simply, "Why do you care for me, Klaus?"

I put my hand back, and this time she let me. My fingers

tightened around the back of her neck, and I tried to control the urge to wrap my thumb around the other side. One hand wouldn't work. It would take both, but she was still holding my left hand, down at my waist.

"Oh, Peg," I said, releasing her. I closed my eyes and took a deep breath. "Every one of us is worthy of affection. Even you. Even me."

CHAPTER THIRTY-SIX

Peg

K LAUS WAS RIGHT, of course. I knew enough about relationships to realize that familiarity led to fondness, and fondness led to love. Was I falling in love with Klaus? Was I capable of falling in love with him? With anyone? This was all moving so fast.

All I knew was that I wanted him to like me, and I could feel my need for his attention and affection growing. I was wearing more makeup now—not a lot, just a little to iron out the wrinkles and give my lips some color. And I was wearing shoes with a heel instead of my usual flats. I could tell it was annoying for him to crane his neck downward to look at me, particularly when we were close together. I was growing fond of wearing my espadrille wedges, which propped me up a solid four inches but looked totally natural, not like I was wearing stilettos. They were also easy to get around in and quite comfortable, and I felt totally steady whenever I had them on.

We talked very little outside of our dates. He wasn't one for texts or phone calls, and I found myself wishing he would put a little more effort into our relationship. Was it a relationship? I still couldn't tell. He'd kissed me the last time

I was there, but it was just a light smack on the lips, maybe a second or two. Better than a peck on the cheek, I supposed. I left shortly after that, after making a lame excuse about needing to call PG&E, too embarrassed and too timid to press things further. I wished that I had more friends around the neighborhood to gossip with. Talking to Alex next door once a month just wasn't the same as having a solid girlfriend I could rely on. Maybe I needed to make some cookies and put a little more effort into coaxing Alex out of his shell.

Yet for now, here I was, lying on my bed, my wedges still strapped to my feet, thinking about whether Klaus and I might have a future together. He always seemed so reserved, so aloof, like he was happy to see me but also a little surprised—vaguely annoyed that I was there, maybe, like I was cramping his style a bit too much. If I hadn't known better—and I did a lot of probing on this front—I would have assumed he was also dating someone else.

Why shouldn't he have been dating someone else, anyway? He was young, successful, and handsome in his own, curious way. What on earth did he see in me? Was he genuinely interested? Bored? Or was he just taking pity on little old Peggle? Every time I came home after an afternoon or an evening at Klaus's, I was more confused than before as to why he'd thought to invite me there. He barely seemed to enjoy my company at all.

Hopefully, he wasn't a serial killer or something.

Right?

CHAPTER THIRTY-SEVEN
Alex

"WHAT THE HELL is this?" I asked Eliza, who was standing at my door, on schedule for our tutoring session.

She jabbed a roll of snowflake-clad wrapping paper into my stomach. "Wrapping paper. You ordered it." She had a big bag of stuff in her free hand, filled with additional rolls of paper and God knows what else.

I grabbed the roll with my left hand. "Here," she said, tossing something else that she'd been holding into the air. I couldn't quite see what it was, but it flew in my general direction. "You bought this, too."

Somehow I managed to catch the thing in my arms. It was a tiny stuffed animal, a polar bear, dangling from a small key chain.

"I bought this? I bought all of this stuff?"

"Yes, you did," she says.

"Jesus, tell me I already paid for it at least."

"Yes, you wrote a check, remember? I mean, I wrote the check for you."

"What about all that?" I asked, pointing to the over-stuffed bag in her other hand.

"No, this is for Peg, the lady next door. I'm dropping it off after."

Sweet relief. "Oh, good," I said. "If she's not home, you can just leave it here. She comes by once in a while."

"Oh, you two are buddies?" she asked.

"No, she just likes to drop by, usually unannounced. Maybe she'll start visiting you the same way someday."

Eliza pushed past me and walked down the entry hall toward the living room, where we always worked. I followed as quickly as I could, dropping the items I'd purchased on the coffee table. Eliza gave them the side-eye but began setting up next to them.

"What are we working on today?" I asked.

"Uh, factoring," she said.

"Polynomials, right?"

"I guess," she said.

"Jesus, if you don't know what you're working on, how am I supposed to help you?"

Eliza didn't answer. She had figured out by now that arguing about what she was or was not supposed to know before she came to see me was pointless. We would get to the important stuff eventually.

The section she was working on was simple. I'm sure she thought it was *impossible*, as she was fond of saying, but she'd get the hang of it soon enough. With these simple trinomials, the easy trick was to just find two numbers that, when added, equaled the multiplier in front of the x, but when multiplied, equaled the final number. So, $x^2 + 7x + 10$ factored down to $(x + 2)(x + 5)$. It took a lot of hand-waving and squiggly line-drawing to get this through her head, but it worked. When it came time to do the homework assignments, she got nearly all of them correct. The bar for this work wasn't exactly at a NASA level. God help me, I knew that the following week they'd be working on problems where one of the numbers was negative, and that was going to be a whole other world of hell. But for now, I was confident that she would ace the pop quiz that would probably be given on Monday. If she didn't forget everything in the next two days.

As the session neared the end and Eliza was packing up her gear, she turned to me and then paused, a quizzical look in her eyes. I knew the face. She was trying to figure out how to say something awkward or vaguely embarrassing.

"What is it?" I asked.

"You know the guy across the street?"

"Not really."

"OK, but you know there's a guy who lives over there, right? In the house with the big turret on it?"

"Yeah, I've seen him."

"He's weird, don't you think?"

"What does that mean, *weird*?"

"I don't know," she said. I could tell she was going to get huffy with me soon. "He's just weird."

"OK, why do you think he's weird?"

"Well, a few days ago when I delivered the paper he bought, he practically slammed the door in my face."

"OK…" I said, waiting to hear more.

"You don't think that's weird?"

"It's not weird; it's rude."

"OK, so he's rude. But he's also weird. I think there was someone in there with him, and he didn't want me to see them."

"Well, maybe he did. I wouldn't want you in my business, either."

"There wasn't any car in the driveway, and nobody showed up in an Uber or anything. I would've seen it."

"Maybe he had an overnight guest," I said. "Or they could've been dropped off in the morning, before you got up."

"And they left after I went to bed?"

"Maybe. Maybe he has a roommate or something. Or maybe you just didn't notice when they came and left."

"I don't think so. There was music, and I smelled booze."

"You smelled booze."

"Yeah, booze. It was spilled on his shirt."

"I really don't know where you're going with all of this, Eliza."

"I don't know," she said, shuffling her feet. "It just wasn't right. He was acting weird, it smelled like booze, and, you know, he's just really creepy."

"I'm sure you say the same thing about me with your little friends."

"No, I don't!"

"Sure you don't."

"I promise!"

"OK, whatever," I said.

"Anyway, he's creepy, and that's that. I think something is going on over there, and I'm going to figure out what it is, and then you'll see."

"Great," I said. "Please get back to me on that."

CHAPTER THIRTY-EIGHT

Eliza

T HE SUN WAS going down already as I packed up my stuff from the tutoring session. Now I could get the big bag of stuff delivered to Peg, the woman who lived next door, and finally my mom would stop nagging me to get it out of the hallway. I probably should have delivered it earlier in the week, considering how much she bought. And Christmas was coming in a couple of months. She seemed like the kind of person who liked to have her gifts wrapped by Thanksgiving.

I trudged up the hill to her house and rang the bell. I swear the door opened before I even pushed the button in all the way, and there she was, this tiny, almost fragile thing with a beaming smile.

"Come in!" Peg practically yelled. "I'm so excited you're here."

Before I could get out a word of my own, she disappeared into the house and into another room. "I've been baking!" she bellowed from around the corner. I followed her and rounded the corner into the kitchen, where an unfathomable number of chocolate chip cookies were laid out on racks, plates, paper towels, and even newspaper. "I hope you'll take some home with you. I think I made too many."

"Uh, sure," I said. Who was going to argue with free cookies? "I have your wrapping paper order," I said, hoisting the bag above my head.

"Oh, what a delight. Can you leave it on the dining table over there?" she asked, gesturing to the one visible surface that wasn't covered in baked goods.

"You got it." I dropped the bag on the table while trying to keep the paper rolls from spilling onto the floor.

"So, how's school going?" she asked, continuing her labor of moving cookies from trays to racks. "How are you enjoying the neighborhood?"

"It's fine. They're both fine."

"You've made friends?"

"Yeah, some," I said. "Well, one really. We hang out a lot. The girl who was with me when we were selling this stuff."

"Oh, that's super."

"And school is good. I have a math tutor. Actually, it's the guy who lives next door—in between your house and mine."

"Alex? Really? He's a tutor?"

"He's not officially a tutor. I guess I'm his only student."

"Really!" Peg always seemed surprised. "And is he a good teacher?"

I thought about that for a moment. "Well, not really, but he's better than my math teacher at school. I've got a B+ in the class now, even."

"Wow, Alex is helping you in school! I see him all the

time, you know. He hasn't mentioned it. That's just great." Peg beamed.

I nodded.

"Sounds like everything's working out," she continued. "You like living here?"

"I guess so," I said. "Sure."

"I really enjoyed my time in high school," Peg said. "I was on the drill team. I had so many friends. We'd spend every weekend hanging out at the lake, driving around town, going to movies. We had to get out of the house. We didn't have phones and the internet back then, you know."

"I've heard about this," I said. "Those must have been dark times."

Peg laughed. "So dark, so dark."

"So what are you going to do with all these cookies, anyway?" I asked.

"Well, I'll eat some, and you're going to take some, and I'll give some to Alex," she said, drawing close and lowering her voice to a near whisper, like she was about to share a secret with me, "and I'm going to take some to my boyfriend."

"Boyfriend?" I said, in mock surprise.

"I know!" she said. "At my age!"

"Oh, you're not that old."

"Well that's nice of you to say."

"So who's this boyfriend?" I asked.

"Oh, I've said too much," she said, turning to wash her hands in the sink. No soap. "You don't want to hear about any of that. And in fact, I'm running late."

I took that as my cue that it was time to leave. Peg piled about twenty cookies onto a paper plate and quickly covered them with Saran Wrap, then thrust the plate into my hands. "Enjoy these with your family. And give some to your friend at school on Monday. I think they'll still be good if you keep them wrapped up in plastic."

"Sure," I said, slowly making my way to the door.

"Where are my shoes?" Peg asked, rhetorically, but there they were, right in the entry hall.

"They're in here," I called as I was about to make my way outside.

Peg appeared behind me with another towering plate of cookies covered in a sloppy bouffant of plastic wrap. "Ah, of course!" she said, almost wild-eyed. "I'm such a loopy-loo, you know."

"OK, well, I'll see you around the neighborhood," I said.

"Come visit me any time," she said, putting the cookies down on a small table near the entrance then sitting down to put on her shoes.

I headed out, and Peg shut the door behind me. I found the whole interaction very strange, especially her urgency. A secret boyfriend? Was it her secret or his? It all seemed very suspicious.

I took my time walking home. What was the hurry?

The sun was just about to sneak behind the house at the top of the hill, and it cast long shadows down the length of the cul-de-sac. As I neared our driveway and the thick hedges between our house and Alex's place, I turned back to look behind me. The glare was at its worst right now, and I was momentarily blinded by the light. Someone was there, though. I couldn't see them, but I could sense them, and then they were gone. A shadow I'd just caught the edge of, disappearing into a house or hurriedly vanishing into one of the tree-shrouded driveways.

I thought I heard a door closing somewhere, and I was absolutely sure that someone on the cul-de-sac was playing music.

CHAPTER THIRTY-NINE

Lew

F LETCHER IN MERCHANDISING said his daughter had left her bike behind when she went off to college, and he asked if maybe Lizzie would want it. It hadn't been ridden in years, he said, so I figured, why not? That's what Judy and I had always said, after all, that the cul-de-sac was so quiet you could ride bikes on it without fear of getting killed like you would in the City. And maybe it would finally win me some points with my daughter.

So today, Fletcher brought the bike to the office and we jammed it into the back of the Nissan. He had to show me how to take the front wheel off, and I was pretty sure I got it back on the right way when I put it back together after getting home.

"Everyone, come to the garage!" I yelled, having arrived before Judy had finished cooking dinner. I couldn't tell if she was excited or annoyed as she took off her apron and placed it delicately on the countertop beside her. She was cooking something involving chicken and had a lot of bowls sitting around, way more than I would have thought you would need to make dinner for three people, but I put it out of mind. I was on a mission.

"Lizzie, are you coming?" There had been no response from upstairs, but eventually I heard her door snap open, and her heavy, thudding footsteps grew louder. I knew from the look on her face that I was going to have to sell this big news and sell it hard.

"To the garage!" I yelled as if I was leading a parade. As Judy approached, I pecked her on the cheek and squeezed her arm—as lovingly as was possible in the tiny hallway between the garage and the kitchen.

As we all pushed through into the garage, I called out, "There it is!"

"There what is?" It was the first thing Lizzie had said since I arrived home.

"The bike! Your new bike!"

"Doesn't look like a new bike," she said, rolling her eyes.

"Well it's new to you. And it's barely used, really. I got it from a guy at work."

"Super."

"Thanks, honey," Judy said. "It looks like a great bike. Don't you think so, Lizzie?"

"Sure. Thanks," she said. Then she turned on her heel and walked back inside.

I was crestfallen, but I'm not sure why. I'd played out the scenario in my head for the last hour in the car ride home, and knew with almost exact precision how it was going to play out, and sure enough it did. What did I expect was going to happen? Why couldn't things just be *normal*?

The dinner, let me be frank, was disgusting. It was supposed to be a healthy take on fried chicken—gluten free, I'm sure, but I didn't ask—covered in something that was obviously supposed to be crunchy but didn't come close to turning out that way after half an hour in the oven. The green beans, drowned in oil, were soggy and gross. I ate what I could, without comment.

"Lizzie, I saw that your math grades are up," I said during one of the many quiet moments during the meal. "I guess that tutoring is doing some good, yeah?"

"Yeah," she said. "Pretty good."

"You're feeling confident?"

"So far, yeah."

"Great. Let me know if you need anything."

"I will. Can I be excused?"

She'd barely touched her food and would probably sneak down later to eat a bag of chips and ice cream right from the carton. God, I envied her.

"Sure," I said. "Take your plate."

Lizzie dumped the plate in the sink and disappeared to her room, the door shutting loudly, but not outright slammed at least. It was quiet for a bit.

"Thanks for cooking dinner," I finally said to Judy to break the silence. She had said little over the course of the meal. "I know it's a lot of work." I couldn't bring myself to compliment the food.

"Well, sorry it sucked," she said. "I tried a new recipe, and sometimes it doesn't work out." She seemed equally happy to change the subject. "Thanks for getting Lizzie the bike." Expressing gratitude was something she had recently said we should try to work on.

"Do you think she'll ride it?"

"I don't know," Judy said. "I heard her say something a while back about how only the losers ride bikes to school."

"Ah, wish I'd known."

"Maybe she'll use it for something else, though."

"Yeah, maybe." I played with my food a bit, pushing the remainder of the oil-drenched beans off to the side of the plate. "A paper route?"

Judy laughed. Yeah, right.

CHAPTER FORTY
Jean Claire

"WHAT, YOU BOUGHT a bike?" I asked Eliza, who was sweating/pedaling her way up my driveway. It had been weeks since we'd had a proper hangout after school. It was just too much work to walk all the way to each other's houses, and Mother never gave me a ride anywhere. "Teach me Your way, oh Lord," she would constantly say, "I will walk in Your truth." I didn't know what that was supposed to mean, but she said it any time I asked her to drive me somewhere, even if I was late for school. But Eliza now had a bicycle, which was at least a partial solution to our transportation problem.

"No, I stole it," she said as she hit the brakes, sliding to a slightly awkward stop. Her eyes rolled back in her head. "My dad got it for me. Obviously to try to buy some family points. It's used, though."

"Well, it's a pretty nice bike," I said. Not that I knew anything about bikes, but it wasn't rusty or anything. Someone had taken pretty good care of it, at least, and it even seemed to be the right size for Eliza.

"I guess. It's better than walking," she said. She climbed down from the bike and without a thought just let it fall over in the driveway, right where she was standing. We went inside and walked upstairs, directly to my room. Mother was in the kitchen, muttering some prayer I did not want to get caught up in.

"So, what about Halloween?" Eliza asked. "Are we going to do a group costume or what?"

This was a complicated question. Mother was against Halloween, as she felt it to be "a crass celebration of paganism," but she knew there was no way to eradicate it completely as long as I attended public school (which she was also against, but also too poor to send me to private). However, costumes were completely banned. I had dodged the subject with Eliza for weeks, but now Halloween was just a few days away, and I'd have to face the issue directly.

"How about cheerleaders?" I asked. It was a costume I could get away with pretty easily by just wearing a sweater over the top and removing it once I got to school. It'd also be a cheap one to pull off if I could catch a ride to the Goodwill.

"Ugh, gross." Eliza grimaced.

"Lifeguards?"

Eliza stared at me like I was an idiot. "What about hippies, like from the seventies?" she suggested.

Too complicated, too hard to hide. "What if we go as teachers?" I said. "Like, wear that striped blouse Barbie G always has on and some nasty slacks?"

"I seriously doubt anyone would get that. They would just think we're nerds."

"We are nerds, Eliza," I deadpanned. I was joking, but

only sort of. Eliza didn't respond either way.

"Superheroes?" she asked. Ugh, no. Way too expensive.

We weren't getting very far here. We went back and forth for longer than I care to think about, but finally we settled on a decent compromise: Daphne and Velma from *Scooby-Doo*. Of course I would have to be Velma because of my height, but I figured I could dig up an orange sweater and some fake glasses without too much trouble. Mother wouldn't think anything of it.

After a discussion about where we would meet before school—Sunset Market, of course—the conversation moved to other topics, which was a blessing.

"What's all this computer stuff?" Eliza asked, looking through a collection of Amazon-boxed packages in a corner of the room.

"That's my new job," I said. "Or at least it's how I'm making some extra money. You know, another side hustle."

"What are you talking about?"

"I buy something on Amazon, then I write a really bad review about it. Then the company emails me and begs me to take the review down. Sometimes they just refund the purchase, sometimes they even pay me in addition to the refund."

"You're shitting me," Eliza said, her face aghast. "Why would these companies do that?"

"Because Amazon reviews are everything for these companies. If they get one bad review, it really hurts their business. They have to have good reviews or they won't sell anything. So it's win-win."

"Why not just get them to pay you to write good reviews then?"

"I've read that it's possible, but it's harder to do. I guess that's a business you can build, but I'm just starting out. Anyway, after they give me the refund, I sell the product on eBay. Most of the time I don't even open the box, so I can list it as brand new."

"How much have you made doing this?"

"Five hundred so far, but I just started."

"You are *shitting* me! Why didn't you tell me about this?" she said.

"I dunno. I thought you'd think less of me, I guess."

"Well, yeah, it's pretty shady, but five hundred. Come on!"

"My goal is to get to ten thousand by the end of the school year. It's ambitious but doable—as long as Amazon doesn't find out about it, anyway."

"So, why do you need ten thousand dollars?" she asked.

That was the big question. How to answer it? Say that I wanted to buy a car when I turned sixteen? That I was saving for college? Or the truth?

"I'm building a nest egg," I said finally. In the silence, I could hear Mother singing one of her hymns downstairs, but only barely.

"A nest egg for what?"

"For the future," I said, then finally relented. "Someday I gotta get out of here."

Eliza snorted. If she caught my drift, she didn't let on. "Yeah, don't we all?" she said. "Well, maybe you'll win the drawing for the Money Machine and get even more money."

"Yeah, but we would split that."

"Right. Well, if you ever need help with this Amazon, uh, *business*, let me know."

"Sure, but it's something you can do, too, without me. It's pretty easy."

"Nah, I'd get in trouble," she said.

We sat around for a while watching YouTube clips and TikToks. Eliza said we should try to make a dance video of our own, but that seemed like too much work, and neither of us had any rhythm. Eventually it was time for her to go. Mother would only tolerate visitors for so long, and the days were getting shorter. After Halloween, daylight savings would end, and then it would be getting dark at, like, five o'clock. We'd probably have to hang out on weekends unless someone gave one of us a ride. I knew that traveling by foot or bike much after dark would be difficult to sell to any of the parents.

As she was strapping on her pink bike helmet, Eliza said, "You know that neighbor of mine, the nice old lady? Peg?"

"Yeah," I said. "I remember."

"She was acting really weird when I dropped off her wrapping paper."

"Weird how?"

"Like she was all giddy. Like she was in love or something. She was making all these cookies, and she gave me a bunch to take home."

"It sounds like you're saying you didn't bring me any cookies."

"Oh, sorry," she said, insincerely. "I didn't think you'd like them. They were awful."

"Uh-huh," I said. "Anyway, what about this lady?"

"I dunno. She basically said she had a secret boyfriend she couldn't talk about."

"Creepy," I said, "but you know that old people are weird."

"That's true."

"She probably met someone on Tinder."

"Old people don't use Tinder."

"No?" I asked.

"Oh God, what if she's getting catfished?"

"Oh man, that would be the worst," I said. "You know all the perverts out there trying to take advantage of older women. Do you think she has any money?"

"I don't know. But anyone who owns a house around here has to have some kind of money. Maybe I'll keep an eye on her. See if anyone strange pays a visit to the cul-de-sac."

"Sounds like a plan," I said, "but next time bring me some freakin' cookies."

CHAPTER FORTY-ONE

Lupe

"LUPE!" MR. PERCY hollered. "What's for dinner?"

Nothing was for dinner, because I'd asked Mr. Percy what he wanted for dinner right after lunch, and he didn't say anything. He just fell asleep in his recliner, and I left him there so I could have a moment of quiet. He slept for hours, and then I forgot all about it. Now it was getting dark out.

"Oh, Mr. Percy," I said, rushing into the living room where he was still half lying on the couch, half sliding onto the floor. "We're out of food. What do you want?"

When I first started working for Mr. Percy a year ago, I'd used my broken-English trick with him, pretending to understand little of what he said. It had worked beautifully well with former clients to get me out of doing the jobs I didn't want to do. They would get frustrated and just shake out the rug themselves. With Mr. Percy, it didn't get me anywhere. When he wanted something, he just repeated himself over and over, each time in a louder voice. It drove me insane. Eventually, I relented and gave up on it and started using my normal speaking voice with him. He didn't even notice the change.

"Lupe, don't be a fool. If I don't tell you what I want, it's your job to figure something out."

"I need to run to the store then. How about a salad?" It was worth a try.

"A salad? How about ribs?"

"Mr. Percy, there's no time to make ribs. It's getting late."

"You can buy the ones they already cooked and just heat them up. Not as good, but it'll do. I'm hungry. Get some macaroni and cheese, too. Potato salad."

"I'll take the car, OK?"

"Yeah, go ahead. Be quick about it."

I picked the keys up off the hall table and rushed to the garage, climbed into Mr. Percy's 1972 Ford pickup, and turned the key. *Click. Click.* Nothing at all. The truck wouldn't start. This was terrible, terrible news, as it was the only vehicle we had to get around in.

I slumped back into the house and found Mr. Percy exactly where I'd left him.

"Mr. Percy, the car won't start."

"The car won't start, you say?" He turned in my direction for dramatic effect, even though he couldn't see me. "Well, I guess you better get to walking."

"It so late, Mr. Percy. Can we order delivery?"

"Order delivery?" He was so aghast I thought he would fall the rest of the way off the couch. "I guess you want me to take the fee out of your paycheck?"

It was tempting, but delivery fees were so high, and deliveries took so long out here. I'd rather just suck it up and keep the ten dollars. "I'll just walk. I'll call Triple A tomorrow for the car."

"Hurry up then. I'm hungry."

"Yes, Mr. Percy."

I slung my purse over a shoulder and hit the road. It wasn't really that far to Sunset Market, but it was getting dark and there were no lights along the stretch of road between the cul-de-sac and the store. But if I hurried I could at least get back before it was completely dark outside.

I was halfway to the market when I realized the sun was going down faster than I expected. I quickened my already fast pace, almost jogging the three-quarters of a mile to get out from under the trees and into civilization. No moon tonight, not yet anyway, so it would be very dark in the next fifteen minutes.

Finally, I rounded a gentle bend and saw the streetlights that indicated I was coming up on the shopping center. Fortunately, I needed only a handful of items and they were all in the same place, right in front of the deli. Saucy ribs, macaroni, potato salad. I paid with cash and was out the door inside of two minutes.

Still, I wasn't fast enough. Now it was almost completely dark, and I knew Mr. Percy would soon be fuming that food was not on the table—or, at least, on a plate in his lap.

As I walked, carefully keeping to the shoulder of the road, a noise startled me. It was a bell—*jingle jingle*—and I instinctively turned around. Just what I expected: a bicycle coming up the road. At first I thought it had a small headlamp on the handlebars, but as the rider approached, I could see it was actually a cell phone flashlight, crudely clutched between her hand and one of the handlebars so she could find her way. The bike approached quickly—it was the teenage girl from across the street. I stopped and watched her zoom by. I raised a hand to wave—or at least to acknowledge that I'd seen her. She smiled at me, I think, though it was hard to see for sure in the dark. She chimed the bell again, and off she went, disappearing around the gentle curves and the enormous oak trees.

I resumed my walk back to the house, though for some reason I felt I had lost the sense of urgency, and my pace slowed. It was not going to get much darker than this, so what did it matter? Mr. Percy could wait for his dinner a little while longer. It's not like he would be any less surly if I magically appeared at the doorstep right now with a plate of hot ribs in my hands.

A minute or two passed. I considered the darkness and the trees, trying to calm the nerves I always felt when I had to be alone in the night. I thought about Mr. Percy, always alone and always in the night no matter what time it was. How sad it all must have been for him.

Maybe I should hurry up.

I quickened my stride and hoisted the paper bag by its handles to propel myself forward, then disaster abruptly struck. One of the handles on the bag broke off, causing the bag to rip and nearly spill open. I instinctively kneeled down in an attempt to limit the damage and hopefully avoid losing everything on the road. Since everything was already cooked and packaged in plastic takeout containers, I was sure that they had burst open upon impact, which would mean going back to the store for more food *and* having my paycheck docked for the replacement meal. *No gracias.*

But I had saved it all. My maneuver had worked; I had clutched my free arm around the bag just in time, preventing anything from spilling out. It was going to be awkward carrying it in a bundle like this without ripping further, all the way back to the house, but better than the alternative.

In the chaos, I hadn't noticed the car coming up the road, driving surprisingly slowly. The headlights illuminated the scene, which must have been quite amusing for whoever was driving.

"What do we have here?" called a man as the car pulled up beside me, the passenger window rolled down. "Do you need help?"

I peered into the car but couldn't see the driver at all. The engine rumbled, destroying the silence of the early autumn night. I said nothing, just looked into the darkness of the car, hoping my eyes would adjust.

"We are neighbors, I think," he called. "Do you live on the cul-de-sac?"

"Yes," I said, a bit relieved. "Who are you again?"

"Some late-night shopping, I see!" he said, laughing. "Perhaps I can give you a ride this last half a mile?"

"Oh, it's not far," I said. "I'm OK."

"You don't look OK," the voice said. "Put your items in the back seat. I'll have you home in sixty seconds."

I could feel the bag continuing to rip. The ribs were heavy and unbalanced and determined to push their way out the bottom of the sack. This was stupid. Why not take a quick ride from the neighbor and save myself the headache of potentially dropping everything? I hoisted the bag a bit, and it ripped further. I was about to lose it.

"OK," I said.

I opened the rear door of the car and carefully put the ripped bag on the seat to avoid spilling its contents further. The car was incredibly clean. It wasn't new, but it smelled new. As I opened the passenger door, I noticed that the interior light didn't come on, but I could see the driver a little better because of the lights on the dashboard. Older but distinguished. Graying hair, kind of slicked back, wearing a button-down shirt and a blazer. He moved a briefcase from the passenger seat and slid it into the back. He looked, I don't know, harmless. Just a guy on his way home from work.

"What's your name?" he asked as I settled into the leather seat. It was a nice car. Comfortable. I immediately felt better.

"Lupe," I said.

"Hello, Lupe," he replied. I could make out a toothy smile in the darkness. "I'm Klaus."

CHAPTER FORTY-TWO

Peg

HALLOWEEN WAS NEVER much of an event on the cul-de-sac. There were no children on the street (and new girl Eliza was probably too old), and even if there were kids around, their parents would have driven them to greener pastures for trick-or-treating. I don't remember the last time I saw a single Halloween decoration on the block. Not a string of orange lights, not a single cardboard ghost. You were lucky if you saw a Christmas decoration around here, not including my own living room, of course.

As usual, Klaus and I were sitting in the kitchen. He was talking distractedly about whatever wine it was he'd opened. I would have liked to have paid attention, but I found myself rather annoyed and was letting my mind wander.

"Well, Peg, you certainly seem to have enjoyed it!"

I was shaken out of my daze by Klaus's voice. His accent and exuberance were bothering me today. The wine was better than the usual ones he served—as it turned out, I'd already drunk the whole glass—but I didn't think it merited this much chatter. But what did I know about it?

"Oh!" I said, trying to switch gears and get back into the moment, like they say in yoga. "Yes, definitely."

"You don't think it's got too much oak? Chardonnay often does."

"Hmm," I said. "No, I don't think so." I helped myself to another glass and walked out to the deck that overlooked Klaus's forested backyard. The sun was going down, but it was still warm. It was a pretty sunset, a layer of burnt orange on top of the dense, shadowy landscape underneath. The sunlight never quite pushed through the thicket of woods to the point where it could reach the ground. The area could probably be cleaned up and manicured by a professional, but I'm sure it would be very expensive. Besides, Klaus had told me he liked it *verwildert*—wild and natural.

"Do you think the fires will be bad this year?" I asked, gazing at the sky as I leaned over the railing. We were positioned one story above the ground level, and I figured you could jump off the deck if you had to—like if there was an emergency—because the endless mounds of fallen leaves below would probably break your fall. The overgrown, almost primal landscape had some hippie appeal, but it was a bit too much for me, and in the twilight it all looked a little scary.

"They say they will be," Klaus said. "No rain this season at all."

"We had some rain. When was it, August?"

"But that was over three months ago. And one or two days of rain really don't matter, I think."

"Hmm." I took another sip from my glass. "They say that PG&E may shut off the power on purpose this season. Have you read that?"

"I have heard about that."

"What does that have to do with the fires?" I asked. "I don't understand."

"Because last year many of the fires started when electrical lines fell down in heavy winds. When the lines fall down, they can make a *funke*—um, a spark—and that catches the dry grass on fire, and before you know it, the whole state is burning. They say it happens very quickly." He snapped his fingers and smiled.

"I see. So if they turn off the power, the lines can't spark."

"Right."

"Are you ready for a blackout? Candles, canned food, bottled water?" I asked.

"Well, I certainly have enough reading material," he said, laughing. "But yes, I think I am quite prepared. And even if the power goes out, we'll still have water."

"Sure, right. Of course."

"Speaking of the fires," he said, "do you know what happened to the house next door to yours? Did you live here when it burned down?"

"I did."

"What was it like? Did anyone die?" Klaus asked, looking intensely over the railing at the ground below us, as if he was searching for something he'd lost.

"No, no one died. No one was home at the time," I said. "The woman who lived there, I have to say I didn't care for her much. She was a divorcee who moved here from the City, and the moment she arrived she began complaining about things. My hedges were too tall. My trees were dropping leaves in her yard. Our shared fence wasn't nice enough, and could we split the cost of redoing it? Well, one day I told her, I don't mind the fence at all. In fact, I rather like the fence as it is, I said. And you know what, Klaus? That fence is still standing today. It didn't even get damaged when her house burned down."

"How did the fire start?"

"They say it was oily rags that just burst into flame. She had been redoing her floors, and that kind of thing is always a danger. Something like that." It was basically the truth.

"Of course."

"Anyway, they put out the fire pretty quickly, but as you can see, the house is not inhabitable anymore, and I think someone needs to come tear it down. There was a lot of finger-pointing about blame, and the insurance company wouldn't pay her out. I think the whole thing is still in court. Meanwhile, we're the ones who have to suffer with this…this eyesore."

"It is a truly ugly thing," Klaus said. "Maybe we should finish the job together."

"Yes, burn it to the ground!" I said, half-jokingly.

He turned back to me and smiled, saying nothing, swirling and sipping from his glass.

I considered the man standing before me, idly swirling his wine. "Klaus, why are we always over here? You never come to my house."

He looked at me, his face blank. "We can go to your house, of course. Should I bring the wine?"

"That's not what I mean," I said. "You have never even dropped by my house. Never asked to visit. Never been inside. Are you not curious about where I live? What my home looks like?"

"Of course I am curious. We can go right now." Somehow, I didn't really believe he'd go through with it.

"Klaus, I don't want to drag you to my house right now," I said, growing frustrated. "I want you to *want* to come to my house."

"Of course, *mein liebling*. I understand." He sipped at his wine again. "I do want to go to your house. Why wouldn't I?"

An old, familiar feeling rose up in me, and I found myself oddly annoyed. "Klaus, what is this?"

"What is what?" He looked back at me. We were face-to-face.

"What are we doing?"

"We're drinking wine on Halloween," he said. "Waiting for the children who will never come."

"I mean, what are we doing with each other? What is our future?"

Klaus considered this for a moment. "I don't really know," he finally said. "I will be honest with you, Peg. I greatly enjoy our time together, but I haven't given our long-term future together significant thought. Have you?"

"It's something I think about all the time."

"Oh, I see. Well, I'm a cautious person, as you know, just taking things slowly as this relationship evolves. Is this disagreeable to you?"

"No, I guess not."

"I'm sure things will become altogether clear to both of us very soon, and I appreciate your patience. You are patient, aren't you?"

"Klaus, you know I am not patient," I said.

He laughed. "Yes, but you can *be* patient when you have to?"

"When I have to."

"Just a bit more time," he said. "I think everything will work out for all of us just fine. What is it that people say? *Everything happens for a reason.*"

CHAPTER FORTY-THREE

Eliza

O K, TRUTH: TRICK-OR-TREATING was way better in the suburbs than the City. More houses were open for business, and people were less stingy with the goods. It was so bad in San Francisco that when I was younger, my parents would have to drive me two miles away so we could go door-to-door. Here, it felt like just about everywhere was doling out the treats—except for our cul-de-sac, I guess. It was just as dead here as it was on any other night.

I knew this was probably the last year I was going to be able to pull off trick-or-treating, but I think Jean Claire and I got away with it because, due to her height, people probably thought that I was her big sister, escorting her around town. People were pretty happy to give her a few pieces of candy, but when I held out my pillowcase, I sensed some hesitation more than once. They always gave out the candy in the end, though. Better not to potentially anger a vengeful teenager and risk having your house egged or something.

It was dusk, and I was riding home from Jean Claire's neighborhood on my bike, my bag of candy tied to the handlebars as securely as I could rig it. But when I hit the turn that led to the cul-de-sac, the bag began to come loose, and even though it was just a few dozen yards to my driveway I figured it was best to pull over before everything went spilling into the street in the near dark. I didn't want to lose all that hard-earned candy, and I couldn't bear a lecture the next day from my dad about *what was all this garbage in front of our house and who would pick it up.*

That's when I saw him, the old man who lived in the house across the street, sitting in a rocking chair on the front porch. I'd only ever seen him once before, when Jean Claire and I had tried to sell him the holiday merch and he'd shooed us away.

He was a lot quieter now than he was back then, just rocking back and forth in the warmth of the autumn air. I stared at him for a bit as the rocking slowed and finally stopped. I don't know what it was, but there was definitely something off.

"You OK?" I called out to him.

"Am I OK?" he hollered back. "Why wouldn't I be OK?"

"I don't know," I replied. "You don't look OK."

"Well, I'm fine. My helper Lupe's gone is all."

"Oh, right, I remember her," I said. I stood there with my bike wedged between my legs, watching him in silence for a moment. He didn't seem to move at all. Things were getting a little awkward, so I asked in a loud voice, "Are you expecting her back soon?"

"I don't know," he said. "Probably not."

"Well, I live right across the street. If you need any help, I'm sure my mom can call someone."

"I already called," he said. "But thank you for the offer."

"OK, see ya." I began walking my bike up the hill, the

tires creaking on some grit on the pavement.

He called out one last time. "If you do see Lupe, tell her to come home soon."

I didn't respond and moved along into our driveway. As I was approaching the garage door, I heard it. That music, wafting down the road from somewhere deeper in the cul-de-sac. I'd heard it before. It was old-people music, like from the eighties. It wasn't unusual in this town or on this street, but something compelled me to drop my bike against the garage, leave my candy behind, and take a walk to check it out.

I crept up the cul-de-sac's incline, which was illuminated by a sole street lamp about halfway up the hill. I didn't have to walk far before the music grew louder and louder, and soon I was able to pinpoint its source: the house of Klaus Fischer, officially the creepiest guy in the world.

His house was built so that the living area was on the second floor, over a garage I guess, and there was a balcony off to the side, overlooking what some people might call a yard. My dad called it a mess that *somebody ought to take better care of*, but I could understand if you just weren't the gardening type and didn't want the hassle.

The overgrowth, however, did create a pretty effective shield between Klaus's balcony and the street, but I realized that if I got into just the right position, I could see through the branches and leaves to get a look at the balcony, and even a peek of the room inside the sliding glass door, which was apparently a kitchen. And as I adjusted my view from side to side, that's when I saw it: Klaus and Peg, on the balcony, and they weren't just hanging out. They were kissing.

CHAPTER FORTY-FOUR

Jean Claire

E LIZA TEXTED.

old guy across the street is just
sitting on his porch, waiting

> waiting for what?

for his nurse to come home. I guess
she quit or something

> and he's just sitting there?

just sitting there. he's blind

> that's weird

so weird

we met her once, you know

latinx girl, when we were selling
christmas stuff

> oh yeah, the old guy too
> when are they going to do the
> money machine anyway?

i dunno, we should ask barbie g

soon probably

what are you doing tonight?

                  nothing. eating candy in my room

yeah same

oh btw i know for sure now that
lady peg is seeing the creeper up
the road

                        really?

i saw them making out

                    what, where?

outside, on his balcony

                omg that is so gross

so gross

              what is wrong with her

guess she's lonely

                    but still

it's a pretty good excuse

                  is it, though?

                  creeper for real

yeah

It was at that moment that Mother burst into the room.

No knock, and when the door flew open, it smashed into the wall with such a huge noise, I literally threw my phone into the air. It landed behind my bed, where I had stashed an obscene number of candy wrappers.

"What the hell!" I yelled, mostly out of shock.

"Do not curse at me!" she yelled back. "Why is this door closed?"

I was still in a high-key panic. My heart was racing, and I knew this was a bad situation for me to be in when having any kind of discussion with Mother. But she had started things by crashing into the room, and at that point I guess I knew we were going to get into it.

"I'm not cursing at you—you surprised me by busting in here!"

"Why is the door closed," she demanded. It wasn't a question.

"For privacy, obvs."

"In my house, you have to earn privacy, and you have not earned it." Finally, she appeared to see my yet-to-be-eaten Halloween candy stash, which I was strictly not supposed to have in my room. "And what is this?"

"Just some snacks," I said, trying to low-key shove the fun size Snickers wrappers and Sour Patch Kids bags under my pillow.

Mother shook her head, looking me up and down. "This is unacceptable, and you know it. Keep it up and you will lose your door."

"What are you even talking about?" I asked.

"I'll take your door off the hinges, then when you cry

about *your privacy*, I'll be able to hear you down the hall."

"You wouldn't," I said.

"I would and I will," she replied. She looked down at my shorts, which were admittedly too small, but that's what happens when you try to limit your clothing budget. "Look at you," she spat. "You are a whore. You have lust in your heart."

Mother was often out of control, but this was really going too far. I could tell things were getting worse, and I was starting to worry that another three and a half years of this would drive me insane. There was a reason my brother Will had yet to visit once after graduating last year. Good thing I was saving every penny I could from my Amazon gig.

"What do you want from me?" I asked.

"I want what I have always wanted," she said. "I want you to clean up this pigsty, dress yourself appropriately, and prepare to come downstairs for worship. If anyone needs to repent and ask for forgiveness today, it is you."

"We all need to ask for forgiveness. Right, Mother? That's what you always tell me."

"Yes, Jean Claire. We all need forgiveness, but some of us need more than others. Now prepare yourself."

She turned on her heel and left. It was definitely time to double up my Amazon efforts. But first I had to find my phone.

CHAPTER FORTY-FIVE

Alex

THE DOORBELL RANG, almost certainly Eliza here for her tutoring session, and it was another slog to the door to let her in. When I arrived, she was staring at her phone, oblivious that I had even opened the door. To my great surprise, her hair was combed and her clothes looked clean, but her outfit was more ridiculous than usual, a pink T-shirt tucked into a pair of beige pants that barely went below her knees. In lieu of a belt, she had some kind of rope around her waist, like something you would tie back your drapes with.

"What's this outfit?" I asked, breaking her rapt attention to TikTok or whatever it was she was staring at.

"I borrowed some of it from Jean Claire," she said, looking up finally and smiling.

"You look like the scarecrow from *The Wizard of Oz*," I said.

"What's that?" she asked.

"From the movie."

"I haven't seen it."

"Then your parents have failed," I said.

She shrugged. "I guess."

It was another few weeks until the end of the semester, and the work was getting harder. Quadratic equations were particularly tricky for Eliza to understand, and I could tell she wasn't really engaged in the work. She did the assignments but sloppily. I think she understood how to get the answers—she just didn't care.

I had her work on some practice problems, but she seemed distracted. Maybe the week off she would be getting soon for the Thanksgiving break would be good for her and would get her ready for finals soon after.

"You know your next-door neighbor, Peg?" she asked, finally.

"Yeah."

"I saw her at the house across the street, kissing that German guy."

"Really? How'd you see that?"

"From the road. At the right angle, you can just barely see the balcony."

"Dedicated, I see."

"What? They were right there, like they wanted everyone to see."

"Mm-hmm."

"I'm *ser*."

"Ser?" I asked.

"*Serious*." Eliza rolled her eyes.

"Sure, OK. But why do you care?"

"I dunno," she said. "Because she seems like a nice lady, and that guy Klaus is totally gross, like I told you before."

I vaguely remembered the conversation.

"I bet he's taking advantage of her."

"Maybe she's taking advantage of him. You ever think of that?"

"Um, right," she said. "She makes cookies, and he's probably a Nazi or something."

"Oh, so you know about the Nazis?"

"Well, that they were bad."

"Yeah, they were also around seventy-five years ago. I'm pretty sure he's not a Nazi."

"You know what I mean."

"No, I have no idea what you mean," I said. "Nazis didn't bring ladies up to their balconies for make-out sessions. They burned books. Invaded Europe. Exterminated Jews by the millions."

"Well, all I know is, he's gross and she shouldn't be with him," she said.

"I don't suppose you've shared your opinions on this with Peg?"

"Of course not—that would be nosy."

"Well, this is all very interesting," I said. It was indeed very interesting, and I was a little annoyed, though not surprised, that Peg had not mentioned her little dalliance during one of her visits. Surely, I could be trusted with her secret more than anyone else she knew. But I let it go for the moment. "I'm sure you'll keep an eye on things and make certain I'm informed when they decide to get married."

She made a face. "Ew, that is so gross."

"That's romance, Eliza."

She shook her head, disgusted.

"Listen," I changed the subject. "Do you think it would be weird if I gave you a key to get in here? It's not easy for me to get to the door sometimes and, you know, it would just be easier if you could let yourself in. Also, I guess it's good for a neighbor to have a key in case something happens. Emergencies and all." I don't know why I felt embarrassed by the discussion. I guess because somewhere in my repressed subconscious, it felt wrong for a grown man to be giving a teenager a key to his house. Anyway, I produced the key from my pocket and placed it between us on the coffee table.

"I guess," she said. "I don't even have a key to *my* house, though."

"What are you talking about?"

"I just haven't needed one since we moved here. My mom is always home and the door's almost never locked. And I can go in through the keypad on the garage if it's a crazy emergency. Maybe you could get, like, a smart lock or something and give me the code."

"Can you just take the key?" I asked, frustrated. "Look, you can put it on that polar bear key chain I bought from you, so you don't lose it." I pointed to the little white bear, which was still sitting untouched on the coffee table, right where I'd left it weeks ago.

She shrugged, grabbed the bear, and clipped the key onto its key ring, something I would not have been able to do. She then dropped it into her cesspool of a backpack, which I was sure meant it would never be seen again.

"You can use that next weekend when you come over for tutoring," I said.

"OK," she replied and turned her attention back to the last couple of problems on today's worksheet.

"Try not to lose the key, OK?" I said again, but she wasn't paying attention.

CHAPTER FORTY-SIX

Klaus

I SNIFFED AT the smoke in the air. Just a few days prior the first fires of autumn had erupted, about fifty miles away, and the local news reported on the hour about how large the fire had grown. The sky was starting to show a little haze, but not much. The smoke wasn't bad enough to require a mask, yet, but you could smell it if the wind was blowing the right way. It would only get worse, though. Soon enough, everyone would be encouraged to stay indoors for weeks on end due to the worsening air quality, and the sky would be a sick shade of orange.

For now, I could still work, though the ground was harder than ever and the digging was absolutely *schwierig*. It had to be done at night, because the cul-de-sac now had too many eyes. Not just Peg, who could show up unannounced at any time, but also the young girl down the way, who always seemed to be coming, going, and lingering on the street. I didn't believe she knew about my relationship with Peg. We were both very discreet, and the secluded nature of my home made it impossible to see inside.

Digging the grave in advance was both a risk and an asset. It was a risk because, of course, it could be discovered and would be difficult to explain. (I had already planned to say I was putting in an irrigation system should anyone question me and had purchased much of the equipment that would back that up.) On the other hand, the grave was an asset, because of course I would not have to do the work after she was taken. I was still racked with indecision on that front. When to do it or if I should do it at all. Lately, I had been leaning against, but, well, you never know when the winds will change. It was better to be prepared, just in case.

The Mexican girl had proven that. My primary memories of the night afterward were sadly limited to the hard work of digging in the dark, as that had been an impromptu event. It really ruined theexperienceand created a rushed unpleasantness around the whole thing. It was better to take your time, not have to worry about witnesses, and more fully relish the hours that followed. With the Mexican girl, the night was marked by nothing more than a small crucifix pendant as a souvenir, resting in my pocket at the moment, her remains a decaying memory under a pile of dirt a few feet to my left.

The recent time change meant that it was very dark, but my eyes had adjusted to the moonlight and, let's be *offenherzig* and honest, this was not work that required very much attention to detail. Dig as deep as you could, cover the body with quicklime and dirt, and if possible put a dead animal on top in order to throw off any cadaver dogs that might come sniffing around. That wasn't a real risk unless you were a suspect, of course. There wasn't anything to connect me to any of these women, and even with the Mexican girl it was unlikely that anyone would bother knocking on my door, asking if I knew anything about her disappearance. And if they did, I could always just pretend to be away and avoid the issue entirely.

I still hoped that the Mexican girl would be the end to my murderous adventures. The thrill when she climbed into the car had been electrifying, but she had barely even struggled when I put my hands around her neck and pushed my thumbs into her windpipe. You never want a brawl to erupt—which is why I had told her to put on her seat belt, smiling inwardly with the knowledge that she was unwittingly restraining herself and putting herself in a position of vulnerability that would make it harder for her to get away. No, you don't want a fight, but you do want some kind of challenge to get the blood pumping a little. Father had said the same about his work during the war. Killing an undesirable offered no excitement if they simply stood there silently. It was especially unrewarding to simply shoot them in the back. You needed to see the tears if it was to count.

The count now stood at seven, which was a fine number, but I knew in my heart that the Mexican girl just wouldn't be a proper grand finale. It simply would not do, this limp and decidedly uncompelling conclusion. I needed a fighter, a challenge. If not a physical one, then an emotional one. Peg was hardly a fighter, but I knew I would have to overcome my own emotions about her, because I did enjoy her company, and I would miss her when she was gone. Even if she presented no real physical struggle, I would have a struggle of my own to contend with. And that perhaps would be worthy of her placement as number eight, the final page in the book.

But then again, perhaps she was not the one. Too much risk, too close to home. But if not Peg, then who?

I refocused my efforts on my shovel and the ground below my feet. This decision would have to wait. At the moment, there was work to be done.

CHAPTER FORTY-SEVEN
Alex

I HAVE TO say, I was developing a sense of pride about the girl. No longer did she struggle to multiply six by seven. No longer did I have to explain how parentheses worked in an equation. She did most of the work without having to involve me at all, and she even appeared to be washing her hair regularly. I pretty much just pocketed the cash and looked at my phone, answering occasional questions when she had them. She would ace the final; I was sure of it.

And that was for the best, because something was feeling off for me. I was having more and more trouble concentrating on the subject matter, and I found myself staring out the window, almost like I was looking at my body from outside the house.

"Explain to me how logarithms work again," she said. "Alex? Hello?"

I was aware of a sheet of paper being waved in front of my face. Things were fuzzy. I tried to wave off the intrusion, but nothing seemed to be working right. My arm wasn't responding, and this metallic taste suddenly hit my tongue.

"You OK?" Eliza's voice sounded hollow and distant.

Something was very wrong, and as a sense of panic and

doom began to set in, the world disappearing from the outside in. I quickly became aware what was happening, as this wasn't the first time.

"I'm having a seizure," I yelled at her. Or at least I tried to. All that came out was a pathetic *bleaaaaargh*. And then I toppled over, my head fortunately hitting the couch instead of the floor or the coffee table, and everything went black.

CHAPTER FORTY-EIGHT
Eliza

ALEX CRUMPLED MORE than he toppled. After yelling—louder than anything I'd heard come out of him before—he began to shake and moan and make all kinds of disgusting sounds. The couch we were both sitting on started rocking back and forth. And while the drooling was always a problem, this was crazy. He wasn't just dribbling a little—he was high-key projectile spitting.

The four hours of babysitting training I took two years ago hadn't prepared me for this. You were supposed to make sure he didn't bite off his tongue, right? That's what they said on TV. But how? Should I hold his mouth open or something? I thought for a second about trying to somehow wedge my math workbook between his teeth, but he was flailing around so much that I'd probably just make matters worse.

I couldn't get help from my parents, as they were out on some kind of couples-only day trip, so I figured the next best thing would be to get another responsible adult involved. I ran out the door, not even bothering to put my shoes back on, and headed up the cul-de-sac to the house next door. If anyone knew what to do here, it would be Peg.

I rang the bell frantically and banged on the door. *Please please please be home*, I chanted, barely under my breath. I rang again.

It didn't take her long to answer, and she immediately picked up on my distress. "What's the matter?"

"It's Alex," I blurted out. "I think he's having a seizure!"

She didn't hesitate, quickly following me back to Alex's house and through the door I'd left wide open.

As we rushed to the couch, I could see that the seizure was already over. The spasms and shaking had stopped, and Alex was simply lying there, unmoving.

"Oh my God, he's dead!" I screamed.

Peg was right behind me, whipping around the couch and dropping to her knees on the floor. She said nothing, putting her fingers to his neck, feeling for a pulse.

"He's not dead," she said. "His pulse is actually pretty strong. Call 911."

I fumbled for my phone and unlocked it.

"No." It was Alex. His voice was feeble, but it was at least a voice. I froze before hitting the green "call" button. "Don't call."

"You need to go to the hospital," Peg said.

"I know," Alex said, still lying in a sort of cashew shape. "But no ambulance. Can you drive me?"

Peg looked at me. Could we? Should we?

"Please," Alex moaned.

Peg pet Alex's head as if he were a child, or a puppy, maybe. "I'll pull my car up."

I sat with Alex while Peg retrieved her car, which fortunately was a four-door. She got the car as close to the front door as possible and opened the back so he could lie down inside. She left the car running as she hustled back into Alex's house. Alex said nothing throughout, breathing gently and calmly.

"Now what?" she asked, looking at me again. "Do you think we can carry him?"

"I don't know what else we can do," I said. I turned to Alex, saying, "We're going to have to prop you up, unless you want us to drag you out of here."

He didn't say anything either way, so I maneuvered my body to his side. Peg got behind the couch, and together we pushed and pulled to get him into a basically upright position. Peg then came around the front and we each got on one side of him, hoisting him up by his shoulders and each putting an arm around his torso. He was nothing but bones underneath his hoodie, and he was so light that moving him around was no trouble at all. Maneuvering around the coffee table was the hardest part, but it was otherwise pretty easy to get him down the entry hall, out the door, and into the car. He seemed a little more together by this point, and he was able to help us out by wriggling himself into the back seat, where he remained curled in a fetal position.

I ran back inside and looked around. What would we need at the hospital? His wallet. His phone. His shoes. His cane. I collected them all and ran back outside. Peg was in the driver's seat, buckled up and ready to go.

She drove to the hospital—the only one in town—fast but under control. Mom would have been swerving all over the place and probably would have had to pull over, broken down in tears. But Peg had an intensity that scared me almost as much as what was going on with Alex in the back seat.

"He's not going to die, is he?" I asked, sweating.

"No, I think he'll be fine." Peg was oddly calm. "Are your parents not at home?"

"No, they're out for the day."

"Maybe you should let them know what's going on."

"Yeah, yeah. I'll text them." I hastily put together a note to Mom. She was terrible with texts, though. She probably wouldn't see it until tomorrow.

At the hospital, Peg ran in, and a beefy orderly came out with a wheelchair. He had a lot less trouble getting Alex into the chair than we'd had getting him into the car—just picked him up and plopped him down like a bag of groceries. They wheeled him into the back and left Peg and me with the paperwork. Fortunately, they were understanding of the fact that we were just neighbors, not relatives. His driver's license and insurance card, both in his wallet, were enough for them to work with. He was already in the system, as this wasn't the first time Alex had been here for a seizure.

"Is he going to be OK?" I asked.

"I think he'll be fine," the kind intake nurse said. "We'll give him an IV drip for a few hours, then he can go home. There's medication for his condition, but I don't think he takes it."

"Why not?" I asked.

She shrugged. "Some people just don't want to do what's

best for them, no matter how hard you try to explain it."

"That sounds crazy," I said.

"Happens all the time," she said, smiling through resigned eyes. "But maybe you and I can work together to make sure he does."

We waited in the lobby for close to an hour. Peg and I didn't discuss staying. It just seemed like the right thing to do. Finally a doctor appeared and told us mostly stuff we already knew. Alex had had a seizure. He was going to be fine. He really needed to take his medication. It'd be a few hours, but there was no need for him to stay overnight. After his IV was done, he could get a ride home on the local Med-Ride bus, which would take him straight to his door.

"No, we can wait for him," Peg said. "Or, at least, I can wait for him." She turned to me. "I can run you home if you need to go. Or want to go."

I had more homework to do, but it wasn't much. For some reason, being at home alone now sounded a little scary. "I'll stick around, I guess," I said.

While we waited, Peg and I flipped through old magazines, checked our phones, made small talk. I wanted so badly to ask her about Klaus, but I couldn't muster the courage. She didn't hint about it, and I never spied her texting anyone. Maybe it wasn't serious at all. I mean, if they were boyfriend and girlfriend, she would have told him about this big adventure immediately, right?

"You did the right thing in coming to get help, Eliza," Peg said at one point. "You have a good head on your shoulders. I don't know what I would have done when I was your age."

"Nah, you're the one who's so calm and collected," I said.

Peg looked me in the eye and smiled. "I guess we're just a good combination to have around when there's a crisis."

"Teamwork, right?" I asked.

Peg nodded.

✖

"DOES IT ALWAYS take this long for him to come to the door?" Mom asked me, standing outside Alex's house.

One day after the trip to the hospital, the smell of smoke in the air was worse, and Mom was starting to cough a bit here and there. But it still wasn't overwhelming, and they said we could still do outdoor activities within reason. No one had canceled P.E. or anything. Barbie G said that it was only a matter of time, though, and that soon enough we'd need to stay indoors or wear masks to protect our lungs until the fires cleared up or the wind shifted. Mom said she'd ordered survival masks on Amazon.

"Yeah, usually," I said. "I can hold the soup if it's too heavy. Though I don't know why you didn't just heat it up at his house."

"That would be rude, Lizzie. You can't just show up with cold soup."

I rolled my eyes. "You can show up with soup from a can, though?"

"It's not from a can!" she protested. "It's Whole Foods

turkey and wild rice, freshly prepared."

I shook my head and said nothing.

Finally the door opened. "When are you going to remember that I gave you a key?" Alex asked, propped up by his cane.

"Oh gosh," I said. "I'm sorry."

Alex dabbed at his lips with a tissue. "I see you brought your mom. And Mom has a pot."

"Soup!" she announced. "Lizzie told us about everything that happened yesterday, so I figured we should check on the patient. Plus, you know, a thank-you for all the help you've given Lizzie with math."

"Well, come on in, then," Alex said.

He leaned on his cane heavily as he shuffled back into the house. I realized Mom had never been inside the house or even seen Alex take more than a couple of steps. What was she going to think of the place? Of him, now that she was getting the full Alex experience?

"Are you hungry? Do you have a bowl?" Mom asked as we slowly made our way to the kitchen. I breathed a sigh of relief that it was generally clean, as was the adjacent living room. The housekeepers must have just been here.

"Maybe I'll have some later," he replied. "I don't really like people watching me eat."

"Understood. I'll just leave it here on the stove. Lizzie can bring the pot home next weekend."

Alex didn't take long before moving into the adjacent living room area, plopping himself into his well-worn couch divot. I sat in my usual spot without being prompted. Mom shuffled around the coffee table to sit in a chair adjacent. The TV was on, and Alex reached for a remote to shut it off.

"How are you feeling?" Mom asked, her face lined with worry.

"Fine," he said. "These things leave you tired, but I get over them quickly enough."

"The doctor said you weren't taking your medication," I said.

"Yeah, it makes me nauseous and gives me a headache," Alex said.

"OK, but still," Mom said. "Those episodes can't be good for you."

"Probably not."

"How often does this happen?" she asked.

"Depends," Alex said. "A lot more if I have stress in my life. But lately, not very often. A couple of times a year."

"Maybe you need one of those Life Alert necklaces so you can push a button for the paramedics to come if something happens. My mother had one, and it really gave me peace of mind," she said.

Alex didn't look up. "Yeah," he said. "I'll think about that. I hate ambulances, though. Worse than the seizure."

A moment of awkward silence before Mom changed the subject. "Well, Lew and I are really impressed with all the work you've done with Lizzie," she said. "I didn't think she would ever do well in math, but it looks like she could even get an A this year."

"If I do well on the final," I said.

"Oh, you'll do fine," Alex said, looking at me. "I think

you have this stuff down." He dabbed again at his mouth and pulled himself up in his seat a bit. "By the way, I'm happy you and your mom came over, Eliza. I did want to say thank you for what you did yesterday."

It was an exceedingly rare moment of vulnerability from the man.

"Oh, I didn't do anything, really," I said.

"Sure you did. Getting Peg to drive me to the ER was pretty genius. You're good at thinking on your feet."

"Well, I tried," I said.

"You succeeded," Alex said. "And if I can ever return the favor, I will."

CHAPTER FORTY-NINE

Alex

I T HAD BEEN no more than an hour since Eliza and her mother left when I heard the doorbell ring. I had been on the verge of falling asleep on the couch—or perhaps I was already asleep and hadn't realized it. Sometimes I found it difficult to know the difference.

Given they rang only once and waited patiently for me to come to the door, I was not at all surprised to discover Peg standing in the threshold. She was carrying a steel pot with a lid on it, propped atop a colorful hot pad.

"I brought you soup," she said. "How are you feeling?"

"Soup! Well, come on in," I said. "Maybe you can put it in the kitchen next to the other pot."

Peg looked taken aback. "You made soup?"

"No, the girl next door brought it. With her mom."

"Oh my God, Eliza is so sweet. She really helped out with your incident yesterday, you know." Peg hurried into the kitchen to drop the soup off, calling out, "This one's chicken noodle. I hope you like it."

"Sounds wonderful," I said. It was possible I'd take a sip from one of them, but not likely.

"Should I get you a bowl now?" she asked.

"Oh, I'm not very hungry. I'll have some later," I said.

I took my seat back on the couch, finding myself more tired than usual. Peg returned quickly from around the corner and stood to my side. "So?" she asked.

"So what?"

"You didn't answer me. How are you feeling?"

"Oh. I'm fine. Not great. But not awful. Still tired."

"Yeah, that kind of thing must take a lot out of you."

"Everything takes a lot out of me."

"I feel so bad for you sometimes. Isn't there anything they can do for your condition? They said there was medication."

"Ugh, yes, I'm taking it." I sighed. I rubbed my eyes in frustration, wishing for anything to make this conversation go away. So I changed the subject. "By the way, Peg, Eliza told me she knows all about you and your little friend across the street."

Peg's eyes nearly jumped out of her head, and her mouth popped open a bit. "What?" she stammered.

"Your boyfriend, the German guy. I don't remember the name."

"Boyfriend? What? I… She…" Peg was grasping at straws.

"Hey, it's OK with me. I don't know why it needs to be a secret. I'm glad you've found someone you can relate to that's not me."

Peg blushed, then looked away.

"Eliza doesn't like him, though," I said.

"Well, she doesn't know him like I do," Peg said, her

attitude turning on a dime. She could do that.

"There it is," I said, smiling.

"Fine," she relented. "We've been dating for a few weeks now. It's very casual, though."

"Sure it is."

"I mean, nothing's happened. Nothing *really*."

"OK."

"We're taking it slow. Klaus is a very private person, and I'm just trying to respect that."

"You don't have to explain yourself to me," I said. "I'm just curious, that's all. If you're happy, then I'm happy."

"I *am* happy," she insisted.

"Me too," I said. "I won't say a word. When are you seeing him again?"

"Tonight," Peg said. "Just a quick drop-in before Klaus has to leave town for business."

"Have fun."

"I will," she replied.

Peg left and I pushed my head back, sinking farther into the couch and closing my eyes. I resolved not to answer the door again that day and tried to give myself a mental note to set the dead bolt later. But for now, a nap.

CHAPTER FIFTY

Peg

"I HAVE TO leave for the airport in a few hours," Klaus said as we stood in our usual spots in his kitchen, sipping a wine he'd poured from a long, thin, green bottle. Gewürztraminer, he'd said. No snacks tonight. Just the booze.

"Where are you going, again?"

"Seattle. Not far. Three days, I'd think. Should be back by Monday at the latest." He made a point to show me a boarding pass on his phone. The departure time looked awfully late.

Something seemed off. Klaus wasn't his normally verbose self, and he kept walking over to the window, staring down into the trees below, a habit that seemed to be more and more common in recent weeks.

"What's out there?" I asked.

"Nothing," he said. "Just admiring the sunset."

While the sunsets were beautiful thanks to the smoke, the sun had actually gone down almost completely by this point. If there was a sunset, there wasn't much of one to see now. Plus, he was facing east. The sunset was the other direction. I let it go.

"The fires are definitely coming our way," he said. "They say we should be prepared to evacuate at any time."

"That's what I've read," I replied.

"Anyway," he said, changing the subject, "that incident with the neighbor last weekend. Sounds *verrückt*."

"Yeah, pretty verrooked," I said playfully.

"Oh, you are making fun of me?" he asked. I couldn't tell if he was being serious or not.

"No, of course not. Just having fun with languages. You know I love your accent."

"I have something for you," Klaus said, turning on his heel. He disappeared into another room and returned in a moment. He was carrying a small box, wrapped in gaudy green and gold paper. I realized it was Christmas wrapping he'd bought from Eliza. "Just a *zeichen*, you know, a small token of my affection."

I was genuinely surprised—and flattered. It was the first time Klaus had given me anything at all, at least something you couldn't eat or drink. Was he hoping to take things to the proverbial next level? I began to feel a bit flushed at the thought of it.

I tore into the package quickly and found a jewelry box inside. My heart was racing. What would it be? I quickly opened the box to reveal...a simple gold chain. Curious. It seemed nice, but nothing extravagant.

"It's for your locket," he said. "The one you keep in your purse. In case you would like to wear it as a necklace."

"Oh, maybe," I said. It was a strange gift and a strange idea. I didn't particularly want to wear the locket as a necklace, as it was more of an occasional sentiment I wanted than a daily reminder, but putting a chain on it couldn't hurt, I supposed.

"Here, let me put it on the chain," he said.

I fished the locket out of my purse and handed it to Klaus. He quickly threaded the chain through the eyehole and handed it back.

"Would you like to try it on?"

"Oh, maybe later." I set it on the countertop and took a sip from the wine. "Thank you so much."

"Certainly," he said, coming in for a kiss. I closed my eyes.

Klaus's hands were warm on my arms, his palms quite sweaty against my skin. It was disconcerting, really. They weren't just sweaty, they were downright wet, almost dripping. I started to pull away. None of this felt very good.

Klaus surely felt my hesitance, and he quickly relaxed his grip. The kiss nearly over, I opened my eyes, only to find his eyes wide open and staring intently and directly into mine, some glare from the overhead lights reflecting off his glasses. Something was off, very off.

"What's the—" I began, when suddenly I found I could no longer speak. Klaus's hands were wrapped around my neck, tightly, though still slippery with sweat. I thought for half a second that he was joking, but that quickly shifted to panic. He wasn't kidding around. He was choking me, and I was having trouble breathing.

Instinct kicked in, and I began to fight back, though I then realized that Klaus had positioned himself in such a way as to gain extra leverage, and I was pinned between his body and the kitchen counter. I tried to kick but found there was nothing I could hit, though at least my hands were still free. I used them both to beat against his back, though I could tell my weak hits were useless. Adrenaline is supposed to make you stronger, but it was like I was in one of those dreams where your punches just bounce off the monster. I tried to squirm away, knee him in the balls, trying desperately to remember the lessons from that self-defense class I'd taken three years ago. As my breathing became labored, I imagined Klaus laughing at my uselessness.

Klaus, however, said nothing, making only a low moaning noise unlike anything I'd ever heard before. It was like a groan, a low and guttural creaking sound that felt as if the earth was opening up, about to swallow us both.

I was able to gasp little snatches of air, his sweaty hands working against him to prevent a perfect chokehold on my throat. But it wasn't enough help. He didn't move, never shook me from side to side, never hit me or kicked me. He just maintained the chokehold, steadily squeezing as hard as he could, standing in one place.

I was fading. My eyesight was getting blurry, and when I tried to scream, I found I couldn't make a sound. The pain from Klaus's hands wrapped around my neck was unbearable. My attacks hadn't done any good to start with. Now they were having even less of an impact as my energy faded to almost nothing. This was it. I was going to die, choked to death by a man who I'd thought was my boyfriend. Why?

And then, in an instant, everything went black. At first I

thought I had died, that my neck perhaps had snapped and I'd gone blind. But I could still feel the rest of my body, and in fact Klaus abruptly relaxed his grip. Clearly, he was just as surprised as I was by what had happened.

The power had been shut off, a preventative measure against the fires knocking down electrical lines—just as Klaus had said would happen a few weeks prior.

I gasped for air, and Klaus made a fresh grab for my neck. The influx of oxygen and a final rush of adrenaline gave me some much-needed energy. My arms reached backward, my right hand brushing against something cold and smooth—the bottle of Gewürztraminer wine we'd been drinking, now about half empty.

I grabbed it by the neck and swung it around as quickly and purposefully as I could. It was now pitch-black—no street lights, no time display on the oven, nothing at all to see by, not even any moonlight. But I knew where Klaus's head had to be, and I aimed the base of the bottle the best I could. It connected and felt like a direct hit, and I knew it had to be his head. It was hard but not rigid like if I'd hit the cabinet or the wall, and it moved after the impact. I felt the reverberation run up my arm. The bottle didn't shatter like glass always does in the movies. It just landed with a dull but loud thump, the remainder of the wine sloshing out from the upturned bottle all over the both of us and onto the floor.

Klaus's grip relaxed again, and he screamed. He let loose with some German obscenities, and I brought the bottle around again. His voice helped me aim this time, and I felt that I got another solid hit, impacting somewhere on the side of the head with another *thunk*.

Clearly angry but disoriented in the dark, he released my neck entirely in order to try to grab for the bottle, which he wrested from my hand. But just as he got the bottle, he suddenly fell, landing on the tile floor with a loud crack. He must have slipped in the wine now puddled beneath us. The bottle fell to the floor too, but it still didn't break.

Klaus was now moaning in a different way—in pain. The fall perhaps had hurt him more than the bottle strikes, or maybe it was the combination of them that had done some collective damage. He wasn't getting up.

Should I run? Should I call 911? I reached for my purse instinctively and fished out my cell phone to use as a flashlight. I backed away and fired up the flashlight with a few taps, aiming it in Klaus's direction. He was still writhing on the ground, lying on his back in a puddle of wine, has hands holding his head. My guess was, the crack I'd heard had been the back of his head smacking against the tile. Maybe he had a concussion. There wasn't any blood that I could see.

"What's wrong with you!?" I screamed at him, still trying to catch my breath. I was dripping wet from the wine, and my hands were shaking badly, giving the cell phone light a sort of strobe effect. The words just came out of my mouth unbidden. "You're a monster!"

Klaus kept moaning, and it looked like he was about to try to get up. *Call 911 now, tell the cops what happened as you run back to your house.* But what if he got up and came after me? Wait in my house in the total darkness and hope the inevitable knock on the door was the police instead of Klaus coming to finish me off? Surely the cops were going to be overloaded with calls in the aftermath of the blackout. How long would it even take them to get to the cul-de-sac, which was about as far from downtown and the police station as you could get? Maybe they wouldn't even believe my story.

I walked back to Klaus's position, aiming the phone's flashlight down at him from directly overhead. "I hate you," I said, still winded. My neck was sore. "You're a terrible human being."

I raised my foot and placed it directly on his neck. I can't explain why I did it, but it sure felt good. My foot was small, and it fit perfectly under his chin. Klaus was beginning to get his wits back, and he brought his hands down from his head, wrapping them around my shoe. His grip was weak, barely there. "Please don't," he groaned pathetically.

I pressed down, shifting my weight to one foot like we did in yoga with the Warrior 3 pose. I calmed myself the best I could, tried to control my breathing. *Inhale the future, exhale the past.* I pushed harder, lifting my left leg off the floor entirely, placing one hand on the countertop for balance. Klaus stopped making any noise. I could feel the cartilage in his neck crushing under my foot, even through the leather of my shoe. It felt like when acorns on the sidewalk pop when you step on them.

I no longer really needed the light, so I put the phone down, the flashlight illuminating the ceiling instead of the floor, but the slight reflection made things visible enough. Klaus was no longer struggling, and his hands finally went limp, his grip eventually failing completely. At last I stepped off of his neck and picked up my phone again. I aimed it back at Klaus to assess the situation, and it didn't look good. His neck had all but collapsed, flattened by at least an inch. His eyes were closed, but his tongue was lolling out of his mouth like a dog's.

I didn't bother to take a pulse. He was dead, all right.

CHAPTER FIFTY-ONE
Jean Claire

T HAT WE EVEN had school today was a surprise, considering the wildfires nearby and the power going out last
night. But this morning everything was up and running like
normal. I mean, they'll cancel school for pretty much any
reason at all—last year they canceled school in the entire
district for two days because it was raining harder than
usual—but not today. The Money Machine was finally fixed,
and today was the big day.

We all huddled in the gym, sitting on the bleachers and
spilling out onto the basketball court in front of them, the
Money Machine towering before us like some kind of
monument from the future. It was even bigger in real life
than I'd imagined it would be, but the money scattered on
the floor didn't look like it could have been all that much.

Principal Edwards had slips of paper bearing the names
of all the kids who'd sold ten items from the catalog in a
baseball cap—probably fifty in total. Chatter, chatter, chatter
in the audience as he stirred them up with his hand, trying to
build suspense. I can't speak for the rest of the school, but I
was on the edge of my seat.

Edwards drew a slip of paper from the hat, then held it

up over his other hand. "OK, are we ready?" he called to the crowd, trying to pump them up.

"*YES!*" we all roared.

He lowered his hand and read the name: "Our next contestant for the Money Machine is...*Jean Claire Fervola!*

My jaw dropped, and I almost lost my gum. I let out a yelp and jumped up. Eliza next to me began screaming uncontrollably. People were hooting and clapping—all for me! This was it!

I made my way down to the floor from our seats in the center of the bleachers, the audience parting as I carefully stepped down through the rows. I was embarrassed but excited, and as I looked down I realized that I'd already broken the first rule of the Money Machine: I was wearing my usual leggings instead of sweatpants. The stash technique wasn't going to work. I was just going to have to try to hold on to whatever cash I could in my hands.

Edwards shook my hand and said, "Congratulations on selling ten items in our fundraiser. Now it's time to collect your reward." He ushered me into the booth, the bills crunching beneath my feet.

"Sixty seconds on the clock!" he yelled to some helper who I couldn't see. A bright red LED display inside the Money Machine lit up, displaying the number sixty.

"You know the drill," he said. "When the timer starts and the fan fires up, grab all the money you can. Whatever you don't drop is yours to keep. And here is the hundred-dollar bill!"

Edwards waved a crisp bill in the air at the crowd like it

was the cure for cancer, then dropped it into the chamber.

"Ready?" he asked.

I nodded and swallowed. I was intensely nervous, but this was going to be great. He shut the door and tapped it twice with his palm, then stepped a few feet away. I looked out at the crowd and caught Eliza's eye. She gave me a double thumbs-up, and I smiled.

"Go!" yelled Edwards.

The fan kicked in, and I found myself immediately blinded by all the paper swirling around me. They don't tell you about how the wind gets in your eyes, too. It was hard to see, but I don't know if that even mattered. I just grabbed at the cash, reached into the air all around me. I could tell that a lot of the money was hovering up near the top of the Money Machine as the fan blasted it upward, but nothing pushed it back down, and so much of it was completely out of my reach because I just wasn't tall enough. I couldn't hear a thing—the fan was so loud—but I'm sure everyone in the school was laughing at me.

After flailing around for a few seconds and not coming up with much, I switched tactics and tried clapping my hands together to catch the bills between them. I managed to grab a few dollars that way. I shoved what I could into the little pocket in my leggings that was designed for a cell phone, which fortunately I'd left back in the classroom. Eventually, I found better luck using my arms to pull money clouds into my chest, then kind of shoving whatever I caught up into my armpits. I hoped at least some of it would stay in place. Still, progress was slow. None of this was going according to plan, and as desperation set in and the clock went into single digits, I made one last maneuver, pushing my back against the rear wall of the Money Machine, hoping to trap a few bucks that way.

Before I knew it, the fan stopped and all the money in the air fell back to the ground. I carefully retrieved the money out of my armpits—unbelievably sweaty now—and fished out the bills trapped between my back and the wall of the Money Machine. Edwards opened the door with a big smile and let me out. I handed a softball-sized wad of cash to him, which he handed to a teacher to take over to a table to count.

I forced my best smile while I waited for the tally, fully on display for everyone to gawk at. My hair was a huge mess, blown out by the industrial fan at my feet. I tried to pull myself together while the students went back to chattering amongst themselves. Eliza gave me another thumbs-up. Only one hand this time.

After about a minute, the teacher handed the stack of smoothed-out bills to Edwards and whispered something into his ear. He walked back over to where I was standing and raised a hand to quiet the student body again.

"OK, here's the total," he pronounced. "Jean Claire is going home with...*eighty-four dollars!*" He handed the cash to me with a grin. "Congratulations, Jean Claire!" Weak applause from the crowd—except for Eliza, who was losing her mind.

Eighty-four bucks. That's what I'd gotten all worked up over? This was probably going to go down in history as the

210

lowest amount that anyone had ever won from the Money Machine.

I folded up the cash and hung my head, slunk back to my seat, and then it dawned on me: not only was it a pitiful amount of money, but I was going to have to give half of it to Eliza because of our agreement from the beginning of the school year. A deal's a deal.

CHAPTER FIFTY-TWO

Peg

A DAY LATER and still none of it seemed real at all. Klaus laid out on the floor in his kitchen. The inky blackness of the sky. The stench of burning wood everywhere. And the quiet. Throughout the night I had heard nothing. Not a car turning into a driveway. Not a bird chirping. Nothing at all. It was as if the entire world had shut down when the power had been cut off, only to claw its way back to life the following morning.

I hadn't slept for even a minute, my neck in agonizing pain despite the series of eight Advil I'd downed with a can of Diet Coke over the last several hours. I had yet to change out of the clothes I'd been wearing during the attack, though the spilled wine had eventually dried in the night. Were they evidence?

My mind wouldn't stop spinning over what to do about all of this. I knew the proper answer: call the police, tell them my story, and deal with the fallout. There would be interviews at the police station, examinations at the hospital, and people from the news asking questions and taking pictures. It would probably last for weeks, as the headlines—*poor, lonely widow fends off a killer*—would be hard to avoid. Would

Oprah call? It sounded truly awful. I was not prepared to be in the limelight, nor interested in it. If I asked the police nicely, could they keep this all a secret? Not likely.

But calling the authorities presented an even bigger problem than publicity, seeing as I was the one who had done the killing. Could I prove that it was self-defense? I thought so. But there was no video of what had happened, no history of violence against me by Klaus. The police would have to thoroughly investigate my story—and there would be many questions about how exactly a tiny woman had fended off a vicious killer, seeing as she was older, smaller, and clearly not as strong as the man lying dead in his own kitchen. The more I thought about it, the more the whole thing felt unlikely and suspicious: Klaus was killed in his own home, but I was claiming that *he* attacked *me*? It all sounded farfetched and made up, and I had the sinking feeling that when everything came to light, I would be the one under the microscope, not Klaus.

The situation was increasingly mortifying and grotesque. Time to get some CBD oil or some St. John's wort, maybe. I just wanted to put it all behind me and move on with life.

Learn from your mistakes, Peg.

Count your blessings, one by one. Being alive: that's the first. OK, don't worry about the other blessings.

Breathe in. Breathe out.

I meditated for a while to try to find some peace, but it never came. I guess that was the point when I started to wonder what I should do about the body.

CHAPTER FIFTY-THREE

Alex

A DOORBELL RING at this hour of the morning usually meant an overeager Amazon driver or a random UPS or FedEx delivery, but by now most drivers knew not to wait for a signature from me. Once they saw a guy with a cane, they took pity and signed for any packages, even though they technically weren't supposed to. Besides, would they really want to come back the following day?

The ringing was insistent. Twice, then a third time. Now I was getting annoyed.

I made my way to the door and cracked it open to reveal Peg.

"Hello?" I asked, clearly confused. She had just been by yesterday, and the multiple rings were unlike her. "Are you here for your soup pot already?"

"Can I come in?" she asked. I took a good look at her and, damn, she looked like hell. Big dark circles under her eyes—and no makeup to try to hide them—her clothes wrinkled and mussed, a lengthy scarf wrapped several times around her neck. Peg wasn't a woman who was normally what I would consider "put together," but this was a little sloppy even by my piss-poor standards. It was pretty clear that something was very wrong.

"Sure." I swung the door open the rest of the way. "Two visits, two days in a row. Unprecedented."

She ignored my quip. "I have a problem, and I need to talk to you about it."

Oh great, hopefully it wasn't going to be about the grass in the backyard or my TV being too loud. I shrugged and turned to head back to the couch. "Mind if we sit?"

I didn't wait for a response. She hurried inside, shut the door behind her, and followed me to the usual seating area.

Should I offer her a drink or something? Maybe that would ease the pain of whatever complaint she was about to deliver. "Would you like anything to drink? You can feel free to help yourself in the kitchen. There's tea."

"No, no, I'm fine," she said. I'd said as much myself yesterday when nothing was fine at all, and her tone made me very much doubt her condition also.

"OK then, what's the problem?" I said, bracing myself.

She looked at me through incredibly sad eyes. "I don't know how to say this, but I thought you might understand."

"Understand what?"

"Klaus is dead."

"Klaus is dead," I repeated, somberly. "The boyfriend?"

"Yes!" She looked like she was about to burst into tears.

"Oh, damn. I'm sorry to hear that. Was he sick?"

"I don't think I'm making myself clear," she said. "Klaus is dead, and I killed him."

None of this made any sense, like she was either playing an elaborate joke or had gone completely insane. But if she was truly nuts, the last thing I wanted to do was set her off. Better to play along. "You killed him? How? Why? What are you talking about?"

"Because he tried to kill *me*. It was self-defense."

"What, do you have a gun or something?"

"No, when I was at his house last night, I hit him with a bottle and he fell down. Then I crushed his neck until he was dead. With my foot."

My eyes popped open. That was a very specific claim, and a very disturbing one. "What did the police say?" I asked.

"I haven't called the police."

"What?" I recoiled. "You need to call them now. You should have called them yesterday."

"I can't. I don't want to get involved with the authorities and have my life turned into a circus. I was sure you would understand."

"I don't like cops, but this isn't the kind of thing you can fuck around with. They're going to come knocking at some point, and they're going to have a lot more questions later than they are if you call them yourself now."

"There's not really anything tying me to him. Just some phone calls. Can't we just throw his phone away and wipe up the fingerprints?"

"I don't think it works like that, Peg. Phone records aren't just on the phone—the phone company has them. And now they can find DNA from like twenty years ago on anything. If there's a dead body over there—and it sounds like you're telling me there's a dead body over there—

eventually, they're going to want to talk to you."

"What if there isn't a dead body over there?"

"What do you mean?" I asked.

"What if we got rid of it?"

"You keep saying *we*. *We* are not going to do anything of the sort."

"I can't do this myself, Alex. And if we do this, it helps the both of us. You don't want a bunch of reporters and police officers camping out on the cul-de-sac, do you?"

"No..." I said hesitantly.

"And Klaus had it coming! I didn't do anything wrong. I was just protecting myself." She was becoming downright manic.

"So you said."

"Yes—and it's true."

"Look," I said, "I don't really want to get involved, but what is it you want me to do, exactly?"

"Just come over to the house and take a look and help me clean up a little. Give me some advice on what I'm forgetting. If you don't touch anything, there's no DNA for them to find, right?"

I had to admit that morbid curiosity was getting the better of me. I didn't really believe there was a dead guy across the street. Maybe they had a fight and she slapped him and he left in a huff. But the whole thing about crushing his neck? This little person? It all seemed really unlikely. Practically impossible. Maybe she'd had a full-scale mental breakdown and imagined it. And yet she was awfully insistent.

"Well?" she asked. "I don't have anyone else, and I don't know what else to do."

I realized I had been silent for far too long, just staring at her wild eyes. "This all seems surreal, Peg," I finally said. "It can't possibly be true."

"Well," she replied, "does this look surreal?" With that she unwrapped the scarf around her neck, revealing a grisly collection of black-and-blue bruises, punctuated throughout with bright red broken capillaries. The more I stared, the more I could make out individual finger imprints, but that was perhaps my imagination.

"Jesus, he did that?"

She nodded.

"And you just need me to take a look?" I asked.

"Yes," she said. "Remember, you owe me a favor." This much was true.

I supposed there wasn't much harm in looking at the scene to see how much of what she was saying was legit— and hopefully convince her to call the cops if by chance any of it was true. It's not like I had anything better to do. I'd need to steel myself for this escapade, though.

"OK," I said. "Get me my pills."

CHAPTER FIFTY-FOUR

Peg

A LEX DIDN'T WAIT long for the medication to go into
effect before shoving his feet into his shoes and fetching
his cane. I briefly wondered if the pills were really a placebo
or if he was overplaying his condition in order to get sympa-
thy—or to be left alone. We went to the door together, and
he seemed much more expedient than I'd witnessed in the
past, but maybe that was just the adrenaline. Or morbid
curiosity.

We instinctively looked both ways on the street, but of
course no one was coming from either direction. Not even
an open curtain as far as I could see. We scurried across the
road and up the hill a bit to Klaus's driveway, Alex still
moving quicker than I expected, enacting a sort of lurching
shuffle with his cane for leverage. In less than a minute we
were up the steps and standing at the front door, which I
instinctively reached down to open, turning the knob and
stepping inside.

"You left the door unlocked?" Alex asked.

"I don't have a key," I said. He rolled his eyes, saying
nothing further about it.

"Wait, take off your shoes," he said before stepping

through the threshold.

"Why?" I asked.

"I dunno. Footprints. Fibers. Better safe than sorry. It's not like I tamper with a crime scene every day."

I slipped off my sneakers and Alex did the same, leaving his shoes—and his cane—outside the door. Probably didn't want to leave cane prints in the house, either.

"OK, show me."

We walked gingerly down the hall, Alex steadying himself on my shoulder. We stepped through the living room and rounded the corner into the kitchen. From this angle, the scene looked completely normal. Had I imagined the whole thing? Of course, deep down I knew the truth, and as we walked around the island in the center of the room that had been blocking our view, the unsettling scene slowly revealed itself, beginning with Klaus's feet and slowly revealing the rest of his body.

Klaus's skin appeared shiny all over, and the situation with his neck was far more disturbing in the light of day than it had been last night under the glow from my cell phone's flashlight, though it's possible the situation was getting worse as the blood in his body settled toward his backside. They say a body started to decompose immediately after death; it would only get worse from here.

I'll give Alex credit. He took this all in for close to a minute, never letting go of my arm as we stood a few yards away from the body. Finally he said, "So tell me again what happened."

I felt like I was going to be sick, but I took a few deep

breaths, closed my eyes, and the wave of nausea finally passed. "We were drinking wine," I said, pointing to the bottle still on the floor. "He told me he was leaving town for a few days, and he showed me a plane ticket. Then suddenly he just starting choking me, out of nowhere. I fought for my life, but it wasn't until the power went out that I managed to break free. I guess he was surprised enough to let go for a few seconds. I grabbed the bottle and hit him with it, then he fell down at some point."

"And then you decided to crush his trachea instead of running for your life?"

"Well, yes. It was dark, and I panicked. If I ran, where would I go?"

"And you didn't think to call 911."

"I thought that if I tried to call for help, I'd be dead long before they got here. I don't even know if the cell phone towers were working with the power out."

Alex shrugged and then nodded, maybe agreeing with me.

"Why do you think he did this?"

"I have no idea. We were going to go on vacation together, even."

"Sounds like you were set up," he said. "This was probably the plan all along."

"Why do you think that?"

"Why else would this guy live out here in the boonies unless he didn't want any prying eyes on what he was up to?"

"Well, he has a lot of books," I said. "He needs the space."

"Oh, please. The guy was a psycho. And I'd bet anything you weren't the first."

"What do you mean?" I asked.

"I mean this guy did not just decide last night that he was going to start strangling women. That's not how people behave. How did you two meet?"

"At Sunset Market."

"Random meeting, I bet."

"Um, yes. He helped me reach something in the produce section."

Alex closed his eyes and shook his head slightly. "He'd probably been stalking you for months." He looked around the kitchen. "You spend much time in this house? In the other rooms?"

"Sure, here and there. But mostly here and on the deck outside." I pointed to the sliding glass door.

"Well, let's go on a little tour. But don't touch *anything*."

Outside of the kitchen, everything was immaculate, as it always was, all the books on the shelves arranged carefully by height and/or color, depending on the section of the house we were in. If anything, Klaus certainly hadn't lied about his book collection, but Alex ignored all that. We made our way through the bathroom and Klaus's office, nothing really standing out. Eventually we landed in the bedroom, which had its curtains drawn tightly. Alex pulled the sleeve of his hoodie down over his hand and used it to flip the light switch.

Again, the scene was completely pristine and tidy, with the exception of a small duffel bag on the bed. We could see inside that it was carefully packed with a small toiletry bag and a few changes of clothes, but since it had been left open, it appeared as if he hadn't quite finished the job. "Guess he really was going to take that trip after all," Alex noted. We turned the light off as we left the room.

"What's downstairs?" he asked.

"Some other bedrooms, I guess. The garage. I haven't really been down there."

"Let's check it out."

Again, we slowly made our way downstairs, Alex steadying himself by holding on to my shoulder while also using a sleeve-wrapped hand on the banister. The spare rooms downstairs looked like they'd never been used except to hold more books and the occasional piece of furniture. Finally we entered the garage and turned on the lights, a battery of fluorescents flicking on overhead.

Klaus's BMW was parked right where you'd expect it, but Alex's attention was immediately drawn to the side of the garage, near a plastic work sink. It was clear that Klaus had recently spent some time here. Against the wall leaned a pickaxe and a shovel, both quite dirty with fresh, brown earth, next to a pair of very muddy work boots and some equally dirty leather gloves. A long piece of new irrigation tubing, held in a coil with zip ties, was propped up against the wall, and a twenty-five-pound bag reading "Fast Acting Lime" was lying on the floor next to the equipment.

"You know what this is?" Alex asked.

"Isn't it to help dead bodies decompose?" I asked, a chill running up the back of my neck.

"No. That's a common misconception, though. It's really to help cover up the smell that comes from a rotting body in a shallow grave. You know what this all means?" He gestured toward the little diorama in the corner.

"What?"

"There's a grave dug somewhere that he meant for you."

I swallowed and said nothing.

"It's probably on the property, too. This doesn't seem like the kind of guy who's going to drive around in his super-clean car and get mud all over it."

It didn't take us long to find the grave, though Alex said we'd probably have to burn the shoes we'd put back on after tramping around in Klaus's backyard. While we clomped through the overgrown trees, Alex used a fallen branch in lieu of his cane.

Instinctively I knew right where to look. Klaus was always staring down from the deck into the wooded area below, even though there was nothing to see. The empty grave wasn't visible until you got within a few feet of it; from even a small distance it just looked like another little hill, some upturned earth piled next to a small depression in the ground hiding behind it. It was only about four feet long, and it wasn't very deep. Maybe three or four feet at most.

"That's why he needs the lime," Alex said. "Grave's not deep enough. You would have started to stink after a while."

I didn't appreciate the gallows humor but said nothing.

"The real question," Alex continued, "is how many more graves are out here?" He looked me in the eye. "You know, full ones."

CHAPTER FIFTY-FIVE

Alex

I SENT PEG back to her house to get some towels. I didn't want to track mud into the house, leaving footprints, and needed time to think about how to deal with all of this. The best plan of attack seemed to take advantage of the work that had already been done for us: dump Klaus's body into the grave and cover it up, then try to wipe the house as clean as possible. If Peg had really been visiting here for weeks like she'd said, that might be difficult, but that would be a discussion for later.

Peg hustled back with the towels—promotional beach towels from some Mexican resort she'd visited almost twenty years ago, she said—and which seemed perfect for our purposes.

"Put the towels down at the back door," I told her. "We'll need to take off our shoes whenever we go into the house."

Peg had also procured yellow rubber gloves from her kitchen at my request, which I figured was all the protection we would need against fingerprints and the like, especially when dealing with the body.

Was I really going to do this? Dispose of a corpse? I'd

done worse back in the day, but the ask was still huge. That said, I was already committing a crime by failing to report what had happened. Pushing him into the grave and tossing some dirt on top—well, if we got busted, it wouldn't make a hell of a lot of difference. And Peg could still play the victim card if she needed it.

She was right about one thing: a media circus on the cul-de-sac would be no good for anyone. The last thing I needed was reporters digging up my past all over again. In my current state, I wouldn't make nearly as sympathetic a character as I'd trumped up all those years ago, and who knew what some enterprising journalist would be able to uncover. Fortunately, all that business back in the eighties wasn't well represented on the internet now—I googled from time to time to see which old archives had been put online—and my name hadn't been printed in the newspapers at the time anyway. But still, you never knew. The gory details were out there somewhere. Most of the time, the truth can't be deleted no matter how hard you try.

Still, I knew once I put my hands on a corpse, I was going to be in a whole other world. Having information about a crime and being an accomplice to a crime—those are two different things. But what the hell? At the very least, now I could call in unlimited favors from her for the foreseeable future.

After surveying the outdoors carefully, we found ourselves back in the kitchen, hovering over the body again.

"Do you think he looks puffy?" Peg asked.

"I don't know. I've never really seen him before now."

"I think he looks puffy."

"In another day it's going to get way more disgusting than this, I promise you."

Peg grimaced and turned away.

"Listen," I said, "all I figure we need to do is get the body out onto the patio, over the railing, and drop it into the yard below. From there it's only twenty or thirty feet to the grave, and we can easily drag him the rest of the way."

"Drop him off the balcony?" she asked.

"I don't see another way. And the ground down there is pretty soft. I really don't think he'll pop."

Peg made a face like she might throw up, but she held it together. I continued, "The hard part is going to be getting him over that railing." I pointed out the sliding glass door. "Neither of us is exactly a Schwarzenegger, you know. But I think between the two of us we can get it done."

She nodded somberly.

"First, though, we need to get everything else ready. Mainly, his phone. Is that it?" I pointed to a handset lying face down on the kitchen counter.

"Yes." She fetched the phone quickly and handed it to me. We were both in our kitchen gloves now, so I wasn't worried about prints. As I expected, the phone had a password on it, but it was an old iPhone with a thumbprint scanner, so that would probably be easy to bypass. I tapped the screen with my elbow to wake it up. He had plenty of texts and a few missed calls. We'd need to go through all of it to see who was already wondering about his whereabouts.

"You know his password?"

"No," Peg said. Of course not.

"Is he right-handed?" I asked.

Peg nodded.

"Put his right thumb on the scanner. It ought to work."

"Even if he's dead?"

"Yeah, you have a day or two before the prints start to go south."

She delicately tried to maneuver the phone under his hand without actually touching the body, but I could tell straight away this wasn't going to work.

"Just pick up the arm," I instructed, through clenched teeth. "We need to get this done."

Finally she relented, attempting to lift his arm.

"Ugh, he's cold. And stiff." She grimaced and made retching faces.

"Yeah, that's rigor mortis. He'll probably be like that for the rest of the day."

As she pulled on the arm, the whole body tilted to the side. She wasn't lying. He was stiff as a board, and the scene of pushing him around like a mannequin was particularly macabre. It took her a few tries to position the phone under his thumb, but eventually she got it done, and I could see the screen unlock.

"I'd say we should change the PIN so we can get into it later, but we're going to destroy this thing today, so there's probably no point."

"Why?"

"This is the first thing the cops are going to check. We need to get it off the network immediately. Frankly, you should have done this last night."

Peg was just staring at the phone with no clear direction about what to do. I knew I'd need to take over. "Give it here," I said. She was happy to comply.

I took off one glove—I'd have to clean the phone thoroughly later—and went to work. First, a couple of missed calls from Seattle. One voice mail, also from the Seattle number, to the effect of "Hey, we were expecting you today, what happened?" The trip had probably been arranged as an alibi, but unfortunately it was a good one. If this was a work engagement, it was only a matter of time before they called the police, trying to find him.

I found some text messages from the same Seattle number, with variations on "missed you today" and "you OK?" plus messages from United Airlines about his flight boarding last night. Nothing additional of substance in his email, but the work client was tenacious in trying to track him down.

"I'd say we have a week, tops, before they call the police," I said.

"Should we write back, say Klaus got sick or something? Or maybe tell him he had to quit the job. He was a consultant."

The sick ploy wasn't a bad idea, and it would buy us some time. Would they buy it? I didn't see the harm in it, though I knew it would only add another layer of guilt if we ever got caught.

"We can't say he quit. They might have paid him already, and they'll want the money back. But the sickness idea…yeah, I think we should do it."

I tapped out a text message reply:

So sorry, came down with terrible stomach flu. Been very sick all night and still in bad shape, out of it. I will reschedule with you asap.

The reply came back swiftly.

OK, feel better. Call when you can.

And with that I shut down the phone completely.

"We need to smash this a few times with a hammer, then I need you to throw it away in a trash can as far away from here as you can easily drive," I said. "Make sure there aren't any cameras wherever you end up going, but wear a hat all the same and don't touch the phone with your bare hands. Put it in a paper bag or something. Don't go across any bridges or anything with a toll booth, and leave your own phone inside your house while you're making the trip. This guy needs to disappear, and you can't be connected to that in any way."

Peg nodded with each suggestion. I knew there was more we could do—we ought to just burn all of this stuff and douse the entire house in bleach—but I knew there were limits to how much advice she was going to take.

Anyway, we were putting off the inevitable. It was time to deal with the body.

CHAPTER FIFTY-SIX

Peg

THE CHOKING STENCH of the forest fires in the distance, getting worse by the hour, made the whole thing even uglier than it would normally be; I was sure. Things would certainly get no better as the day wore on, so I knew I should pay attention to Alex and try to expedite our efforts the best we could.

The first order of business was getting Klaus's body over the railing and into the yard below.

"I think we can use this rigor mortis to our advantage," Alex said. "We probably can't lift the body, even working together, but I'm betting we can prop him up. Really, we only have to lift about half of his body weight if we leave his feet on the ground. Because he's so stiff, we should be able to maneuver him to where he's leaning against the railing. Then we just push."

"It's worth a try," I said.

The first step was dragging him outside. I thought we'd just drag him by his arms, but they were down by his sides and they weren't budging, so instead we went with the legs. This wasn't easy, either, since his body wouldn't bend at the waist, so we had to hunch over and drag him along the ground—our gloves firmly on our hands—maneuvering around the kitchen counters and through the sliding glass door and out onto the patio. It was slow work, especially because I had to do 80 percent of it; Alex just didn't have enough strength or balance to make much of an impact. Still, I was happy he was trying.

We had Klaus about halfway through the threshold of the door when Alex paused to take a break, sitting down on the ground where he'd previously been standing. We had barely moved the body ten or twelve feet, but he was huffing and puffing like he'd just finished a marathon. "Halfway there," he said, between gasps, wiping the sweat off his forehead with his sleeve.

I considered Klaus while I waited, my earlier waves of panic and nausea subsiding as I focused on the task at hand. He looked more pathetic than ever, his shirt riding up from being dragged across the floor, obscuring some of the damage I'd done to his neck. His face was still contorted in pain, though, his mouth agape and his tongue slightly visible. I felt sorry for him, then disgusted. He was going to murder me, but for what? Had I really been destined to be the next victim of a serial killer? Who else had he killed after plying them with wine and promises?

Finally Alex was ready to continue, and we doubled our efforts, dragging Klaus through the sliding door and onto the wooden balcony, situating the body so his left side was aligned with the balcony wall.

"Now's the hard part," Alex said, sitting down alongside the body. "I think if we lift him up a little, you could wedge one of those chairs under him." He pointed to the patio furniture. "From there we ought to be able to get him the rest of the way up to the railing."

The plan worked. I pulled the chair up next to Klaus's head, and together we lifted the body. I lifted the shoulders, and Alex worked in the middle, kneeling on the ground. Again, it was awkward, but ultimately it took just a couple of good heaves and we had Klaus propped against the chair, his body turned into an obscene and surreal plank. We then pivoted the feet away so that he was facing the railing and we could both get access to one of the arms. From there it was another easy lift to rest his shoulders against the railing, his head sticking out over the ground below.

The very picture of this man was unsettling, stiff as a board and propped up as the long side of a perverse triangle. I tried to imagine what I would say to someone who happened upon this scene. We understandably didn't want to linger in this state, so we quickly moved back down to the feet, lifting the legs up as high as we could until he simply slid headfirst over the railing, disappearing out of view. A second later we heard the thud as the body hit the ground, muffled by the whooshing of leaves piled below. I rushed over to see Klaus's body lying there, expecting to see it crumpled up in a heap, but no. This rigor mortis stuff was no joke. He was still a plank, only now lying face down in the dirt.

Alex sat on the ground where we'd lifted the feet, exhausted. "OK, now we just gotta get him into the grave."

We returned to the outside, ensuring the towels were in

place, putting our shoes back on, and fetching the shovel we'd seen in the garage. There was only one, so I'd be doing all the work. "Get the lime, too," Alex ordered, sitting on a fallen log. I didn't argue.

In the yard, we worked together as we had inside, dragging the body by the shoulders this time toward the gravesite some twenty feet away. The dried-up leaves on the ground actually made it easier to slide him along, providing some kind of natural lubrication, and Alex had to rest only one time before we finally had Klaus in place.

The next problem was soon evident. "The grave's not big enough," I said.

"Yeah, I see that," Alex replied. Why was the hole so small—not even big enough for me to fit in lying down? "We'll just have to make it a little bigger," he said. "I mean, unless you want to cut the body in half."

I retched a little and didn't reply. I just got to work digging out a small channel on one end where I figured we could wedge his legs. I spent about a half hour digging out a narrow trough a few feet deep—very little to show for my labors—my arms all but giving out along the way and my hands completely raw beneath the kitchen gloves, which were now dark brown from dirt.

It wasn't hard to push the body in from that point. Alex was well rested by then.

"Let's get rid of his duffel bag, too—bury it with him. Easier than trying to throw it away in some dumpster somewhere." Klaus's keys and wallet should go into the grave as well, he said.

I carefully returned inside, retrieved the bag, and came back out, throwing it all into the hole in the ground with the lifeless body. I then dumped all the lime from the bag we'd taken from the garage, covering everything with a fine white powder. I tossed the empty bag into the grave as well.

"Now we just cover him up," Alex said, coughing from the smoke in the air. My hands were so tired they could barely grip the shovel, but this part was much easier work than digging the hole. The body disappeared underground quickly. I didn't even think to say goodbye.

Alex instructed me to arrange leaves on top to make it look as undisturbed as possible, and we both pushed the underbrush back into place as best we could to cover up the drag tracks we'd made. I was really quite amazed at how effective the whole thing was. Even if you looked closely, there was barely any hint of the previous night's unpleasantness.

"Now we just clean up inside, and then we're out of here," Alex said. Our shoes came off again, and I gave each of us a fresh pair of rubber gloves for the next stage of work, stowing all our dirties in a plastic garbage bag. I also cleaned up the shovel, carefully wiping it down, then tossed it deeper into the underbrush on the other side of the property, where it promptly vanished beneath the leaves.

"Tonight, all of this stuff—the towels, the clothes, your shoes from last night—either needs to be washed with bleach or burned," he said. "I'll do the same."

I nodded.

Inside, we spent the better part of an hour wiping everything down, starting of course in the kitchen, where Klaus had died and where I had spent the bulk of my time in the house. While we worked—or rather, while I worked and Alex watched, sitting on a clean towel draped over one of the kitchen chairs—he reminded me yet again about how the plan was supposed to work.

"I think it'll be a while before anyone calls the police, but eventually someone—probably these Seattle people—is going to wonder what's up. Eventually the cops will come out to the house, and soon enough they'll get inside to see if he's here. That could be a few days; it could be months. Whatever happens, we want them to find absolutely nothing. Klaus was here, and then he left, and he could have gone anywhere. Just vanished without a trace. If he doesn't have any family—that's what you said, right?—then that will probably be the end of it." Alex produced a tissue from his pocket and dabbed at some drool forming on his mouth. I could see he was getting very tired.

"The cops are going to knock on your door at some point, and probably mine, too, but they're definitely going to want to talk to you because they will know you had some kind of regular communication with Klaus," he said.

I looked up from cleaning duties. "But we're going to get rid of the phone," I said. "Can't we just delete all the calls and texts?"

"Yes, but it doesn't matter. All of those call records are available through the phone company. You can't delete them. They're there forever. You're just going to have to explain to them that you were only casual acquaintances and that he told you he was going to Seattle and that's the last you heard from him."

I didn't like the idea of having to talk to the police at all. "Can't I just hide like you said? Not answer the door?"

"Did he call you yesterday, before the murder?"

"Yes," I said.

"Then you're the last person who saw him alive. The police will know that."

I shuddered.

"Fortunately you look completely harmless, and as long as you don't have blood on your hands when they come to the door I think you'll be fine."

"You think."

"That's the best I can do," he said, pointing toward the sink. "You missed a spot. The faucet handles."

I scrubbed and scrubbed, then did the same in the bathroom, and, at Alex's behest, wiped down every doorknob I could possibly have touched, both inside and out. Places I hadn't been—like inside Klaus's car—we were careful to leave untouched and as is. If there was DNA or something that could possibly point to other people involved with his disappearance, Alex felt we should leave that all behind to give the police something to investigate. Made sense.

"Aren't they going to be suspicious about how clean the kitchen is?" I asked.

"Probably, but he's a neat freak, you said. And we don't really have a choice. You can't have been in here lately. He just called you to say goodbye and said that he'd be back in a few days, *and that's all you know.* If they ask you anything else, like how he was getting to the airport, *you don't know."*

I nodded, then kept spraying 409 and wiping things down with a rag.

The house was looking clean, cleaner than my house anyway, and Alex continued with his lecture. "You need to make sure you don't do anything stupid from this point on, Peg. Don't call and leave messages for him. Don't come back to the house for any reason. Once we leave, we are locking the door behind us and never coming back. We're going to walk through the backyard one last time to do a thorough check to make sure you didn't do something stupid like forget your purse or your car keys, then we're gone forever. Whatever you do, don't go on the internet and search for his name or do something like Google 'how to get rid of a body.' You didn't do that already, right? It's like the phone records. That kind of thing is tracked, and they will use it against you." He pointed in my direction. "Hey, what's that there on the counter?"

I followed his finger. "Oh, that's my locket. I almost forgot it."

Alex's eyes rolled back in his head. "Are you kidding me? Jesus Christ. What else are you forgetting?"

I pocketed the locket and looked around. "Nothing, I think." My eyes landed on the wine bottle—the murder weapon. I picked it up and held it in Alex's direction. "I cleaned it carefully, but what do I do with this now?"

Alex frowned. "Take it home," he said. "Throw it in the recycling."

CHAPTER FIFTY-SEVEN
Eliza

I T WAS ALWAYS good to get to go somewhere other than home after school, but the color of the sky, smeared orange from the fires, and the stink of burning wood made everything seem weird and not at all fun. Jean Claire's mom was being super freaky today, too. There was only so many times I could watch Jean Claire roll her eyes at the woman, who today was complaining endlessly to no one in particular about the commercialization of Christmas, even though it wasn't even Thanksgiving. I hadn't seen any ads or decorations around yet.

"What are you going to do with your half of the money?" Jean Claire asked in a moment of peace while her mother scrubbed kitchen counters and double-checked to ensure all the windows were shut tightly to keep the smoke out.

"Uh, blow it on snacks and stuff, probably," I said.

"Maybe they'll cancel school tomorrow," she said, changing the subject and gazing at the amber sky out the window.

"Maybe."

Jean Claire didn't seem eager to chat much, so I finally started putting my stuff back in my backpack. "I should probably go home," I said. "I bet my mom is worried."

"Yeah, probably." Jean Claire never changed her gaze.

I knew the ride home well, about fifteen minutes if I took it easy, which I did because the smoke made it hard to breathe if I pedaled too fast. My bike knew the way—autopilot—and before I knew it I was making the final turn onto the cul-de-sac.

As I made my way up the hill, something felt off, and not just the smoke and the hazy, orange sky. I soon realized there was quite a bit of noise coming from the wooded yard next to Klaus's house. It was shuffling in the leaves. An animal, maybe? Curious, I stopped pedaling and walked my bike slowly toward the sound, then began to hear people talking. I was sure I recognized the voices but had trouble believing my ears.

I dumped my bike next to my house and walked the rest of the way on foot. The closer I got, the clearer I could hear them, though I couldn't quite see anyone yet. It was definitely Alex and Peg. *What on earth?*

I heard snippets of their conversation, and it was mostly Alex doing the talking. "What's that behind that log?" "Fluff up those leaves over there." "Grab that scrap of paper—it could have fallen out of his wallet." This made no sense at all to me.

As I approached closer, I took care to walk gingerly and minimize the sound of my footsteps. I had to know what was going on here, and I knew that meant seeing it with my own two eyes.

I crept nearer, peering among the trees until finally the scene came into view. There was Alex, leaning against a tree, all but ordering Peg around the yard, pointing at something with a long stick. "Look over there," he said. "Make sure we didn't forget anything next to the house." Near the wall were several large trash bags and a mountain of dirty towels. It was then I noticed that they were both extremely dirty—like, covered in actual dirt—which is something I wouldn't have thought possible of either of them.

I watched the scene intently for several minutes before I finally decided it was time to reveal myself. Once Peg had returned from Alex's bidding and was standing close to him, I took a few steps forward. "What are you two up to?" I called out.

They both stopped dead in their tracks, completely frozen. Neither of them said anything. None of us moved. I felt like we were all frozen in time, or—thanks to the sky—maybe transported to some other planet where time moved at one-tenth the normal speed. This was getting weirder by the second.

Finally I took another step toward them. As I began to move, Peg jumped a little, almost falling down. Alex moved, too, and began rubbing his forehead but continued to lean against the tree. He looked exhausted and numb. The closer I got, the dirtier they appeared. Absolutely filthy. Neither said a thing, just staring at me in silence.

"What's happening here?" I asked both of them. "Why are you both in Klaus's yard, covered in dirt? This is making me really uncomfortable."

Alex looked dead on his feet and ready to collapse, but he finally spoke.

"I dunno, Peg," he said, making eye contact with her. "Do you want to tell her what we've been working on all day, or should I?"

CHAPTER FIFTY-EIGHT

Alex

P EG HURRIED US all into her house, locking the door behind us and making sure the curtains were drawn tightly. She rushed into a back room with all the towels, to a laundry room I guess, and reappeared with fresh ones. She said nothing as she laid them out on the couch: one for me, one for her. Eliza just stood nearby, saying nothing, her mouth slightly agape.

"Are you going to tell me what's up?" she asked at last, after Peg and I had both taken a seat. I desperately wanted to lie down, but that would be inappropriate, in large part because I would probably fall asleep on the spot.

Peg, on the other hand, was a bundle of energy and showed no signs of slowing down, even though she clearly hadn't slept last night and had just completed hours of manual labor.

"Does anyone want some tea?" she asked. "Water?"

"No," Eliza said, "and I'm getting a little freaked out."

I shook my head. "Just get on with it," I said.

"OK," Peg said, looking down at her dirt-stained hands, then pressing them into the towel underneath. She finally looked up at Eliza. "You know, Eliza, sometimes when a man and a woman really like each other—"

"Oh my God," I interrupted. "You're not going there, are you?" I couldn't believe what I was hearing.

"What?" Peg said. "I was starting at the beginning. No?"

"No. Let's jump ahead a little," I said.

"OK, um…" Peg's voice trailed off, as if she had no idea what to say next. I guess because that was true. She was pretty far out of her depth here.

I took over. "Eliza, you know that Peg has been seeing that guy across the street, right?"

"Right," Eliza said, turning to Peg. "Yeah, I saw you together once."

Peg looked a bit bug-eyed but said nothing.

"Well," I continued, "that guy Klaus is a real asshole, it turns out."

"Yeah, I could tell," Eliza said. Peg looked mortified.

"In fact," I said, "he's such a huge asshole that he tried to strangle Peg to death last night."

"What?" she said in abject disbelief. It wasn't even a question. Her eyes looked ready to pop out of their sockets.

"It's true," Peg said. "See?" She untied the scarf still wrapped around her neck—only now it was stained brown with dirt—showing off bruising that looked even worse than it had this morning.

Eliza recoiled. Peg should probably take pictures of the injuries, just in case things went badly later and she had to prove what happened. First things first, though.

Peg continued. "So then there was, well, kind of like an accident, and Klaus died." Eliza's expression didn't change.

"It wasn't an accident," I said. "You were defending yourself. That's what you told me."

"Right, but, well, I didn't mean for him to die."

I didn't want to get into it. Looking at the body with its crushed windpipe, she had surely known what she was doing.

"So are the police coming?" Eliza asked. Naturally.

"Well…" Peg stammered. "No."

Eliza looked perplexed.

"You know, if we called the police then that means a huge investigation, a lot of questions, and then reporters would come." Peg looked at Eliza through sad eyes. "It would just be so disruptive—and really, what would the point be?"

"Uh, I guess."

"You don't want the cul-de-sac to turn into a destination for weirdos who want to see the house where this guy got killed, do you?" she asked.

"Yeah, it'd be all over TikTok," I said, jumping in. "Your house, too."

"See, even Alex thinks it's a good idea."

I bit my tongue. This was all a very bad idea, but I had been hopeful we would get away with it until Eliza caught us in the street.

"*What* is a good idea?" Eliza asked.

"Well," Peg stammered again, "we buried the body in his yard. In the grave Klaus had already dug for me."

"You're kidding," she said, now in a state of some sort of shock.

"I am not kidding. We think he even might have done

this before. So really I am doing the world a favor."

"If you say so," Eliza said.

"I do say so."

"OK, well, that's all pretty crazy, but I guess I understand."

"Good."

"So what happens now?" she asked.

"Well," Peg said, "you can't talk about this. None of us can talk about any of this to anyone. Hopefully, the police won't come, but if they ask you anything, you just say you don't know anything about any of it. Teamwork, remember? Like when we had to get Alex to the hospital, you and me."

I wasn't sold. "The police *will* come," I said. "Someday."

"Your parents may not even let you get involved," said Peg. "That would be even better."

"But don't bring it up," I said. "Basically, you have to forget that you saw us today. We'll get cleaned up, we'll do all the laundry, and it'll be like this never happened."

"And for you," Peg said, "nothing did happen."

"I guess," she said.

"We're a team, remember?" Peg reminded us all.

"Trust me," I said. "With time, this will all fade into the background of your mind. Every day that goes by will make this memory hazier and hazier, until it eventually feels like a dream, and someday you'll wonder if it was real at all."

"It already feels like a dream," Eliza said, staring at both of us.

CHAPTER FIFTY-NINE
Peg

THE FOLLOWING DAY, the police had still not come to the cul-de-sac. I checked religiously every half hour, peering out through a crack in the curtains to make sure a cop car wasn't parked across the street. Meanwhile, I was washing the clothes I'd worn the night of Klaus's death for the third time in a row.

How long would it take? Another day? A week? Months?

I felt so terrible about the whole thing. Completely sick to my stomach. Maybe I had been wrong about the attack. Maybe Klaus hadn't really intended to kill me but was just playing an aggressive game that I didn't wholly understand. Maybe it was all a joke, and I was the one who took it too seriously. Or maybe he was having some kind of episode, and I should have felt sorry for him instead of fighting back. But now he was gone, and he had no ability to explain himself. When the police eventually came, there would be only my word—and whatever evidence they could get from Klaus's house. And what if they found the body? I was starting to wonder if we had made a huge mistake in burying him in the backyard. Was it too late to dig him up and take him into the woods somewhere and try again?

Of course, we had involved a third person in our sordid little tale also. I felt even worse about that. Eliza had moved to the cul-de-sac to get away from the crime and drama that comes with living in the City. Now she had more than she probably ever thought she'd have to deal with in her life. This poor girl, just starting out in life, and now she had to keep my secret. I didn't have any doubts that she'd be able to do it or even that she would do it. She'd proven her resilience well enough to me already, and Alex seemed to trust her completely.

What would I have done if I'd been in her situation as a teenager? I couldn't even imagine it. The big dramas when I was a kid were about Vietnam and Watergate. That stuff felt real, but it really wasn't the same as having a dead body buried across the street and the person who killed him living two doors down. How did she feel about the situation? How did she feel about me?

I reached into my purse and retrieved my locket. Thank God Alex had pointed it out on Klaus's countertop. It still had the chain Klaus had purchased for it attached. I thought for a moment about removing the chain but decided against it. The locket would remind me of Jack, and the chain would be a reminder of Klaus, for better or for worse, a tragic symmetry. At the very least it would remind me not to be such an idiot again, and to make better choices about who I socialized with. If I ever left the house again, that was.

I put the locket back into its little pocket in my purse and fished around for another item, removing it. I held Klaus's cell phone delicately in my hands, wishing I could know the secrets that must be buried inside it. I knew turning it on would be a bad idea because it could lead the authorities to me, and without Klaus's fingerprint or password, I wouldn't even be able to see the pictures on it. Was there a photo of me on the phone somewhere? I didn't think so, but I couldn't really remember if he'd ever snapped one. If he had taken a photo, it was possible it was out there in the cloud, even. Another thing to worry about.

Alex had insisted I smash the phone then drive it far away and throw it in the trash. That seemed like a lot of effort to get rid of something no one could track, and was a better reminder of the last few days than that gold chain would ever be.

Plus, it was something that might be useful to me if the shit eventually hit the fan, excuse my French.

CHAPTER SIXTY

Alex

S ATURDAY HAD ARRIVED and still no sign of an investigation into the mysterious disappearance of Klaus…Klaus what? Had I forgotten his last name or did I not ever know it? No matter anymore, I supposed.

It was still early, though I had managed to get a quick shower and brush my teeth. I hadn't seen or heard from Eliza since the fateful discussion at Peg's house earlier in the week. Tutoring would be this afternoon, but I wondered if she would show up.

Suddenly there was a ring of the bell followed by an insistent knock at the door, and I knew without even getting up from the couch who it had to be. Sure enough, from my vantage point I could see Peg's silhouette through the curtains, which I'd closed tightly to make it impossible to see inside. If the police showed up, I simply wouldn't answer. But that trick wouldn't work if they knew I was home. I was keeping the TV volume down low for the time being.

Again a knock at the door, louder this time, and I hadn't even stood yet. I attempted to expedite things and made it to my feet, hustling down the hallway as quickly as possible. I opened it to reveal Peg standing there, rather disheveled and looking extremely tired, dark circles visible under her eyes. She was still wearing the scarf. I supposed the bruises had yet to fully fade. I ushered her inside quickly and closed the door behind us.

"Jesus, Peg, you look like hell," I said. "You need to pull yourself together and get some sleep. And really, no one should see us together for now. Try to imagine what would happen if the cops showed up right this moment."

"I know, I'm sorry." She seemed out of breath, though I assumed she'd only walked here from next door.

"What's going on?" I asked.

"When are the police going to come? No one has called me. No one has come to the door. I can't stand the wait."

"The wait is good," I said. "The longer this takes, the colder the case gets."

"Alex, they solve cases that are thirty years old or more all the time now. Haven't you ever seen *Cold Case Files*?"

"No."

"Well, you should."

"This isn't a cold case, really. Remember, this is a case of a guy who decided to leave town and didn't tell anyone where he was going."

"That's what you want them to think, but you and I both know he's buried across the street."

"I don't think anyone's going to find that body, because no one is going to look for him. Not there, anyway."

"Don't you think we should go check to make sure the grave hasn't been dug up by an animal or something?"

"No!" I protested. "Don't go anywhere near that house

ever again!"

"What about the mail? I can see from my front door that the box is already stuffed full."

"Do not get the mail. Don't even think about it. Remember, he left town—of course he can't get the mail. It's got nothing to do with you."

"Maybe we should have put a hold on it."

"Maybe. But it's too late now. You got rid of the phone, right?"

"Right, like you said."

"Good. Let me see the bruise on your neck."

Peg took her scarf off and showed me the damage. It was improving—at least you couldn't see the outline of Klaus's hands anymore—but it probably still had a few days to go before it was fully healed.

"It looks better, but you still shouldn't let anyone see it if you go out in public," I continued. "If the police do come, probably best to pretend you're out until it's completely gone."

Peg nodded.

"Remind me again what to say when the police do come."

I sighed. "Keep it simple. Cops are stupid. Just answer their questions as simply as possible."

"Like what kind of questions, do you think?"

"Did you know Klaus?"

"Yes."

"What was your relationship like?"

"We saw each other socially from time to time."

"When's the last time you saw him?"

"Oh geez, what do I say?"

"Tell the truth, mostly. You saw him last Sunday night. He was packing to take a trip to Seattle for work. They'll probably ask where you were in the house, what you did. Just keep it basic."

"I don't know. I'm nervous."

"The cops don't know anything, and you won't be a suspect. It won't even be an investigation because there's no evidence of a crime. Eventually, when they do pull the phone records, they'll see that you were telling the truth. I think the whole thing will go away in a matter of days—*but you have to get your shit together* and stop acting crazy."

"I worry about what's on the phone. What if there were pictures that, you know, he put on the cloud?"

"So what? As long as you don't claim that you don't know the guy, it'll be fine. Pictures only back up your story."

"What if there are other victims, though? I feel bad for their families. Shouldn't they get closure if they have a loved one who's gone missing?"

"Oh Jesus, Peg," I said, rolling my eyes. "Cry me a god-damn river. If he killed someone else, that had nothing to do with you. In fact, maybe you stopped him from killing again. I've done plenty of things I'm not proud of in my life, but this isn't one of them. And you have done nothing morally wrong here."

"Why does it feel wrong, then?" she asked.

I sighed and backed off a little. "It's understandable that you're feeling guilty. This is all very fresh and raw. Hell, you still have the bruises from where you were attacked. But with time you'll see this with a new perspective, and that feeling of guilt will wane. Meditate or do some deep breathing, I don't know. You just need to find a way to let it go, otherwise this situation will consume you completely. Maybe you should get a weed delivery and knock yourself out with some sativa. It works for me."

"Seriously? You get marijuana delivered?"

"Of course," I said. "It's the only good thing left about living in California."

CHAPTER SIXTY-ONE
Eliza

I HADN'T SEEN Alex since the day he told me about...Klaus. Not that I was avoiding Alex. We just never saw each other or spoke unless it was a tutoring day. Now that day was here.

I rang the bell as usual and waited, thumbing through TikToks mindlessly, knowing it would be at least a minute or two until Alex appeared to open up. Eventually I heard the lock turn and his face appeared.

"When are you going to remember you have a key?" he asked. "Every week it gets more annoying to have to make this walk."

"Jeez, I keep forgetting," I said. "Sorry."

Alex sighed and let me in. As usual, I walked ahead of him to the couch, while he took his sweet time following me, finally parking himself in his regular spot.

"Finals are coming soon, right?" Alex asked.

"Yeah, a couple more weeks."

"How are you feeling about them?"

"Pretty good. Not much more new material to learn at this point. And I think I'm solid on what we've been working on so far."

"Good to hear."

I produced a worksheet from my backpack—a little crumpled but not too bad—and smoothed it out on the table. I worked on it mostly in silence. Honestly, it didn't seem very difficult. Alex flipped through his phone, saying nothing.

After a few minutes, I put my pencil down and leaned back on the couch. "Are we going to talk about...you know...the thing?"

Alex put his phone down. "The thing?" He gestured with his thumb toward the door. "I don't see why we should."

"I just don't understand it," I said. "How could Peg kill a guy? And you didn't call the police? You just helped her bury him in a hole?"

"Peg didn't do anything wrong. She doesn't want a spectacle. I get that. I think even you can get that."

"It sure *sounds* like she did something wrong, which is why we aren't supposed to talk about this at all."

"You didn't tell anyone, did you?" Alex looked a bit panicked.

"No," I said. "But I'm not sure it's doing the right thing to keep this secret."

"Listen," he said, his eyes getting bigger and intense. "You *have* to keep this secret. This could be the most important secret you ever keep, because now if the police get involved, Peg could get in trouble. Not for defending herself but, like you said, for not calling the cops. I could get in trouble because I helped her out a little. And you could even get in trouble. So could your parents. It would be a disaster."

"Now I really don't feel good about it."

"And I can respect and understand that. This is just one of those things that isn't going to give you happy feelings when you think about it. And guess what—there are going to be plenty of those moments throughout your life. In fact, the older you get, the more you're going to have. I'm sorry this has to be your first taste of adulting, but honestly it could be a lot worse."

"I don't see how."

"You'll just have to trust me, I guess."

I took a breath and shuffled my papers, thinking. "I don't think I could talk to my parents about any of this anyway," I finally said. "I am pretty sure they have zero experience with the ins and outs of burying a dead body."

"Well, you never know," Alex replied. "Everybody's got secrets. Everybody."

CHAPTER SIXTY-TWO

Eisenstein

O<small>UR WORKSPACE ISN'T</small> anything like you see in the movies. Fresh carpet, cubicles, each desk with family pictures and tchotchkes—it looks more like a corporate office than a police station. It was nice to have my husband and kids on my screen saver. I was sure most units wouldn't allow it.

The call was patched through to my desk on account of I was the only one in the office. Most of the time it was empty like this, since we have just forty-five cops of various ranks on the street, six in leadership, and then the admin folks. Budget cuts out here in the sticks are just as bad as in the city. No one wants to pay for anything, but if a minority knocks on the door, they want you there to deal with it *toot suite*.

The other three detectives were all out working cases—domestic abuse, a burglary, and an urgent graffiti issue—while my caseload was pretty light at the moment. Chief always liked to keep one of us at the station in case of emergency, which made sense to me.

The phone rang again, and the little red light kept flashing, insistently. I picked it up.

"Detective Eisenstein," I said, my usual greeting.

"Oh, hello," said the voice on the other end. "The person who answered said you could help me?"

"I can sure try. Who am I talking to?"

"Jonathan Wan, I'm a vice president at Illuxis."

"Illuxis?"

"It's a tech company." He spelled it out. I wrote everything down.

"What's your address?"

He gave me the corporate location, based in Seattle.

"So how can I help you?"

"Well," Jonathan Wan said, "we work with a consultant from time to time, and he's based in your town. His name is Klaus Fischer." He spelled that, too, carefully noting the C in Fischer. "He does computer configuration work for us and was supposed to be up here a week ago, but he never showed up."

"OK, and you're concerned about him?"

"Well, yeah. He sent a text that said he wasn't feeling well, and that's the last I heard from him. Emails, texts, and calls have all gone unanswered."

We went through the history of his relationship with Mr. Fischer. This would have been his third trip to the Illuxis—*barf*—offices, and he had been professional and on time as expected the other two trips. Always communicative with Wan and his team. Didn't seem like the kind of guy to just disappear. "I'm worried that he's sicker than he let on in his text."

"So you'd like us to check on him?"

"Yeah, if it's not a problem."

"It's not a problem, but normally it's family that initiates this kind of request. I don't suppose you have any information about Mr. Fischer's family, do you?"

A long pause. "No, I don't think so."

"And you're not even his employer, it sounds like. He's a consultant, you said? Independent?"

"That's right."

"I understand," I said. "It's not a problem. I can definitely send someone to his place to have a look, at least. But I will say that this kind of behavior isn't wildly unusual. People quit their jobs and go on sudden vacations all the time, leaving unfinished business behind. And a lot of times they lie to their bosses that they're sick so they don't get yelled at about quitting. I know you're not technically his boss, but you get the idea."

"Sure," said Wan. "None of that sounds like Klaus, though. He was always very dedicated to his work. Extremely focused."

"Understood. We'll send a car out to his house and have a look-see. Do you have his address?"

Wan rattled off the address for Mr. Fischer and confirmed that the number on my caller ID display was the correct one for a callback. I told him I'd report back with any results of our welfare check.

Wan thanked me and hung up.

I'd had calls like this before, and every time it was someone who had simply decided to leave town—either with a side piece or because of a foreclosure. Fischer's address was in a respectable yet remote area—I had never driven out there and I even double-checked to ensure it was part of our jurisdiction. Given his occupation, I didn't immediately suspect a foreclosure. Anyway, some computer work was in order before we wasted anyone's time by sending them to investigate in person.

A quick call to the hospital found no one under his name. Same with U.S. Customs. Klaus Fischer had not left the country in the last two weeks. I tried calling Fischer's phone number, which Wan had given me, and it went straight to voice mail. The mailbox wasn't full, which was a good sign. I'd need a warrant to obtain the phone's ping records, though, which would reveal a lot more about where he was and had been. Hopefully, we wouldn't need it.

With nothing turning up in the various databases, I figured we should go have that look-see. When my trainee Simmons got back from his call—a security alarm had gone off at someone's house in the middle of the day, surely another false alarm—I'd have him drive us out to the Fischer residence, and we'd knock on some doors and look through some windows. You know, the glamorous side of police work.

✗

YOUNG SIMMONS, BRIGHT and eager but less street-smart than I'd have liked, drove us out to a part of town I didn't even know existed. After taking a left off the main road that would take you to Sunset Market and on to the high school, we wound our way through a wooded area, devoid of houses, until we finally reached this small cul-de-sac. It gave off a creepy vibe, with all its homes quiet and looking completely devoid of life. If not for a bicycle dumped in one yard and a few parked cars in driveways, I could have easily been convinced this street had been abandoned. Hell, one of the houses was partially burned down—and the damage didn't look fresh.

"Fischer residence is up there on the left," I said, pointing from the passenger seat of the cruiser. It was one of the biggest and most ominous houses on the block, a rambling monstrosity painted brown, featuring a Gothic turret that jutted out from the roof.

"Roger," he said, slowly taking us up the incline of the cul-de-sac before turning hard into the angled driveway. The mailbox was stuffed full, and there was a box from Amazon on his front porch. If Fischer was home, he was probably rotting away inside, a thought that made me inwardly grimace. After a dozen years on the force, I'd dealt with thirty or forty corpses in various stages of decay over that time, and soon enough Simmons would encounter his first. "You get used to seeing them," I had told him once, "but you never get used to the smell."

"You think he's dead in there?" Simmons asked as he put the car in park.

"I don't think anything," I said. "I only know what the facts say. And at this point, we have a lot more of those to collect."

I looked the young cadet in the eye after he parked the

car. "Once you start speculating about things you don't actually know, you taint your ability to see the scene objectively. Use your senses, and be prepared for anything—but don't start guessing about what might have happened."

We got out of the car and approached the front door. No sign of forced entry, no broken windows. Just the Amazon box on a nearly pristine welcome mat. I knocked loudly on the door. "Police department," I called out as loud as I could. Thanks to years of practice, I'd learned to project my voice well beyond what my five-foot-four frame would normally suggest. Sometimes it took people off guard, which was entirely the point. "We're here for a welfare check."

No response. While we waited, knocking again a few more times, we both peered inside through the large windows flanking the door. There wasn't much to see in the entry hall, but the side table and hall tree looked unmolested, with a couple of coats hanging on the latter. A small bowl of what was either pebbles or candy was visible on the table.

I had Simmons check the door. Locked.

"Let's walk the property," I said.

The house was built into a hill with what looked like dozens of oak trees surrounding it, covering the area in deep shadow. While the surface level of leaves, a foot thick in some places, was dry as tinder, I could tell everything was damp underneath, as all that moisture remained trapped there with nowhere to go.

Most of the house was on the second or third floor. Aside from the entry, the only other window we had access to was in the back door, which led to the garage. The window was rather dirty, but by shining a flashlight we could see a sedan parked inside. This seemed like the kind of house that would have more than one car, but maybe that was speculating too much. I recorded my observations in my notepad, as did Simmons.

"Don't just use your eyes," I explained to Simmons. "Listen carefully, and use your nose. Is someone hurt and screaming for help inside? Do you smell anything funky? Like a decomposing body?"

I put my finger to my lips, and we both spent a minute listening. I heard nothing. The smell of the underbrush was present, but it was overpowered by the smoke still hanging in the air. The situation had gotten better in the last few days thanks to the wind shifting, but it was still nasty, and some folks had taken to wearing face masks to protect their lungs.

We continued walking and made it all the way around the house. Nothing looked amiss to me. Either he wasn't here, or he was dead in the bathtub or some other area we couldn't see. I walked us over to the mailbox. We went through the stack of mail piece by piece, which mostly turned out to be catalogs and junk, with a couple of bills in the mix. No postcards from Morocco or checks from foreign banks. I put the mail under the Amazon box on the front porch and wedged my business card into the doorjamb.

"What now?" Simmons asked.

"We don't have enough to break in at this point," I said. "Right now we assume he left town and didn't tell anyone, unless we have reason to suspect otherwise. This happens all the time. In fact, it's the most common resolution for these kinds of welfare checks, at least in my experience. Our next stop is to canvass the neighbors to see if they know anything."

And sure enough, they didn't know anything. Most of the houses were dark and seemingly empty, with almost no one answering the door at our knock. A fellow who did come to the door at the top of the cul-de-sac introduced himself as one Darren Charles. He was extremely nervous and pointedly did not invite us in, but he claimed to have only a passing familiarity with Mr. Fischer and couldn't even accurately describe him. He had no information about Fischer's family and didn't know anything about his work, saying Mr. Fischer kept to himself, as did Mr. Charles, but that he knew Fischer traveled quite frequently. He accepted my card and said he'd call if he saw Fischer return from wherever he had gone.

A few houses down, across the street, we got another hit, in that someone actually answered the door when we knocked. It was a middle-aged woman named Judy van Damal, a harmless homebody type typical of the area. Her husband worked in San Francisco and wouldn't be back until the evening. They were new to the neighborhood. She didn't know Mr. Fischer, and in fact said she was surprised to find out that anyone lived there at all. She seemed mostly confused in response to all of our questions, and I got the impression she was still trying to get things settled at home. From our vantage point in the entry hall, I could see there were still pictures waiting to be hung and paint samples smeared on the wall where the family was trying to decide on a color. Again, I gave her a business card. She said she'd bring it up with her daughter and husband at dinner.

No one else answered when we knocked: three no-shows, not including Fischer and not including the eyesore of a house that was uninhabitable due to fire damage. Neither of the people we managed to speak to had security cameras or video doorbells, and we didn't see any of these devices in our cursory tour around the six (standing) houses on the block. These kinds of video cameras have really made police work a lot easier, but we were striking out on this one.

"Well, what now?" he asked.

"Back to the station," I said. "Start a file and type up your notes. If he stops paying his bills or someone else calls to report his absence, we'll roll back out and kick things up to the next level."

CHAPTER SIXTY-THREE

Alex

AGAIN I KNEW who it was before I got to the door. No doorbell this time. Instead, an insistent, low-volume knocking—*tap tap tap tap tap tap tap tap*—whose nervous energy I could hear from the living room. Again, *tap tap tap tap tap tap tap*. Once again.

"I'm coming!" I yelled, which was uncharacteristic but necessary to shut her up for a minute. I turned the dead bolt and the door burst open, nearly knocking me over. I held on to the knob for support as Peg pushed her way inside, then shut the door behind her, again nearly falling to the floor. She locked the dead bolt and peered through the curtains that covered the neighboring window.

"Come on in," I said facetiously, regaining my composure.

"Did you see them? They were at the house," Peg said, still peering through the tiny crack. "Then they came to my house and rang the bell. Did they come here?"

She surely knew the answers to her questions already, but I responded all the same. "I didn't see them, but I heard them at the door. I peeked out the bedroom window and saw the police car, so I just laid low. Like I said, they left eventually. It sounds like you did the same."

"*Yes, I did the same,*" she said through clenched teeth, finally turning my way. "I'm not ready to talk to them. I just don't think I can handle it. Here, they left these in our doors." She produced two business cards for Rachel Eisenstein, Detective, and handed me one. I looked it over and put it in a pocket.

"I saw them," she continued. "There were two of them, walking around Klaus's yard. It was like they went right to it. To...you know, the spot."

"Were they searching the yard or just walking around the outside of the house?" I asked.

"I don't know, maybe both. They were looking for something. They took the mail, too."

I finally noticed Peg was done with the scarf now. Her neck showed no sign of the bruising anymore, which was a good omen.

"Yes, sounds like they were looking for him, but they're not looking for a dead body buried in the yard. They surely just wanted to see if he was in the house, and for now they must assume he's not, otherwise they would have broken down the door. They didn't, right?"

"Not that I could see from my house. Should I go look?"

"God no, don't go over there. We're never going back over there, remember?"

"Right, but just to see..."

"No," I said firmly. "You need to stay in your house, do your shopping, and keep living your life as normally as you can. You did good." It was difficult to comfort her, but I was trying my best. "If they had found anything, the cul-de-sac would be swarming with police right now. They wouldn't have stuck a business card on your door and called it a day, right?"

"Right."

"Try to relax."

"Easy for you to say," she said. "I'm the one on the hook for this."

"Well, we're both guilty, Peg," I told her. "Classic prisoner's dilemma."

"What?"

I did my best not to sound condescending, probably failing. "Two prisoners are both accused of a crime. The police question them separately and try to get them to turn on the other prisoner. The one who turns goes free while the other one goes to jail. If both talk, they both go to jail. If neither talk, they get a slap on the wrist."

Peg's eyes widened. The woman could really turn on a dime in an alarming way. "It sounds like you're saying you're going to talk to the police so you can go free."

I sighed. "No, you're not getting my point. I'm saying that neither of us talk and we all live happily ever after."

"I don't think that's what you're saying at all."

"I promise you it is. Maybe I'm just not being clear." I was really doing my best to pull her back from the ledge.

"It also sounds like you're saying it's best if I talk to the cops."

Now it was my eyes that were widening. "That is definitely not what I'm saying. We stay quiet, and this whole thing goes away."

Peg raised a finger at me. "Don't make me regret bringing you into this, Alex."

"What?" I asked, incredulous. "I'm the one who regrets ever getting involved with you on this."

"Because I will teach you about regret," she snapped.

Jesus, time for another approach. "Everybody needs to chill. We just keep to ourselves for a while and everything will be fine. This will eventually all blow over."

Peg considered me and, after another tense moment, left without a word.

I breathed a sigh of relief and returned to the couch, exhausted from the exchange but happy that I did not remind Peg of the eventuality that Rachel Eisenstein and partner would return—and that when they did they would be a lot more persistent about meeting with the woman across the street.

CHAPTER SIXTY-FOUR
Lew

LIZZIE WAS QUIET at dinner as usual. Judy, on the other hand, wouldn't shut up. I don't blame her, of course. It was a big day.

"Did you hear, Lizzie? *The police* were here today," Judy said.

Lizzie gulped and almost choked on her mashed potatoes, which she didn't like but Judy made anyway and told her she *only had to take one bite.*

"No, what happened?" Lizzie asked, not looking up.

"I told your dad earlier, but apparently the man in the large house across the street is missing. No one knows where he is."

"Uh-huh," Lizzie said, chewing.

"I don't know why they would think I would know anything about it, of course," Judy said.

"See, I miss all the excitement when I'm at work, Lizzie," I said. I turned to Judy, saying, "What kinds of questions did they ask?"

"Well," Judy said as if she'd been rehearsing for this very moment all afternoon, "they wanted to know if I knew him, when I had last seen him, if I'd seen anyone strange on the cul-de-sac recently, or if I'd seen anyone go into or leave his house in the last few weeks. I'm afraid I wasn't of much help, I told them, because I don't know the man, I haven't seen any strange cars on the street lately except for Amazon delivery drivers, and we can't even see his front door from our house, so there's really no way I could have seen anyone coming or going."

Judy looked disappointed with herself.

"What did they say about the guy? Fischer, right? Do they have any leads?" I asked.

"Not really. They said he didn't show up for work and someone called to check on him. They went by his house before they came here, but nothing seemed unusual."

"He probably got sick of his job," I said. "Skipped town." A man could dream.

"Yeah, maybe," Judy said. "Kind of a weird thing to do if you have a big house like that though, right?"

"Maybe he cracked," I said. "Had to drop everything and get away from it." Suddenly I felt like I could understand what might have happened to this guy.

"That's definitely a possibility," said Judy. "Maybe we'll find out the truth someday."

"I hope so," I said, turning to our daughter. "Lizzie, what do you think?"

"Hmmm?" Lizzie responded to her name but appeared lost in thought, still chewing on an undercooked green bean.

"What do you think happened to Mr. Fischer?" I asked. "Have you ever seen him around the neighborhood?"

Lizzie stopped chewing, swallowed, and looked up at me.

She was acting awfully strange, but she was always acting awfully strange these days, so I didn't push it.

Finally she answered: "No."

CHAPTER SIXTY-FIVE
Eliza

I WAITED UNTIL I absolutely knew it was safe. My parents were early-to-bed types—especially now—and you could usually count on them both being fast asleep within forty-five minutes of them closing their bedroom door, max. I gave it an hour and fifteen, then crept down the hall, literally crawling, to see if there was any sound whatsoever coming from their room. Light snoring—my dad for sure. No light coming out from under the door. Mom was done reading for the night as well.

I crawled back the way I came, heading down the stairs backward on all fours, intent to avoid the creaky step that was three down from the top. I know in the movies kids always go out the window to get out of the house, but that wasn't an option for me. There was no roof outside my window to provide access to the ground, and no convenient tree for me to climb down, either.

Step by step I made my way toward the front door, unlocking the dead bolt as slowly as possible, attempting to muffle the *click* by pressing my body against the lock. From there, I carefully turned the knob until the door was open. Thank God we didn't have a security system that beeped every time anyone came in or out.

It was a full moon. Smoky but not terrible today, and getting cold. We'd had "indoor P.E." for the last week because the air was considered too unhealthy for us to breathe outside, which pretty much meant dodgeball in the gym every day. That was fine by me. I just pretended to get hit after a minute or so and sat out the rest of each game on the bleachers. It beat running laps.

I stayed to the shadows the best I could as I made my way up the slope of the cul-de-sac. There really wasn't anyone around to see me—I was sure Alex was asleep, Peg was probably the same, the old man was blind, and the place at the top of the street didn't have a clear view of the road. It didn't take long to make it to the tree line just inside the boundary of Klaus's property. From there, the idea of staying out of the moonlight became redundant. There was no light at all under the canopy of Klaus's densely forested yard, to the point where I wished I'd brought my phone so I could see better.

My eyes adjusted, but still I didn't know what I was looking for. A big, human-sized mound of dirt like in the movies? A skeletal arm sticking up out of the ground? I paced the highly sloped yard, trudging through the thick layer of leaves, looking for some sign that Alex and Peg weren't lying to me about what happened. The cops came to the house. Klaus was gone. Was the story possibly true? That little old Peg had actually killed this guy after he attacked her? I still didn't know what to think or how to feel.

Back and forth I wandered, looking for a sign. But there

was no sign, only dead tree branches and leaves and plenty of them. Was I leaving footprints? I tried to look behind me to see if there were tracks, but it wasn't like when we took that trip to Tahoe and trudged around in the snow all afternoon. Here, the mounds of underbrush opened up beneath me for each footstep, then closed in again after I took each step.

The Fischer guy was buried out here somewhere, for real? Where? Could I be standing right on top of him? It just didn't seem possible.

Eventually, I got tired and went back home, but my mind was racing, and I couldn't get to sleep. I knew then that my little trip across the street had been a huge mistake. I went to the woods because I wished to discover the truth, to settle my mind and no longer live in a constant state of fear and confusion. But the visit had only made things worse. I'd thought I might never sleep again, wondering whether the death of the man was real or some kind of fantasy. Now I realized that it didn't matter, and I didn't want to know anymore.

CHAPTER SIXTY-SIX
Jean Claire

I HADN'T HEARD from her lately, so I texted Eliza.

are you avoiding me?

no

you haven't been saying much

yeah sorry

what's up

just really weird over here with the
police and all

yeah because of the creeper that
went missing, right?

yeah

have the cops come back?

no

do they have any leads?

i dunno, i guess not

probably went out of town to perv
out on some girls, rite?

yeah prob

probably best if he doesn't come back at all

yeah seems like he won't

?

you know cuz he's too busy creeping

haha

can't sleep

why, you think he's going to come
for you next or something?

uh no

it's just too much drama for me

the cops were there for like 15
minutes you said—that's too much
drama?

yes it is. i don't want to see any cops
for any minutes

did they even talk to you?

no just my mom

i dunno sounds like maybe you are
making a bigger deal out of this
than it is

i don't think so. you don't know what it's like

I was getting annoyed by her attitude so figured I'd wrap it up.

> ok well whatever
> i guess i'll see you at school tomorrow

k

Something had been off about Eliza for at least a week, and I was determined to figure out what was up with her. I wasn't going to wrestle it out of her via text, I guessed. Maybe if I sent her a really funny Snap, it would break something loose and get her talking. I mean, that always works with me.

CHAPTER SIXTY-SEVEN

Eisenstein

"A FUNNY THING came up when I was going through the month's call logs to the station," Simmons said to me. It was surprising that he'd invested the time to do this, as the job was tedious and dull, but I appreciated the effort. I made a mental note to indicate as much in his personnel file. It wouldn't hurt when it came time for evaluations and promotions.

"Yeah?" I asked, turning from my computer toward his, directly behind me.

"We got a call a few weeks back from"—he double-checked the computer screen—"an outfit called Helping Hands Caregivers. Missing woman, live-in caregiver. Lupe Flores."

"Mexican?"

"Salvadoran."

"Legal?"

"Not sure. They said she was."

"Surprised anyone bothered to ask. Not surprised they said she was legal, but anyway, go on."

"Yeah, so anyway one day this woman goes missing from her assignment—full-time watching over a blind guy who she'd been taking care of for more than a year. No call, nothing."

"She probably decided to move back home. Happens all the time once these people have earned enough money to live on. No point giving notice and getting a guilt trip from the employment agency."

"Sure, that's what I thought, too…"

"But?"

"But check out the address where she was working."

I squinted at the computer screen. "Huh. That's the cul-de-sac with the missing German, right?"

"Yeah, it's basically next door. I mean, it *is* next door."

"Well, that is a coincidence."

"You think something's up?" he asked, before stopping myself. "Right, you don't think anything. You only know—"

I interrupted. "What the facts say, right. But these facts are at least a little suspicious. Did we knock on the door of that address?"

"Yes," he said, consulting his notes. "No answer."

"We left a card?"

"Yes, but the agency says the guy she was taking care of is blind."

"Guess that's one reason why he never called," I said. "Suppose we should roll out there again and talk to the guy. Maybe take a peek inside his house while we're in the neighborhood."

It was a quick drive to the cul-de-sac, me riding shotgun as usual and noting to Simmons his failure to come to a complete stop at every single sign we passed—the kid was always in a hurry. Simmons bit his tongue at my criticisms but kept rolling through the signs the whole way.

My memory of the house next to Fischer's was fuzzy. The huge, tree-covered yard put at least seventy-five feet between the two places, almost all woods. From the front steps of the blind man's house, you couldn't even see Fischer's place. I didn't know if that was suspicious or not suspicious, but I had Simmons snap pictures and make note of that fact.

I could hear music coming from inside. I knocked loudly. "Police department. Mr. Goodwin, can we have a word?" More knocking and waiting. Finally, some sounds of shuffling inside and, eventually, the door creaked open.

Percy Goodwin was a heavyset man, early seventies, and on the short side at about five foot five. Black, carrying a cane, and wearing dark sunglasses. Inside, the house was minimalistic, which I guessed was how blind people have to keep things, and the radio was on, playing a classic jazz station.

"What's this?" he asked.

"We're here about your helper, Lupe," I said. "I'm Detective Eisenstein, and I'm here with Officer Simmons."

"The girl wants to come back?" he asked.

"Um, no, but we wanted to ask you a bit more about her departure." I avoided using the word *disappearance*.

"So she's still gone," he said.

"Right."

"OK. I called the agency when she left. They said they'd send a new girl. So far, nobody. I don't like making do by myself, but I done it before. Meals on Wheels is shit, but I'll take it."

"Mr. Goodwin, mind if we come in?"

"I guess."

He turned and walked slowly back toward the living room, and we followed.

"Mind if I turn the radio off?" I asked, not waiting for an answer before reaching for the remote next to a worn, almost threadbare recliner. A TV tray with the remains of Goodwin's lunch sat to the side of the chair, into which the man plopped with a grunt.

"Can you tell us more about the day Miss Flores left?"

"Miss Flores? You mean Lupe?"

"Yes, Lupe."

"Well, we were going to eat dinner, but she hadn't made anything, so I sent her to the store. She ain't never come back."

"That's Sunset Market?"

"I suppose. I don't know where else she would walk to."

"She didn't drive?"

"Sometimes. Truck's broken, though. She don't have her own car."

"I see," I said. "And what time did she leave for the store?"

"Well, I can't rightly tell you on account of I don't wear a watch. But it was about dinnertime."

"Of course. And this was October 28?"

"Don't remember, and don't much keep track of the calendar anyway. Something like that, though. It's a long time to go without a helper, you know. That agency is shit."

"We can call them for you if you'd like," Simmons said, chiming in for the first time.

"Sure," Goodwin said. "Maybe you can get them off their damn asses."

Our interview continued down the usual road. No boyfriend. No local family, though she called home periodically. Goodwin didn't speak Spanish, so he didn't understand what she was saying when she was on the phone. He didn't know Klaus Fischer, didn't know anything about Klaus Fischer, and didn't think Lupe knew him either, though how could he know for sure, he remarked.

A quick search of Lupe's room revealed the trappings of a twentysomething without much in the way of assets. Clothes, a small TV, simple bed that had been made. There was an empty suitcase in the closet, and it didn't look like she had planned to leave. No purse, ID, or phone, however.

"Make a note to see if Sunset Market has video footage of the night she allegedly went shopping there," I said to Simmons. "Maybe we'll get lucky. Otherwise, I'm not seeing much to go on at the moment."

I shut the door behind us as we left the room. Goodwin was still sitting in his recliner, fiddling with the remote but with the radio still off.

"Do you mind leaving that room as it is?" I asked.

"For now," he said. "But if I get a new girl, she's gotta live in there."

"Of course, just for now."

"OK," he said. "But you'll call them."

"We'll call them," I replied. We thanked Goodwin again for his time and walked out to the street to compare notes.

"You don't think he had anything to do with it, do you?" Simmons asked. We left the car in front of the Goodwin home and walked up the incline of the cul-de-sac toward Fischer's house. It wasn't far, but the hill was steeper than it seemed. I was huffing a little by the time we made it to Fischer's.

"The blind guy?" I asked, a little surprised. "No. But we'll check him out."

"Sure is quiet out here," Simmons said. All you could hear was the occasional bird chirp and the rustle of a light breeze. It was getting colder, and while there was still a hint of smoke smell, the air was clearing up, as it usually did when the holidays were getting close.

At Fischer's house, the mailbox was once again full. It had been eleven days since our last visit, and clearly no one had been home since. I gathered the mail and went through it, approaching the door just as we had previously. Again, mostly junk. Nothing that looked personal in the slightest. The driveway was now littered with fallen leaves from the nearby trees, and as we reached the house, I could see spiderwebs had formed inside in the corners of the windows.

I rang the bell and knocked loudly. "Police! We're looking for Klaus Fischer! Can you please come to the door?" Three times in total. No response.

"We'll need to break the lock," I said to Simmons. "Grab the crowbar."

"From the car?"

"Yeah."

"Why didn't we drive up here if you thought we were going to need the crowbar?"

I shrugged. "You can drive it up when you come back."

He saluted sarcastically and trudged down the driveway, jogging down the hill to the patrol car. After a few minutes, he was back, parked at the top of the driveway. He fetched the crowbar from the trunk.

"See, that wasn't so hard," I said. Simmons said nothing and handed me the bar. "You ever done one of these?" I gestured toward the door.

"Only at the academy."

"OK, then watch and learn." I wedged the end of the bar into the doorjamb near the lock as deeply as I could, then planted my feet, setting a wide, solid stance. Using my arms and the weight of my body, I pushed forward, hard. The jamb splintered with a loud crack as the bar forced the dead bolt through the wood. Like that, we were inside.

"Police department!" I called out. "Mr. Fischer, are you in the home? We're entering to perform a welfare check. If you're present, please identify yourself immediately."

No response, as I expected. I said to Simmons, "Let's have a look around." The good news: no immediate smell that would indicate a corpse, thank God. I put on my nitrile gloves and gestured for Simmons to do the same. Inside, Simmons took photos based on my direction.

As usual, I started out by seeking out the master bedroom, which is where trouble can most often be found in a situation like this—either there or in the master bathroom. It wasn't hard to find, just a jog to the right, down a hallway, and through a set of double doors. Nothing out of the ordinary here. The closet door was open, but that wasn't unusual. Dresser drawers were closed and, when we peeked inside, looked full of clothes or close to it. Plenty of clothes hanging undisturbed in the closet. If a suitcase was missing, I couldn't tell. A combination safe drew a small amount of my attention, but again that was not an unusual thing to discover in a residence.

The bathroom was clean—not sparkling, but clearly kept up—though dust had settled on various surfaces. It was immediately clear that no one had been in the home for several weeks. Same story in the additional bedrooms—most looked unused—and the office. The computer was turned off.

"What's with all the books?" Simmons asked as we walked down the hallways, which gave the place the appearance of a library.

I shrugged. "Guess the man's a reader."

The living room was much the same, and the kitchen was exceptionally clean. Like a maid had been through it, though again dust was settling everywhere. There were dishes in the dishwasher, which had been run and clearly never opened since. There was still moisture inside.

"It's awfully clean in here," Simmons said. "Is that weird?" He was alternating between taking notes and snapping pictures with his phone.

"Not necessarily. Lots of people go on a trip and like to come home to a clean house," I said. "Pretty standard, really.

Who wants to return to a pile of nasty dishes in the sink?"

He nodded and kept documenting the scene.

"Still," I said, "it's very strange that two people would vanish from the same street at the same time. Something's off here."

"You think they ran off together?"

"I don't think anything yet, Simmons. I only know what the facts say, remember? But I do want to keep digging into this."

We checked the rest of the house—and I was interested to find Fischer's car in the garage. The doors were unlocked, but there was nothing of interest in the cabin or in the trunk, which we popped. We never located Fischer's identification or keys. His cell phone was nowhere to be found, either. Presumably wherever he was, he had all those things with him—and not much else.

We followed standard procedure upon leaving. Simmons fetched a padlock hasp from the trunk of the patrol car along with a fresh padlock and a power drill. We returned to the front door and from the inside installed the hasp across a piece of the doorjamb that hadn't shattered. We locked it with one of the included keys and kept another for ourselves—though since it was padlocked from the inside, it wouldn't do much good unless we figured out another way in. We returned to the garage, left a key and a note about our visit on the hood of the car, and exited quickly as the door came down. It took Simmons a couple of tries of running and jumping to avoid setting off the ankle-height sensor, but eventually he managed.

We stowed our gear in the trunk of the squad car, and I leaned against it, looking out at the street. Two missing people. No contact with anyone. No notes left. And no obvious signs of foul play. It was, to say the least, extremely strange. I didn't want to say anything to Simmons, but something smelled very wrong here, and we had nothing to go on.

"When we get back, let's pull the phone records for both of the missing persons. Talk to the employers again and check with the airlines." Simmons took notes. "Call Lyft and Uber, see if there is a record of either of them taking the service in the last month, since it looks like Fischer didn't leave with a car and Flores didn't have one. Check for credit card charges. You got all that?"

"Yeah," he said.

"And we'll need to talk to all the neighbors again," I said. "Let's start with that one." I pointed.

Directly across the street a blue Volvo was at that moment pulling into the driveway, apparently a neighbor we'd yet to talk to.

"Well, that's convenient," I said. "Maybe this will be our lucky day after all."

CHAPTER SIXTY-EIGHT
Peg

"HI THERE!" A woman's voice came from behind me as I was getting a bag of groceries out of the trunk. I was already on edge, and I was so startled I nearly dropped the bag, spinning on my heel.

My stomach dropped immediately as I saw it was my personal worst-case scenario: two uniformed police officers, a shorter woman walking ahead of a taller, younger guy. "Just home from grocery shopping?" she asked.

I stammered but managed to spit out a word or two. "Um, yes." I turned back to the trunk, trying to get myself composed. Did they know? It looked like they had come from Klaus's house. I had been thinking about this moment for days, but I still wasn't prepared for it. I guess I had no choice. As Alex had predicted, eventually this day would come, and now it was here.

I took a deep breath and turned back. Behind them, I now noticed a police car pulled up in Klaus's driveway. How long had they been on the cul-de-sac? They hadn't been there when I left for the store. Or had they, and I hadn't noticed?

Peg, this is no time to be a loopy-loo, you fool. Pull it togeth-

er.

"Can we ask you a few questions?" the woman said, finally reaching me. "I'm Detective Eisenstein and this is Officer Simmons. We're investigating a missing person. Well, two persons. Looks like we missed you last time we were in the neighborhood." She held a business card in her hand. The woman was barely an inch taller than me, and I could see her trying to stretch herself upward in an attempt to manufacture some tiny bit of additional authority.

"Simmons, can you help her with the bags?" she asked the taller officer. I had only two bags and didn't really need help, but I was so nervous with two police officers standing in front of me, I just nodded and mumbled OK. Simmons grabbed both bags as I fumbled with my keys and shut the trunk before taking the business card. I didn't have to look at it. I knew what it said.

Simmons began walking toward my front door without asking. "Mind if we come in for a minute?" Eisenstein asked.

"Oh, um, sure." I should have made up an excuse why they couldn't, but the words just came out of my mouth unbidden. As if on autopilot, I walked over, unlocked the door, and found both officers in lockstep behind me as soon as I was through the threshold. Eisenstein, the last one in, closed the door behind us. Simmons followed me to the kitchen, and he placed the bags down on the counter. I was happy at least that the place was clean and tidy, but I looked around nervously to make sure nothing was out of place. Nothing *suspicious.*

"Feel free to put your groceries away if you need to," the

detective said. "We don't want your ice cream to melt." She laughed.

"I don't have any ice cream," I said.

"Oh, I don't mean—" she started. "Sorry, just joking."

I guess I missed it.

"Anyway," she continued, "whatever you need to do with your groceries, please go ahead." Simmons was looking around intently, scrutinizing everything in the house. I could tell I was under a microscope. Did they already know everything and were just toying with me?

"It's fine," I said. "How can I help you?" I could feel my hands sweating.

"So we're investigating a couple of missing persons, like I said. A Klaus Fischer and a Lupe Flores. They both lived across the street from you, next door to one another," Eisenstein said.

Lupe Flores? Who was that? What was I missing? I could feel my neck start to sweat.

"Did you know them?" she asked.

"Um, no. I mean, yes," I stammered. "I don't know any Lupe, but I knew Klaus. Casually, of course." I felt like I didn't have control over the words coming out of my mouth, which was quickly clogging up with gunk, all cottonmouth.

"I see. So how did you know Mr. Fischer?"

"He was, well, he was a neighbor. Just a friend, you know. A casual, regular friend."

She began taking notes. "When you say *a casual, regular friend*, what do you mean by that? Did you see each other socially?"

"Um, yes, I mean, sometimes."

"Sometimes? How often is sometimes?"

"Like, maybe once a week sometimes?" I said.

"Maybe?"

"Yes, about that."

"OK, and was this a romantic relationship?"

"Um, no. We were just friendly."

"Got it. So do you know Mr. Fischer's current whereabouts?"

"No."

"When was the last time you saw Mr. Fischer?"

"Oh, gosh, I think a few weeks ago."

"And what were the circumstances of that meeting?"

"He invited me for wine at his house."

"Do you think you could determine the day you went to the home?"

"I'd have to look it up, but I suppose I could."

"Great. Did Mr. Fischer travel frequently?"

"Yes, I know he traveled for work."

"And what kind of work did he do?"

"Computers, something."

"Were you aware of him traveling on or around the date of November 18?"

"Um, I don't think so. Maybe he said something about work? I don't remember."

"Are you aware of any relationship between Mr. Fischer and Lupe Flores?"

Again with this Lupe Flores. Who were they talking about? "No," I said. "I've never heard of her."

"She was a caregiver for a Mr. Percy Goodwin, who lives on the corner of the cul-de-sac, across the street from you. She disappeared around the same time as Mr. Fischer."

"Wow, that's really, um, that's really strange," I said. "No, I don't know anything about her. Or them. Her and him." *God, shut up, Peggle.*

"Have you heard from Mr. Fischer since November 18?"

"Um, no, I don't think so."

"No, or you don't think so? Do you want to check your phone messages, maybe?"

"No, I mean, I definitely have not heard from him."

"So you have no knowledge of a trip or if he's coming back at some time."

"Not that I can remember."

Eisenstein seemed to relax a bit. "It's just so strange, Ms.—I'm sorry, I didn't get your name."

"Peg. Jurgensen."

"Is that with an E?" Simmons interjected, who I realized was furiously scribbling notes the entire time.

"Two Es."

"So maybe you can help me figure this out," Eisenstein continued. "It's so strange that these two went missing at the same time. What do you think happened to them?"

"Gosh, I really don't have a clue."

"You've lived in this house how long?"

"Fifteen years."

"Are you working?"

"No, I'm retired."

"And you live here alone?"

"Yes," I said. "I'm a widow." Simmons raised an eyebrow as he clearly took note of that fact.

"Just getting ready to make some dinner for yourself, then?"

"Right. I should unload those groceries."

"Of course, feel free to do what you need to do. Don't mind us."

Sure. How could I not mind two police officers standing in my kitchen? I plowed ahead and started working on the groceries while Eisenstein looked around and Simmons scribbled. Suddenly, I couldn't remember where I kept the bread. I stared at the loaf in my hand for far too long, detached entirely from what was going on around me.

"What's your theory about what happened to them?" Eisenstein asked.

"I don't have a theory."

"Humor me," she said.

"Well, I guess they went on a trip together, like you said."

"You think they went on a trip together?"

"No," I stuttered quickly. "You asked for a theory."

"Well, how did you come up with that theory?" she pressed.

"I don't know," I said, flustered. "You said something about traveling and, well, I don't know."

She said nothing for a moment. Simmons kept writing.

"If you do hear from Mr. Fischer or Miss Flores, you'll call me at the number on that card?" she asked.

"Sure. But again, I don't know Miss Flores. I barely

know Mr. Fischer."

"Right, you said that," she said, nodding. "But you'll call me?"

"Of course." The bread was still in my hand. Finally, I just put it down on the countertop and picked up the detective's business card from where I'd left it. I affixed the card to the refrigerator with a magnet, proving that I was a good citizen who could definitively be trusted to help the police in any way possible, then I smiled.

CHAPTER SIXTY-NINE
Alex

"THE POLICE. THEY were here. They asked a lot of questions. And apparently there is a girl missing along with Klaus." It was Peg yet again, sweaty and frantic and running her mouth off before I'd even gotten her inside.

"Can you hold that thought, Peg?" I said, trying to calm her down. "Come in, close the door, and take a breath."

She stepped in and hurriedly closed the door behind her. The panic was so immense, I thought she might hyperventilate.

"We can't have these conversations on the front steps, you understand," I said. Maybe I was mansplaining, but she deserved it. At the same time, I wanted to be careful with my language. The last thing I needed was to set her off like last time.

Peg just stared at me with wide eyes. "You heard what I said, though, right?"

"I heard you. You spoke to the cops?"

"Yes! They ambushed me on the street when I was coming home from the store. For all I know they were waiting for me, like, you know, a stakeout."

"OK, calm down. It sounds like it went fine. You're not

under arrest, are you?"

"No."

"Well let's sit down and you can tell me everything they said. I can't do this in the entry hall again. And I want to hear about this missing girl."

I hustled back to the living room as quickly as I could. Peg pushed past me brusquely and sat down in Eliza's usual tutoring spot. I ignored the fact that this meant she was now in my way and kind of shimmied between her legs and the coffee table before sitting back down where I usually did.

Peg then walked me through a lengthy narrative, barely seeming to take a breath along the way. There were two police officers—one of whom was the same cop who'd left the business card before—with questions about Klaus, someone named Lupe, and Peg's relationship with both of them. Like her, I was surprised to discover there was a live-in caretaker for the old blind guy on the corner, who I'd seen once or twice sitting alone on his front steps. I was immediately concerned about the news that she had vanished.

"You didn't kill her, too, did you?" I asked during one of the few breaks in her monologue. Peg didn't find that funny *at all*, sneering at me and plowing ahead with the story.

From the way she was telling it, the police seemed to be working with an idea that Klaus and Lupe ran away together, which felt like something we could also work with. Older man, younger woman, different cultures, forbidden love. Why, it was almost romantic. But lovers, even forbidden lovers, usually don't leave without a trace, not like this. There was no sign of Klaus, and it sounded like no sign of

Lupe, either. So surely the police would have to suspect that something was amiss. I certainly did.

I told Peg as much but kept my worst fears to myself. "Sure, the situation is suspicious, but it's not out of the realm of possibility. And maybe she'll turn up at some point. There's not much we can do about it, either way, though. I still feel like we're pretty well in the clear here."

"We're sure as hell not in the clear, mister," she said. Tensions were rising again, and I could see panic in Peg's eyes start to bubble up. "Whether or not Klaus's disappearance has anything to do with the girl, they *know* something is up. That's why they were asking me all those questions."

I lowered my voice and tried to be as soothing as possible, like I was reading her a bedtime story. "Listen, it's all OK. There's nothing to do, like I said. You don't know anything. You told them as much, and now you can stop talking to them completely."

"That sounds incredibly suspicious."

"If you have to say anything more, just offer simple answers. If they ask you to speculate, say *I don't know*. This isn't rocket science, Peg. The cops are stupid. They only know what you tell them."

"It sounds like they know everything. It's only a matter of time before they figure it all out and start digging in his yard."

"And how are they going to do that?"

"They'll find a fingerprint or something, I don't know."

"You told them you'd been in the house, right?"

"Yes."

"So, of course there will be a fingerprint."

"But what if I'm the only fingerprint?"

"Listen, no one looks at old ladies—sorry—and thinks they killed the guy across the street and then just went on with their lives like nothing happened."

"Sure, but—"

I interrupted. "No buts. You didn't do anything, you don't know anything, and that's all you have to say. How many times do I have to tell you this? I can't believe you answered any questions at all, much less suggested some idea that he ran off with this Lupe."

Peg looked like she was either going to scream or cry. In the end, she swallowed whatever emotions she had. "Maybe I need a lawyer," she said.

"You absolutely do not need a lawyer. If you want them to start investigating you in earnest, then get a lawyer. Remember, right now, they still don't even have a crime. They're still investigating a disappearance, and hopefully that's where it will end."

"You know it's only a matter of time before this escalates, Alex. Eventually they're going to stop picking up his mail. The mortgage is going to stop being paid. The utilities will get cut off. He will be totally vanished or presumed dead."

"Well, let's hope for the first option. This kind of thing is not unheard of."

"I can see them doing that except for the damn Latina disappearing. It's incredibly suspicious. I mean, what are the odds?"

"Jesus, Peg," I said. "I'm not *that* good with numbers."

CHAPTER SEVENTY
Eliza

"Eliza?"

"Huh?" I said, startled by hearing my name. I hadn't been paying attention, miles away again as I thought about the creeper rotting in the ground across the street. What should I do about it? Should I tell the police? My parents? Barbie G?

"Eliza? Are you with us?" Ms. Barbagianni asked. Shit, I was doing it again.

"Yeah, I guess."

"Do you have any thoughts about why Jack covers himself in charcoal and clay?"

Oh, right. *Lord of the Flies*. I was one and a half chapters behind.

"Well, um…" I stalled for time to think a bit. Class participation was 20 percent of our grade. "I mean, to mask himself."

"OK," Ms. Barbagianni said. "Why does he mask himself?"

I hadn't gotten to this part of the book yet, so I was just winging it. "I mean, he wants to hide. He wants to hide because of the things he's done."

"Well," the teacher said, "he hasn't really done anything—not yet. Sorry, spoiler, everyone. He wants to hunt the pig, and this is his method of camouflage."

"Right, the pig."

"But maybe you're suggesting this is foreshadowing the darkness of Jack's character?"

"Yes," I said, firmly. "Foreshadowing."

"That people hide behind masks when they feel they have some reason to hide."

"Agreed."

"Any thoughts on the symbolism of the fire signal going out while Jack and the other boys are hunting for the pig?"

"Um," I stalled again. "I mean, they were distracted."

"Yes, go on."

"The fire went out...so they couldn't cook the pig." I was grasping at straws.

"No. The signal fire was for their rescue." She turned to the class. "I'm not sure Eliza has thoroughly read this chapter and may need to go over it again tonight. Does anyone else want to discuss the symbolism of the charcoal mask and the signal fire being extinguished?"

I didn't pay attention to what anyone said after that, slumping back into my seat, relieved in my assurance that I would not be called on again that day.

People were talking at school. The missing German guy and the Latinx had made the local news, with police asking anyone with leads to come forward. That kind of thing wouldn't normally make the rounds on campus, but someone had figured out they lived across the street from me, and there were suddenly a lot of questions from people I barely knew. "Maybe he kidnapped her..." "Maybe she kidnapped him..." "Maybe Eliza is hiding them in her basement..." We didn't have a basement, but whatever.

Some of the comments were really out there. "Maybe he had his eyes on you next, what do you think? Those kinds of guys usually like young girls." I would always just scowl and walk away. There was nothing to say. "Better watch your back, Eliza! What if he's hiding in the woods!"

Jean Claire was avoiding me or ignoring me, I couldn't tell which. Usually it bothered me, but I was too distracted and exhausted to care at the moment. I was ready for the news cycle to change, the story to go away, to move back to the City—anything, really, to get this over with so I could forget about all of it.

Meanwhile, Barbie G was going on and on about a dead pig and someone with broken glasses. I would have to try to catch up on the reading tonight but was praying for the Christmas break to get here so I wouldn't have to think about anything at all for a couple of weeks.

I DON'T KNOW exactly what made me go to Peg's house after school. Alex had been clear that we needed to act normally and try to put everything behind us, but I just couldn't help myself. The anxiety was eating away at me, and I just didn't have anyone to talk to about it, because Alex wouldn't hear it.

Peg answered the door quickly after I rang the bell. To put it simply, she was a wreck. Sweats on top and bottom, and hair that might have been two days out from a wash.

"Hey, partner," I said. "Can I come in?"

Peg forced a smile and opened the door all the way. She looked around furtively before ushering me in and quickly closing it, then turning the dead bolt.

I remembered the last time I'd been in her house, standing in almost the exact same spot, when she'd been baking cookies and had left plates of them all over the house. She'd been nothing but smiles and happiness then. Now the house was dark and gloomy, with all the curtains drawn shut. Instead of cookies, there were several weeks of newspapers scattered about, each opened to the local news section.

"How have you been?" I asked.

"Eliza," she said with a tragic look on her face, "you know we're not supposed to see each other right now."

"Yeah, I know, but," I stammered, trying to think of what to say exactly. "You know, we're a team and all. I thought we could help each other out again."

Peg softened. "Oh, nothing would make me happier, Eliza. I just don't know if I'm in a state to help anyone right now."

"I've been having a hard time at school. At home. Pretty much everywhere," I said. Whether she wanted to hear it or not, I wanted to get it out. "All I can think about is the man buried across the street."

"A bad man," Peg said.

"Still a man."

"I know, I know," she said, forcing a grim smile. "I think about it all the time, too."

"I can't imagine what it must be like for you, especially with the police coming around all the time."

"It eats away at me from the inside," Peg said. "But I'm just hoping for a day when this all blows over, and everything can get back to normal."

"It doesn't seem like it's going to blow over."

"It has to," she said. "Everything does eventually. People get bored and they move on."

"Do the police get bored?"

"Alex seems to think so. That they'll just assume he disappeared or died in an accident."

I nodded. "Maybe. That would really be nice."

"The problem is we'll never know. It's not like the police will come by and tell us, *Hey, never mind, we closed the case.*"

I laughed nervously. "I just wish I knew how to stop thinking about it, even for a little while," I said.

Peg took my hand and drew me closer, then put her arms around me, pulling me into a sad but tight hug. I didn't fight it.

"Me too," Peg said. "Me too."

CHAPTER SEVENTY-ONE
Eisenstein

LOOKING AT CELLULAR subscriber "ping" records was never a fun part of the job, but with Fischer's case, it took us all of a minute to see that his activity ceased completely on November 18. That matched up perfectly with the last known text message he'd sent to Illuxis that morning, telling them he was sick. His cell phone was either shut off or the battery died shortly after that, and it hadn't been turned on since.

There was nothing particularly unusual in the call or text logs or in the remainder of the pings. A variety of work calls that I had Simmons check out—no one had heard from Fischer in weeks—and a few texts to Peg Jurgensen across the street. Interestingly, there was no communication at all with Lupe Flores. Flores's phone was still unaccounted for, but we had obtained her account information as well. No activity on her phone since October 29, nearly three weeks before Fischer went missing. If the two had decided to vanish together, she would have had to lie low for more than half a month.

"That doesn't make any sense at all," Simmons said, leaning on my desk. "Do you think it's possible she hid out in Fischer's house for all that time only for him to disappear them both weeks later?"

"It doesn't seem likely," I said. "Not a theory I'd give much credence to; that's for sure."

The video from Sunset Market was in, too. She'd paid the bill in cash, but we were almost certain it was Lupe Flores, buying a bag of groceries on October 29, just like Percy Goodwin had suggested she was doing, and walking out the front door, alone. "You don't just go buy dinner and then run away from home without eating it," I said.

"Flores disappeared sometime between leaving the grocery store and getting home. Fischer's last known whereabouts place him in his house," Simmons summed up. "They disappeared within a mile of each other, but weeks apart."

"Either these have nothing at all to do with each other or everything to do with each other," I said, leaning back in my chair. "But right now, none of this makes any sense at all." I looked at Simmons directly. "So what do we need to do next?"

He replied, "Get more evidence."

"Yes," I said. "It's time to head back to Fischer's house."

The return trip to Fischer's house was quite a bit more involved than our first two visits, as we had to arrange for two specialists to come along: a fingerprint technician—who was early—whose job was to process a variety of rooms of the house and the inside of Fischer's car. And a locksmith—who was late—whose job was to cut open the safe in Fischer's bedroom with a circular carbide saw. I had also tapped a photographer to capture everything we saw. This wasn't a crime scene. Not yet, anyway, but it certainly had the potential to become one. Cars both official and civilian lined the street outside.

I warned Simmons that this would be more complicated than the usual calls he'd been on and that he needed to follow the protocol carefully. "We're working on an operating theory that these are two missing persons who likely had some connection we don't yet know, right?" I asked.

"Right."

"So we're looking for evidence of that connection. Or for evidence that contradicts that theory in some way."

I had made a rough sketch of the Fischer house and was adding more detail as we worked the scene, noting points of interest as they came up. The main thing right now was the safe. Presumably, once the fingerprints came back, that might raise other questions we would need to answer. I was regularly checking in with the tech on areas where there were lots of prints—the bedroom, the garage, inside the car—and areas where there were none—namely the kitchen and all the doorknobs. I could hear the camera shutter click and see its flash whenever I was close enough. The photographer must have snapped three hundred pictures or more over the course of the nearly four hours we spent working the house. He even shot pics of every shelf inside the refrigerator.

"I'm old enough to remember when this kind of coverage was impossible because film was so expensive," I said to Simmons as the man captured a photo of a badly decaying cantaloupe.

On the trip we also obtained some personal items of Lupe Flores from her room, which Percy Goodwin had left untouched as we'd asked him to. It would take time to process the fingerprints to see if any of the prints in Fischer's house matched up, but that was work we'd have to send out to one of the state forensic labs. The tech said it would take only a couple of days to get the results for whether any of Flores's prints were present in the house, and at most a few more days after that to see if there were any electronic matches in the IAFIS, the big national database of fingerprint records. If we wanted to do DNA work, that would be a whole other trip with all new specialists involved.

Eventually, the locksmith arrived, looking hungover though it was now close to noon on a Wednesday. But it was the holidays, with Christmas only a week away, so some revelry could be forgiven. He took one look at the safe then headed back to his truck to fetch a saw and a crowbar. "I've done this before," he muttered, putting his safety goggles and earmuffs into place. "This is a pretty basic model."

He got to work spreading out tarps to collect flying bits of metal and other debris and suggested we stay out of the room unless we had ear and eye protection. I set my phone in the corner of the room, aiming it at the scene to record video of the process and preserve the chain of evidence. Then we did as instructed, waiting down the hall while the saw fired up and dug into the metal safe, carving a channel through the steel.

The locksmith was right. It didn't take long, and soon we heard a loud thump as some portion of the safe crashed to the ground. An acrid smoke wafted through the doorway, and we approached cautiously. The locksmith emerged from the bedroom before we got there, his earmuffs around his neck.

"I took a peek inside after I got the hole cut," he said to the both of us, removing his goggles. "I think you're gonna want to see this."

CHAPTER SEVENTY-TWO

Peg

THE CARS HAD been lined up halfway down the cul-de-sac, and more kept coming as the afternoon went on. How could they possibly need this many people to look through Klaus's dumb bookcases? Why didn't they just take what they wanted and leave? Couldn't they tow his car to, you know, the police lot and check it out there? It was all so excessive, and I knew that the police presence would invite outside interest I definitely did not want.

This wasn't my fault, right? If I had known about the missing girl down the street, we would have come up with another plan. Now the odds that her disappearance was a coincidence that had nothing to do with Klaus were growing smaller and smaller with each new car that arrived on the block.

I guess there was no sense worrying about it now, though the good news was that, from my vantage point, peering through a crack in the entry hall curtains, the police seemed to be focusing on the interior of the house instead of the yard. That meant there were still a few options, at least for now. I decided to write them all down—though I knew I would have to burn the paper on the stove later.

They came to me in no particular order.

Option one—Dig him up. It seemed likely that the body was going to be discovered at some point, so why not move it? Get Alex to help again, pump him up on his meds, get to digging in the night, wrap the body up in a sheet, and then take it out to the forest or maybe dump it in the ocean. Was this realistic? There were some problems with the plan, including getting Alex to help at all. And how would we get the body out of the grave and into the car? We'd barely been able to get it over the railing and into the grave in the first place, and it would be a lot harder and more difficult to drag the body from there to a car in the driveway—not to mention much more visible to onlookers. The police seemed to show up randomly, and maybe they were watching the place. If we went back to the scene of the crime—though it was definitely *not* a crime—it seemed awfully probable that someone would see us.

Option two—Burn down the house. I knew well that a fire was a dead certain way to get rid of an awful lot of evidence at once. Burning the house down wouldn't get rid of the corpse out back, but it would surely cause a lot of confusion and set the investigation back months if not years. All that DNA would go up in smoke—if they didn't have what they needed already. I knew I would not be a strong suspect, but I would have to be extremely careful in setting the blaze to make it look like an accident. Again, if police were watching the street, this would be difficult—and it was possible the plan could backfire, causing them to renew their investigatory efforts. Also, burning down the house *would* be a crime. A big one. What if the trees went up, too? It could take out the whole cul-de-sac if I was careless.

Option three—Run. I had plenty of money in reserve. Cash out and hit the road. Move to Mexico or Costa Rica, where there were plenty of other Americans my age. Learn to play pickleball or something. If two people vanished from the cul-de-sac and a third went missing as well, maybe they would think someone else was responsible for all three disappearances. It was very suspicious, but it could work, right? I made a mental note to check whether my passport was expired.

Option four—Don't do anything. Like Alex said, there was no evidence tying us to Klaus's death, and as long as we stayed cool and quiet, we wouldn't be charged with anything. The problem was that this relied on Alex—and Eliza—doing the same thing. What if they accused Alex and he talked? What was it he called it? The prisoner's dilemma. What if he'd snapped a picture of me burying the body when I wasn't looking, something he could use as a Get Out of Jail Free card? Could I trust him? And what about Eliza? This might have been the smartest plan overall, but in many ways it seemed the riskiest because it relied on putting all my faith in two people I barely knew.

Option five—Find someone else to blame. Perhaps the best idea yet. If they found Klaus's body, who could we pin the murder on? Another neighbor? A stranger? Suicide? OK, probably not suicide, but still, like they used to say at work, there are no bad ideas, right? Great concept, but I needed someone else to blame and some kind of evidence to use to point to them. Maybe I could take a piece of someone's clothing and bury it near Klaus's body. They could trace the clothing to the new suspect through DNA, maybe. Oh, what about the neighbor at the end of the cul-de-sac, the guy with the mustache? He even looked the part. Maybe I could just take some of his mail and scatter it around Klaus's yard. Would that be enough to do the trick? I needed to think this one over some more.

Option six—Speaking of blame, what if the cops thought Alex actually did it? Would that even be conceivable? Just thinking out loud here.

Option seven—Confess. If they were going to pin this on me down the road, maybe it was better to come forward before things got too out of control. To be honest, I hated this idea, but I knew I had to at least include it on the list.

Those were all the ideas I could come up with. A solid seven, some better than others, but proof enough that I did have options that didn't involve being arrested. Still, I thought as I held the paper over the gas flame of my kitchen stove and watched it ignite, the exercise was frustrating. Why hadn't anyone heard about the Latina girl before all of this? Gossip just wasn't what it used to be, and that upset me more than anything. I dropped the last bit of burning paper into the sink and doused it with water, flushing the remnants down the disposal.

I opened the junk drawer to my right as I often did on quiet afternoons and considered one of the most prominent items within: Klaus's phone, powered down and laying in stasis. A simple reminder? An insurance policy? A foolish keepsake? I didn't know which of these it represented yet, but I still thought that maybe the phone would be the key to getting out of all of this at some point.

I was so mad at myself that it had all come to this, and to hell with Alex and his stupid plan. Even without knowing about the missing girl, I knew we should've come up with a better story to begin with.

CHAPTER SEVENTY-THREE
Jean Claire

E LIZA WAS STILL being moody. I was happy she'd finally come over—it felt like the first time in months—but it wasn't the same as before. We weren't even hanging out in my room, because Mother was upset that I did not go with her to the prayer circle the previous weekend. I told her I had cramps, but I'm sure she knew it was a lie. She didn't push it then, but she said I would need to stay close by for the rest of the week so she could pray for my recovery. In other words, I was grounded from doing anything in my room except sleep. At least she hadn't taken the door off the hinges.

We were sitting in the formal living room just inside the front door, a room that no one ever used, particularly including the upright piano, which had come with the house. There was discussion of me taking lessons, but when Mother found out how much they cost, she dropped it, thank God.

Eliza sat on the floral-patterned couch. I sat in an arm-chair, same pattern, across from her. No one said anything. We just looked at our phones, not even giggling at the day's TikToks and Snaps. I could hear the audio droning from the TV room around the corner, where Mother was watching the local news. What a waste of time.

"Do you want to stay for dinner?" I asked Eliza, despite knowing that getting permission to have a guest at the table would be a massive hurdle.

She looked up from her phone. "I dunno," she said. "What are you having?"

"Meat loaf."

Eliza grimaced.

"Yeah, I know," I said. "Don't blame you."

"Probably better than whatever my mom is cooking, though," she said.

I mindlessly swiped through a few more clips. "Do you know what you're getting for Christmas?" I asked.

"I asked for AirPods. I think they'll go for it. Probably a bunch of ratchet clothes also, as usual."

"Sucks."

"What about you?"

"Well, we don't really celebrate Christmas." I had assumed she had noticed the lack of a tree or any Christmas décor by now, but Eliza could be a little dense at times.

"Oh really? Your mom is so religious."

"Yeah, well, Mother says it's a pagan holiday and it's blasphemous. We are supposed to fast and pray that day, pray for all the gluttonous sinners who waste their hours at the shopping malls. That's what she says, anyway."

"Ser? Who goes to shopping malls anymore?"

"I dunno. Sinners, I guess."

There was a lull in the conversation, and we returned to our phones for a bit. Eliza had a look in her eye that was hard to describe, but it was like she was intensely uncomfortable. Like she ate too much and had bad gas or something. Something was bothering her, and it clearly had been for weeks. I decided to ask her straight out, but as I opened my mouth, Mother walked around the corner, staring me straight in the eye.

"Jean Claire, I need you to come see this right now," she said.

She turned on her heel and marched away. I knew from her tone it was time to follow, quickly, and I beckoned a startled Eliza to come along. God knows what she was going to show me, but if Eliza was there, at least I'd have a witness to whatever insanity was waiting for me.

We marched into the TV room and saw the television on, playing a commercial.

"Yeah?" I asked.

"Just wait," Mother said, pointing to the television set. "They said it's coming up next."

After the commercial ended, the local news came back to life. It was a story about what was going on in our little town.

A woman in a blue dress, seated at a desk with a fake picture of San Francisco behind her: "New information in the bizarre case of two missing persons from the same Bay Area community. Here's Jessica Raska with the story."

Cut to, presumably, Jessica Raska: "Last week we brought you the story of Klaus Fischer, a Bay Area man who mysteriously disappeared only days apart from his next-door neighbor, Lupe Flores. Police were inundated with tips, and now they say they have new leads in the case. We're here with Detective Rachel Eisenstein, who is the lead investigator in both disappearances. Detective, can you give us an update on the case?"

Pull back to reveal Rachel Eisenstein, indicated as such with a subtitle, being interviewed by Raska: "Yes, Jessica. We have been investigating both disappearances and have strong leads that we're now pursuing."

Raska: "Do you suspect foul play, and are these disappearances connected?"

Eisenstein: "There is evidence now that the cases are connected, and yes, we do have reason to suspect this is more than a simple case of two people running off together."

Crummy pictures of Klaus Fischer and Lupe Flores, taken from who knows where and both labeled with their names, pop into the top right of the screen.

Raska: "What's the next step in the case?"

Eisenstein: "We have several persons of interest we're looking to interview in connection with the disappearances. I think we'll have more to share with the public in the next few days."

Raska: "Is there a criminal on the loose? Does the

community have reason to worry?"

Eisenstein: "We're definitely not advising anyone to panic, but we are suggesting residents stay off the streets at night for the time being and to ensure their doors are kept locked."

Raska: "Thank you, Detective, and we look forward to hearing more as you continue your investigation. Back to you, Diane."

The news went on to another story. Mother turned around in her chair to look at us.

"You see this, children?" she asked, sober as I've ever seen her. "There is sin in our world. Sin in our community. Sin all around us, surrounding us. And people are vanishing because of it."

I'm not sure Mother knew that Eliza actually lived on the very block where Klaus and Lupe lived—and that I had actually met both of them—but I'm sure that didn't matter to her. The sin, it was everywhere in her mind.

She went on, "Pray that you have no sin in your hearts, children. Pray for forgiveness, lest we are all taken like these two."

Eliza audibly swallowed.

"And we should all pray for the man and woman who have gone missing. As the Book of Job tells us, 'The eyes of the wicked shall fail, and all refuge shall vanish from them, and their hope shall be the breathing out of life.'"

Whatever that was supposed to mean.

CHAPTER SEVENTY-FOUR
Eisenstein

"SO YOU'VE NEVER met Klaus Fischer?" I asked Mr. and Mrs. van Damal, who were sitting in front of me at their dining table. I'd given Simmons the night off and was handling this one alone.

"No," Judy van Damal said.

"No," Lewis van Damal said.

"And you've never met Lupe Flores."

They both answered no.

"And what about Peg Jurgensen?"

"Not personally, no," Judy said.

"Our daughter has met her," said the dad, who looked like he couldn't wait for this interview to be over. "In fact, I think she's met all three of them, at least in passing."

"I see, and is she home?"

"No, she's at a friend's house," Judy said. "We could call her, but I think she'll be home soon—definitely before dinner."

"Understood. We can talk to her later, or another time."

"Is there anything else you can tell us about what's happening?" Lewis asked. "I thought the two ran away together."

"That was our initial theory," I said, "and while I can't

really comment on too many details, we are now treating this with more severity."

"More severity?" he asked. "What does that mean?"

"We're working under the presumption that at least one of the missing parties is deceased."

Judy van Damal fell back in her seat on the couch, looking stunned.

"What does Peg Jurgensen have to do with any of this?" asked her husband.

"Again, I'm not free to comment at length, but there's substantial evidence of her being in the Fischer home shortly before his untimely disappearance—and she has stated as much. In fact, we believe she may have been the last person to see him alive. And now we have found other items in the home that indicate, as they say, *foul play*."

"Wow, I really don't know what to do with any of that information," he said. "And you think Peg had something to do with it?"

"It's possible," I said, probably saying too much. "It's a theory I keep going back to if for no other reason than Ms. Jurgensen just doesn't seem truthful to me. But you've never met her, you said."

"Right," he replied.

At that moment the front door swung open with a crash, slamming back shut with a grace that could only indicate a teenager had arrived.

"Lizzie!" Mr. van Damal yelled. "Come in here, will you?"

"Yeah, what?" she said, as she rounded the corner to the

dining room. Her face fell immediately when she saw me. "Oh."

"Hi, Lizzie," I said. "I'm Detective Eisenstein. I've been looking forward to meeting you for quite a while."

CHAPTER SEVENTY-FIVE

Alex

I KNEW FROM the tone of the knock that it was Eliza. Rushed and rapid, yet weak in power. Insistent, too. Peg's knocks of late were much more forceful. Still, this was a Friday night, not the weekend, so she wasn't here for tutoring. Plus school was officially out for two weeks for the Christmas break, anyway. I guessed I should answer it.

I shambled to the door. The knocking was getting to be a nuisance. Finally, I swung it open.

"How was the test?" I asked. Finals had been earlier today or yesterday, I couldn't remember.

"Fine, whatever," she said, pushing past me into the house. "I need to talk to you."

"Oh boy," I said, closing the door. "You still have the key, right? Do you need me to show you how it works?"

By now she had made her way to our usual spot in the living room and was fiddling with the TV remote to turn it off. "Can you shut up about the key for one minute?" she asked, annoyed.

This was going to be fun.

I started making my way back to the living room. "OK, lay it on me. What's up?"

"What's up?" she asked. "You know what's up. It's this situation with Peg and the police and the neighbor and the whole thing."

"OK."

"The cops, they came to my house. They *interviewed* me."

This was troubling. "I'm surprised they would interview a minor about a missing person."

"Well, they did," she said, "and it's not a missing person anymore. I'm pretty sure they know he's dead."

"They know or they think?"

"Think, know, I don't know. They said they have evidence that a crime happened, and it's all because that Lupe girl is missing, too."

She was in full panic mode, which was understandable, I supposed. "Slow down and catch your breath. Did they tell you about this evidence?"

"A little. There are fingerprints, and something about a safe."

Oh great, the safe. We'd seen it, but I didn't think anything of it at the time. What had Klaus been collecting in there?

"Well, what did you tell them?"

"Nothing! I told them I don't know anything!"

"Well, basically you don't," I said.

"I know enough, and now I'm lying to the police, and soon they're going to come for me—I know it."

"Ugh, first Peg, now you! You need to pull it together. You're not going to get arrested. You're not going to get in trouble. You will probably never have to see the police again."

"Alex, there were news trucks on the street today. This is becoming a major story, at least around here. People are talking about it at school. It's everywhere."

"By the time you go back after the break, this will probably be forgotten."

"You're delusional," she said.

I was about to respond, but at that moment, a banging on the sliding glass door leading to the backyard erupted. Eliza jumped, and I jumped. What the living hell is happening?

The lights were off outside, but I could make out the figure from the light streaming through the window from the living room. It was Peg, looking even more disheveled than ever.

"Jesus, can you let her in?" I asked Eliza. She scurried over to the door, and Peg rushed into the house.

"What the hell is this?" I asked.

"I climbed the fence," Peg said. "I didn't want anyone to see me."

"Oh my God," I replied. "Eliza, is anyone watching the house from the street?"

"No," she said. "I mean, I didn't see anybody."

"They're out there," Peg said. "I'm sure they're just hiding."

"There's nowhere to hide," I said. "If they were on the cul-de-sac, they'd have to be parked on the street."

"You don't know!" she cried. "There were news trucks

here today, too."

"I heard," I said.

"Well, you should have watched. You watch TV all day as it is, so you don't have an excuse."

"I was just telling him that the police interviewed me," Eliza said. Peg's arrival had done nothing for her mood.

"Oh, great. What did you say?"

"Nothing, just like I told Alex. I told them nothing. But they had a lot of questions about you."

"Oh my God, they know." Peg physically slumped.

"They don't know anything," I said. "If they did, they would have taken you in or something, I'm sure of it."

"It's only a matter of time before they do," Peg said. "I'm going to be arrested. I'm going to prison. They're going to find the body."

"We don't know any of that, but we just have to stay calm, even if they do find Klaus."

"This is exactly what I wanted to avoid," Peg said. "All my worst fears are coming true."

"Well, I told you to call the police in the first place. This whole idea was stupid."

"Stupid? *You're stupid.* Maybe if you had helped me get rid of the evidence better, we wouldn't be in this mess."

Eliza's eyes were bulging out of her head.

"This isn't my fault, Peg."

"Well, I beg to differ, and I bet they're getting their information from you, too."

I was taken aback. "What? I haven't even spoken to the cops once. I told you I never answer the door when they come around."

"Yeah, well, eventually even you have to leave the house. They'll get you one of these days."

"And if they do, I'll stick to the story. *Just like we all need to do*, which I've said since the beginning."

"Your story is dumb. There's a dead body, and they're going to know he didn't commit suicide and bury himself in the yard."

This was going badly. I had to get things back under control and fast. "Listen, this is a tense situation—I get it. Yes, maybe they'll find the body. No, that doesn't mean they will arrest you or have any idea who put him there. Police want to intimidate you because they know you will slip up and make a mistake or do something dumb like confess. When people commit a crime, the cops count on them to get nervous and start talking. They wait for you to change your story. If it wasn't for criminals screwing themselves over, most crimes would never be solved."

"Wait," Peg said. "Do you think I committed a crime? Because I was just defending myself, and now you're talking about a crime. I didn't do anything wrong."

"No, I don't think you did anything wrong. Except that you're spiraling and doing crazy things like climbing over my fence in the dark."

She squared up and looked me in the eye. "I'm not crazy, Alex," she said. "I'm protecting myself."

CHAPTER SEVENTY-SIX

Lew

"I'M WORRIED ABOUT Lizzie," Judy said to me as we prepared for bed on Christmas Eve.

"For once, so am I," I said.

"I thought things were going so well with school and friends. And now she is just so distant."

"Maybe it's a phase."

"Maybe it has something to do with all this police activity."

"You think? I don't know why a few questions would bother her so much. It doesn't have anything to do with her."

"I don't know," Judy said. "I think there's gossip."

"About Lizzie?"

"I don't know. She doesn't tell me. But even I've heard the whispering around town, about how the cul-de-sac is cursed."

"Cursed?"

"You know, bad luck."

"You make your own luck, Judy."

"Well, try telling that to a fourteen-year-old, Lew."

"She'll be fifteen soon, you know," I said. "She'll want a car."

"Of course she will," Judy replied. "I miss the days when she would open her presents on Christmas and be ecstatic about getting a Barbie or a Rainbow Loom."

"What did we get her this year?"

"An iTunes gift card."

"That's it?"

"She asked for AirPods but I didn't order them in time. This is the next best thing."

"Christ, we should at least wrap up some socks or something. Have you seen how ratty hers are?" I asked.

"I'm not putting socks under the Christmas tree, Lew."

"Um, I got socks for Christmas last year."

"You getting socks and Eliza getting socks—those are two different things," she said.

We went quiet as we finished brushing our teeth and such. I could tell right away that Judy had a new nighttime lotion she was going to try out tonight. This one smelled worse than the last, but I resolved to bite my tongue this time and say nothing about it. Eventually we both made it into bed.

"So what do you want to do?" I asked. "About Lizzie, I mean."

"I don't think there's anything *to* do," Judy said. "Except wait for this all to blow over and hope for the best. Maybe if we can get through the Christmas break, things will get back to normal."

"If things could get back to normal," I echoed, trying not to sound mocking. I flipped my phone on because, honestly, what else were we going to do right now? "What a dream that would be."

CHAPTER SEVENTY-SEVEN
Eliza

THE ITUNES CARD was fine. I could pay for Apple Music for the rest of the year and maybe buy a few new apps. Whatever. No AirPods, but at least Mom and Dad didn't try to do something stupid like buy me a Barbie.

There was no point texting Jean Claire. She would be at church with her mom for hours. She'd probably check in in the afternoon, but she would be exhausted, as she usually was after church days, and she wouldn't want to talk. What was there to talk about, anyway? Christmas presents she wasn't allowed to receive? Finals, now that they were finished? What next semester was going to be like? I was one-eighth done with high school, and I knew Jean Claire felt exactly the same as me: When will it be over?

Of course, I was desperate to talk about Peg, the German creeper, and how insane life on the cul-de-sac was becoming. I knew she could tell something was wrong but didn't say anything, and I was glad she didn't. I couldn't tell her the truth. Could I? With all the police activity, it seemed like it was only a matter of time before it all came out. Would Peg get in trouble? Would Alex? What about me? Was I an accomplice now? I don't know why I thought Christmas would be any different. All I could do was lie in bed and wait for the police to knock on the door again, telling me they had more questions to ask and this time maybe I was going to need a lawyer.

Maybe I should tell my parents. They would understand, wouldn't they? I mean, they're my parents, so they don't really have a choice. They would know that I didn't do anything wrong, except try to be a good friend to our neighbors. Wouldn't they?

Were they going to find the body in the woods behind Klaus's house? Why hadn't they found it already? Surely, it was only a matter of time, no matter what Alex tried to say. It just seemed inevitable, which made me even more depressed.

There was no solution. Spill my guts to Jean Claire. Tell my parents. Talk to Alex again. Talk to Peg again. What was the point? No matter who I talked to it would end with disbelief, anger, scolding, or a trip to the police station. Nothing, nothing at all to do.

I tried to put it all out of my mind, as I had been, just like Alex had been saying. It never worked, but I figured I should keep trying. I went back to scrolling TikToks and wondering if maybe I should finish unpacking, a job Mom said a day ago I absolutely, positively, no-buts-about-it had to finish before New Year's.

CHAPTER SEVENTY-EIGHT
Eisenstein

IT TOOK DAYS to arrange for the cadaver dogs from San Francisco—along with their handlers—but I was hoping it would be worth it. It didn't take long to see results. The dogs were curious from the get-go, and they alerted almost as soon as we let them start walking the property. The entirety of the wooded area outside the house was suspicious, to the point where the dog handlers said they had rarely seen activity like it. Simmons took video of the entire scene so we could refer to it later if needed.

Inside the house the dogs seemed curious but didn't properly alert, according to the handlers. The suggestion was to continue to focus on the outside, at least to start. But that would mean a lot more work.

We spent the rest of the chilly, damp morning marking the boundaries of the Fischer property with wood stakes and "DO NOT ENTER" police tape, and marked the most interesting spots, according to the dogs, with red-tipped flags.

Simmons and I reviewed the evidence while we waited for more manpower and shovels to arrive. The items retrieved from the safe had been particularly fascinating, including thousands of dollars and an equal number of euros, a not-yet-used Belgian passport that was clearly intended for Fischer but had been issued under a different name, and quite a number of little trinkets that I was now assuming were trophies. Various pieces of jewelry, a small purse, and, most alarming, an identification card for a woman named Elizabeth Opola, a nurse. A cursory search revealed that she had disappeared after a shift at a Vacaville hospital a couple of years prior. The case was still open but had gone fully cold.

Until now. A picture was starting to emerge that was growing stronger with each passing hour. I was now operating on the assumption that Opola was dead and buried in Fischer's yard, probably along with numerous others—including the Flores girl. I guessed that Fischer was now on the run, living off the grid.

Once extra hands arrived, the work progressed quickly. As I feared yet wholly expected, human remains began to be recovered almost immediately. The ground was hard and difficult to dig in—except in areas where some surprisingly deep graves had already been dug. Someone had put quite some time into digging these out, and here the earth was much softer and clearly disturbed. If not for the thick layer of leaves that blanketed the entire area, the gravesites would have been quite obvious. Once our crew began realizing this, the job turned quickly to raking leaves rather than earnestly digging, as we more easily located site after site where bodies had been put to rest. There were five so far, quite neatly arranged, almost like the rows of a cemetery.

They began with the oldest—she was at least five years in the ground—and ended with the youngest, a very fresh corpse I was certain would soon be officially identified as Lupe Flores. Even though the body was significantly decayed, I could tell she had been strangled at one point, though there was no telling yet if that was how she actually died. The other bodies were all too far gone. The coroner would have to get involved to tell us more.

It was getting late, and people were starting to whisper. This is not the kind of work anyone in law enforcement around here had ever done. A single murder? Sure, once every few years, always related to domestic violence. A yard full of dead bodies? This was new territory for all of us.

Though we had a strict blackout policy against telling anyone anything about the crime scene—not even family—it was only a matter of time before the media would arrive. The good news was that a crowd of locals had yet to materialize. It was as if no one was home at any of the houses on the cul-de-sac, and most of them appeared dark from the street. We'd have to have someone on site twenty-four hours a day to protect the crime scene—at least until the FBI arrived, which would likely be tomorrow. Five corpses officially made this a serial killer case—people were already comparing this to our most famous local killer, the Zodiac—and they would soon be disassembling the Fischer house down to the studs to look for every possible scrap of evidence about his presumed crimes.

Simmons's phone battery had died long ago, and the videos had come to an end. That was for the best. I didn't know how much more of this I could take and did not relish the thought of revisiting any of this on film. As the sun began to set, I leaned against the hood of my car and day-dreamed for a moment of getting as far away from the cul-de-sac as possible, out of my uniform, and into a glass of zinfandel. I was interrupted in this idyll by Simmons, who emerged from the thicket of trees, completely covered in dirt.

"You about ready to go home?" I asked him, hopefully.

"I was ready three hours ago," he said. "But I doubt we'll be done here anytime soon."

"Oh?" I asked.

"We're digging up one more body in there," he said, ex-hausted. "You're not gonna believe this. I think it's Fischer."

WITHIN FORTY-EIGHT HOURS, the police station no longer had any semblance of its prior, sleepy demeanor. Every available desk, including my own, was now commandeered by an agent wearing a blue windbreaker with the letters "FBI" emblazoned across the back. People were chattering and phones were ringing, nonstop. Laptops everywhere connected to extension cords and power strips overloading the meager few outlets in the room—a problem we had long since given up complaining about.

"I only know what the facts say" was straight out the window. *Everyone* now had a theory about what had hap-pened on the cul-de-sac. Some were more plausible than others, but you wouldn't have known it from the depth and intensity with which the agents in the room discussed them.

The most original theory was that Fischer did not kill the women, that someone else had killed them and was burying them in his yard, unbeknown to him. It seemed farfetched at first, but when you remembered that Fischer traveled frequently for work, it was perhaps plausible. Maybe all the murders happened while he was out of town. Perhaps someone had surprised him the night he was going to Seattle, thinking he had already left, there was some kind of fight, and he ended up in the ground.

Of course, this theory had some major holes. It didn't explain the trophies in Fischer's safe and the fake passport, and it didn't explain the new DNA evidence that Lupe Flores had been present in Fischer's vehicle.

That led to a perhaps more credible theory that Fischer was indeed the killer, but he had an accomplice. The two of them would prey on the victims together. That would help ease the difficulty of apprehending someone, maneuvering a body, and so on. Fischer appeared to be in good physical shape, but it wasn't easy to deal with a corpse alone no matter how small it was. They're heavy and awkward and unbalanced. Having a helper would explain a lot.

The problem with that theory was that 90 percent of serial killers—and Fischer was tentatively being labeled such—were solo operators. From what the few people who knew him had told me, Fischer seemed to be gregarious and outgoing. Unlike pop culture would suggest, that also fit the profile of a lone, serial predator. He must have been able to abduct and murder these victims because he had the ability to woo or charm them in some way.

But Fischer was dead and buried in his own yard. This clearly wasn't a suicide, though some ambitious new graduate of Quantico tried to suggest such a theory with a straight face. Someone must have done the deed. Who? Perhaps the most exciting, tongue-waggingest theory to emerge revolved around Peg Jurgensen.

Jurgensen and Fischer had some sort of relationship; that was clear. Could they have been some kind of murderous duo? A sick sex thing where they recruited a willing participant, then killed her? Jurgensen didn't seem like the type, but who really knew what went on behind closed doors? But it was the strongest possibility we had so far, and the feds were doing a massive amount of research into Jurgensen's background to see what dirt they could dig up on her in advance of a formal interview, which would probably happen soon.

Of course, we locals didn't get to do much more than listen in on all the hubbub from the feds. The agents barely introduced themselves to us, and groused repeatedly about the broken door at Fischer's house, the footprints in the yard, and everything else we'd done to destroy the sanctity of the crime scene.

Our job now was to maintain a twenty-four-hour patrol on the cul-de-sac, log who came in, who went out, and ensure no one tampered with anything near the Fischer residence. You know, the kind of meaningful work that represented the real reason I became a police officer to begin with.

CHAPTER SEVENTY-NINE

Lew

"IS THIS SOMETHING we can live with?" I said to Judy, peering out the window set in the front door. A swirl of red and blue lights danced in the cold dark, but it was all eerily silent. I could make out shadowy figures plodding up and down the steep hill of the cul-de-sac, to and from the cars that lined every available parking spot on the street—and one in our driveway, after Judy had told a young FBI agent in a rented Yaris that he could leave it there "for a few hours." That had been at dawn. Thankfully, tomorrow was a work day, so I could get out of here for a little while.

"Hmm?" she asked, distracted, looking at her phone. Surely reading more news and social media commentary on the Fischer case.

I turned around. "I said, how long do you think we can do this? How long can this go on?"

"I dunno, Lew," she said. "Here it says these investigations can take months."

"Jesus Christ," I said, looking back toward the road.

The news crews weren't allowed on the cul-de-sac, so the reporters had taken up residence at the end of the road and along the long woodsy street leading toward Sunset Market.

Normally a dark and quiet part of town, it was now lit up like a twenty-four-hour diner, cameras aimed vaguely in our direction, hoping to capture something to use on the news. Truck after truck, each armed with a telescoping tower and tipped with a satellite dish, occupied every inch of roadway, leaving only a narrow path that one car could fit through at a time, with cops having to direct traffic. There was a constant, unbearable drone of helicopters overhead, surely news media trying in vain to get a peek at the scene of the crime, all but impossible thanks to the thick foliage across the street.

A pair of cops—or FBI, I couldn't tell—trotted down the cul-de-sac toward the police barricade at the intersection. Some reporter was trying to talk his way onto the cul-de-sac again from the looks of it. They had yet to let anyone through, and it was hard to get through ourselves. We had to show our IDs every time we came home, and since I still had our old address on mine, I had been forced to explain that fact twice today. Maybe eventually they would recognize me.

"I don't know if I have months in me," I said.

"Well, what else can we do?" she asked. "We can't exactly move again."

"I don't know, Judy. Maybe take a long vacation. Get out of town for a while, wait for this to blow over. Maybe Lizzie could do school remotely for the second half of the year."

"You're going to work with her on her classes while we ride around the country in a motor home?" she asked.

"People do it all the time."

"And your work is going to give you time off?"

"I dunno, sure. They'll understand."

"I don't guess you have a plan on how we're going to earn money while we're on the road, do you?"

I lost it. "Jesus, Judy, I haven't gotten that far. Maybe you can work with me for once."

I expected her to quickly back down, but she uncharacteristically rose up to fight back. "No, Lew. That's always been your problem. You want to dream about foolish things while I have to deal with the reality that's right in front of us. Your plan is unrealistic, and you know it. Your little midlife crisis about being an absentee father isn't going to be solved with a ridiculous idea like this."

That one stung. "Maybe if you worked with me, we could figure out a more realistic solution. All you want to do is shoot me down."

"All I want to do is live in the real world, Lew. The solution is to keep our heads down and focus on what matters: getting past all this with our family and our new life here intact."

I turned back to the window and idly watched the swirl of red and blue lights in the street. "Well, our new life sucks."

"Yeah," she grumbled. "Tell me about it."

CHAPTER EIGHTY

Peg

THERE WAS NO way I was going to be able to dodge the police anymore. They were on the street twenty-four hours a day, clearly watching my house. Exit the front door and I'd be spotted immediately, and probably followed. So this time, when they came knocking, I gladly greeted them at the door with a smile forced on my face, having steeled myself with repeated internal incantations that I had nothing to hide.

But I hadn't slept in days, and anyone could tell. Makeup could only do so much to hide the dark circles under my eyes, and my hair simply wasn't cooperating.

Sure enough, my appearance was an immediate topic of conversation.

"Not sleeping, Ms. Jurgensen?" asked a man wearing a suit and a navy-blue, weatherproof jacket. "You are Peg Jurgensen, aren't you?" Another identically dressed man, who might as well have been his twin brother, stood three steps behind him.

"No, how can I sleep?" I asked. "What with all of the commotion out here." I gestured to the street.

"Yeah, we're sorry about that. I'm Special Agent Davis,

and this is Special Agent Harlow. We're investigating the deaths of Klaus Fischer, Lupe Flores, and the other victims you have probably heard about on the news."

"Of course you are. How can I help?"

"Detective Rachel Eisenstein has given us some background on her discussion with you," he said, holding up a manila folder filled with papers. "That's been very helpful, but maybe you can help us fill in some of the gaps we still have in our understanding about your relationship with the deceased."

"Oh, I'm sure I told them everything I know," I said, playing along.

"Certainly, Ms. Jurgensen. Peg—can I call you Peg?—it's just that we've had a lot of movement in these missing persons cases in the last few days, so I think a fresh look at the facts might help us out."

"Sure, OK," I said.

"Sure is cold out here. Mind if we come inside?"

He stepped through the doorway before I could answer, and before I knew it, both agents were in the house. I could now see the huge yellow FBI insignia emblazoned on the backs of their jackets.

"I guess they don't want anyone to be confused about where you work," I said, indicating the yellow text.

"No," Agent Davis said, "I suppose they don't. Where can we sit?"

I closed the door and led them to the kitchen, the same place I'd met with Eisenstein and Simmons. I could see her card still stuck to the refrigerator. Would the FBI agents think that was a good or a bad thing? We sat around the table, and both men retrieved notepads from their pockets. The one called Agent Harlow started an audio recorder and placed it between us.

"So as you probably know, we have uncovered a number of bodies buried right across the street from your house."

"Mm-hmm." I nodded.

"A number of women, including Lupe Flores—as well as Klaus Fischer."

"Right, I have heard that."

"So," he said, sizing me up, "I guess my first question is, how can all of this happen across the street from you without you ever noticing it?"

"Yeah, I understand. I guess it's because the trees are so thick there. You really can't see anything happening more than a couple of feet in."

"But surely you would have noticed people coming or going, right?"

"No, I really like to keep to myself. I don't much pay attention to what's going on outside."

He pressed on. "But you knew the deceased intimately, and in fact you were a regular visitor at his home, correct?"

"Right. Well, not regular. Sometimes," I hedged. "An occasional visitor."

"And possibly on the night he died."

I swallowed. This was getting uncomfortable. "I don't really know anything about that."

"No?"

"No."

There was an awkward silence as no one spoke. I knew this was a stupid police tactic to get me to talk, and I had to fight hard to prevent it from working.

Finally, Agent Davis broke the silence. "What would you say if I told you we had a witness who placed you at Fischer's house after his disappearance?"

I could feel the panic deep in my stomach. Had Alex cracked? Eliza? Or maybe it was the creepy guy at the top of the hill—had he seen something?

"What?" I stammered, hoping to buy time and regain my composure.

"What would you say," he said, "if someone said you were at Fischer's house after he disappeared—or died?"

"Uh, maybe it was someone who looked like me."

"Hmm," he said, "have you seen anyone at his house since his death?"

"Only a hundred policemen," I said.

"That's a good point," he said. "But it sounds like you are paying attention to what goes on around the cul-de-sac."

"Maybe I am now, but not then."

"Not then?"

"When he disappeared."

"Which you didn't know anything about."

"Right," I said.

"Because how could you?"

"Right."

More silence. I sat with my hands in my lap, trying to keep my feet from tapping and my arms from shaking. My palms were sweating.

Finally, Davis spoke again. "Peg, I want to lay this all out for you. You have to understand the situation we have out there. There's a field of bodies in the ground, some of them several years old. One of them is Lupe Flores. And one is Klaus Fischer. And those two are particularly new. They're fresh. These are not accidental deaths. They're all murders. And that means someone did all this killing. Now, I'd like to believe that Fischer did all this, but that leaves me with a big problem, because Fischer isn't just dead, he's buried in his backyard alongside all the other victims—right in a row. So whoever buried him must have known about the other graves, right? I mean, that makes sense to you, doesn't it?"

This was not going well. In fact, I didn't think it was possible it could be going worse. It was probably time to shut up, but I knew that would only make me look even more suspicious. Should I ask for a lawyer? That would only make me look guiltier, wouldn't it? No one had read me my rights. Was any of this legal? How bad could it be? I realized the silence was stretching on for quite a while.

"Peg, I can see you're nervous, and I want you to relax," Davis said. "I'm not saying you had anything to do with any of these deaths, but you were the last person to see Fischer alive, and I think maybe you know more than you realize. You definitely know more than we do—though that won't last forever. We have a team of forensics investigators working around the clock, and they're busy pulling prints, DNA, you name it, from the crime scene. So sooner or later the truth is going to come out. It's really just a matter of time."

I said nothing. What could I say?

"But in the meantime, I'm hoping you can give us something to go on," Davis said. "Because if you're not involved in this, I think maybe you know the person who was."

CHAPTER EIGHTY-ONE

Alex

I HEARD SIRENS in the distance and decided to take a peek to see what the status was. The trip to the front door this time wasn't as difficult as I'd imagined it would be, but curiosity had gotten the better of me again. Perhaps it was the adrenaline. Nervous energy about the world of shit in which I was now firmly immersed. I dared not spend too much time glancing around the curtains at the parade of police outside, a parade that now included the FBI, swarming the Klaus Fischer residence.

Who could have predicted this guy had a full-on cemetery in his backyard? Well, maybe I should have, given the fact he had dug a grave for Peg in anticipation of offing her. The situation was a full-on disaster now. Twenty/twenty hindsight, right?

Regardless, you can't turn back the clock or erase the past, and I now knew I was completely out of my element. It was one thing to have dealt with a cretin like Steve Williams as I had as a teenager—decades ago before everybody had a camera in their pocket and when forensic investigations were still rudimentary. Hell, I hadn't even had to dispose of the body. Looking back, the whole thing seemed quaint in retrospect.

But this, this was an entirely different thing, as I should have known, and I could tell that the feds were keeping a particularly watchful eye—though not a blatantly obvious one—on Peg's house, based on how they had positioned their vehicles and stationed various personnel. She was clearly under suspicion, and all I could do was hope she hadn't cracked and spilled her guts already. I knew I would not be able to dodge interrogation myself for much longer. Officers of various sorts knocked on the door at least three times a day, and my front step was now littered with business cards that had fallen after being wedged into the doorjamb.

Eventually, I'd need to leave the house. For one thing, I was due for a dialysis treatment in just two days, and if I skipped it, things would quickly go south. Also, I was running out of food and would soon need to go buy more or arrange an Instacart delivery, but either way that would be the point at which they'd swoop in and want to know why I hadn't answered in so many days.

Thank God Peg had not tried to communicate with me in any way lately. No phone calls, no more surprise visits over the fence, and most of all no knocks on the front door. Had she finally learned how to just lay low? Stay quiet? Feign ignorance? Perhaps it was too much to ask.

Regardless, things were not going in the right direction, and while I was reasonably confident I would avoid any immediate fallout, I couldn't say the same for Peg. The question I was wrestling with now was what would happen if—or, really, when—she was arrested, and how my involvement would be perceived if she decided to run her mouth off. Would that somehow reopen questions into the death of Steve Williams so many years ago? I had mastered overplaying the cripple card pretty well by this point and was reasonably certain that I would not be prosecuted even if everything we had done came to light. In the face of my severe disability, the D.A. would surely relent. Still, the headache that would ensue and the risk of my complicated past brought back to light by some nosy reporter—well, I'd simply rather not deal with it.

What then to do about all of this? Peg was a liability, and turning her in, confessing to save my own skin, was a possibility. In many ways, it could be the best possible outcome, as Peg would surely become a hero of sorts, especially to other women, for standing up against a potential murderer, and I could conceivably corroborate at least some of her version of events. Again, though, it would open me up to scrutiny, which I really didn't relish.

Perhaps it was insane to wonder if Peg should herself go the same way as Steve Williams, as Klaus Fischer. It would have to be abrupt. An accident or a suicide—and getting that done would take some thinking, and that was admittedly far from easy these days. Could I get my hands on cyanide or strychnine without leaving the house? Amazon Prime, perhaps? I would need to put my mind to this problem in full, to be sure, starting out by taking my medication to help me concentrate.

Anyway, it was dawning on me now that this entire endeavor was exceedingly stupid. I never should have gotten involved with Peg in the first place. Note to self: stop answering the door for anyone.

It was at that point in my thoughts that a huge ambulance—lights and sirens and the whole works—rolled past my house, up the cul-de-sac and on to the end of the street.

CHAPTER EIGHTY-TWO

Jean Claire

MOTHER HAD RALLIED Eliza and me around the television again. When she wasn't praying, she was watching the news. That was really it now. On the screen I saw a reporter, standing in front of the barricade that stopped cars from driving up the cul-de-sac where Eliza lived. I could see her house in the background, while blue and red lights swirled off camera.

A woman in red was standing at the end of Eliza's block.

"Jessica Raska, KNOV-TV, in the field again with Detective Rachel Eisenstein, with new information surrounding the Klaus Fischer case, this time involving one of his neighbors. Detective Eisenstein, can you explain the situation to our viewers?"

Eisenstein: "We're getting new information every hour, and our understanding of the situation is still evolving. But I can say that in the course of our interviews with Klaus Fischer's neighbors, we discovered a troubling situation in one of the homes."

Raska: "Tell us more."

Eisenstein: "When we visited the home of one of Fischer's neighbors, we learned of the presence of Agatha Charles, a woman we had not yet met during our investigation. Ms. Charles was confined to a bed in an upstairs bedroom, unable to stand because of her significant body weight. We're performing an emergency extraction to get her into immediate medical care."

Raska: "What is her weight?"

Eisenstein: "We aren't sure yet, but the doctor we're consulting with estimates she could be over seven hundred pounds. Because she is unable to walk, we're moving the bed entirely, which means we're going to have to remove part of a wall of the Charles's residence as part of that process."

Raska: "You said she's on an upstairs floor. How are you managing that part of the removal process?"

Eisenstein: "We're still working that out."

Raska: "I assume Ms. Charles does not live alone?"

Eisenstein: "No, she's married, and we currently have her husband at the station for questioning. We don't think this is a criminal issue, but we do want to understand how this situation developed, as Ms. Charles is facing an incredible number of health conditions and is at risk of imminent death due to her extreme weight."

Raska: "Does this have any relationship to the Fischer case? My understanding is that he potentially kept some of his victims hostage."

Eisenstein: "No, we think this is unrelated. There's no evidence that either of the Charleses have ever had any dealings with Fischer."

Raska: "What updates can you give us on the Fischer investigation?"

Eisenstein: "I can't talk at length about it, but I can say we're confident in the new evidence we've uncovered that we'll be able to make an arrest soon."

Raska: "An arrest? As in, an accomplice?"

Eisenstein: "That's our working theory, yes."

Raska: "And your advice to residents of the area?"

Eisenstein, to the camera: "Stay inside. Lock your doors."

Raska: "Thank you, Detective. Back to you in the studio."

The scene switched back to two talking heads behind a desk in the TV studio. From one of them: "Thanks for that update, Jessica. We'll keep following this story as information develops. Up next, a new warning from the World Health Organization is hitting social media, reporting on a mysterious cluster of pneumonia cases in Wuhan, China."

Cue the commercial.

Mother muted the television with the remote control. "Look," she said, not looking at either me or Eliza, who was now spending every afternoon here, often until well after sundown. Her parents understood why, I think. "You smite down one killer and another rises in their place. God is vengeful, but people...people are worse."

She muttered prayers under her breath as the newscast switched to a commercial.

"Can we go now?" I asked.

Mother snapped her head to look at me directly. "Can you go? I *demand* that you go," she said. "Go to the den of sin that you call a room and consider the evil in your heart, as it is evil like yours that allows people like these to exist." She gestured at the television.

I was taken aback even more than usual. "You think *I* am the reason for these murders?" I asked.

"You, your friend, all of your generation. Your evil begets more evil. And you are directly responsible for these incidents. My attempts to raise you properly have obviously failed, and you are clearly incapable of learning anything I attempt to teach you. Now we are all doomed to be victims of evil for our lifetimes—and beyond—because of my inability to set you on the correct path."

My blood was boiling, and I attempted to bite my tongue. Eliza was aghast but, I could tell, a little numb from everything that had happened over the last few weeks.

"Fuck you, Mother," I said sharply. It was the first time I had ever cursed at her, and I was on the verge of tears.

She rose from her chair and grimaced. "How dare you," she said, then lifted the back of her hand as if to hit me across the face, but she paused, holding it back. I didn't think she would do anything, and I called her bluff, staring her in the eyes. That must have pushed her over the edge, because she steeled herself and brought her arm around, faster than I could react. The hard back of her hand—small but bony—caught me right on the cheekbone. I heard the dull thud as it hit, and my head spun quickly to the left. Eliza gasped and stepped back. I lost my balance and almost fell down, going down to the carpet on one knee. It had hurt when she hit me, and a second later it was hurting even more.

Mother stood over me, shaking. Her hand was now up near her face, bound in a tight fist.

Against my will, I began to sob. Quietly, but with tears I could feel running down my cheeks.

"Apologize," she commanded.

"No," I said from the floor.

"Beg for forgiveness."

I looked up and screamed at her, "Never!" Eliza had backed all the way into the corner.

"Beg for forgiveness from me, and from God."

"I will die first," I yelled again, finally rising to my feet and backing away. Her fist was still in the air. "Come on," I said to Eliza.

Eliza responded quickly—I can't imagine how horrified

she must have been—and followed me as I rushed out of the room, down the hallway, and up the stairs to my bedroom. We got inside, and I shut the door. There was no lock; Mother had removed it years ago. But I had a piece of wood I'd found that could hold the door closed in an emergency by jamming it underneath the door. I tested the door and it held shut. Hopefully, Mother would not follow us upstairs, but I wasn't about to take any chances now.

"Oh my God," Eliza said. "Are you OK?" She sized up my cheek, looking at it closely.

"I don't know. It hurts."

She took a hand mirror from my desk to show me. My face was a mess of tears and smeared makeup, both atop a bright red mark on my cheek. It looked cartoonish. I gingerly patted my cheek to see if anything was broken. It hurt to the touch, but I didn't think she'd done any real damage. I'd get better soon enough, but would it last? I could tell Mother was increasingly spiraling out of control.

"I don't feel safe here anymore," I said.

"Yeah, tell me about it. I'd invite you to come stay with me but..." Eliza's voice trailed off. "I don't know if I can go home."

"The reporters and cops will be gone soon enough," I said.

"No, it's not that," she said.

"What?"

"The story about the killer—the two killers—it's true."

"What do you mean?" I asked.

"There are two killers. I know what happened."

I sat down on the bed. First Mother, now this. I was stunned. I said nothing. Better to let Eliza get it out of her system.

"It's Peg. She was at Klaus Fischer's house, and they got into a fight or something. She killed him and buried him."

It sounded made up, but I played along. "How do you know about that?"

"Because I saw her coming out of the yard afterward, covered in dirt. She confessed to me. She told Alex—you know, the tutor—what happened."

This was almost too much to stand. "Do you believe her?"

"Yeah," she said. "I mean, I don't have any reason not to. They were filthy from the burial."

"They?"

"Alex had to help her do it, I guess."

"Jesus Christ, this is insane. How did she kill him?" I asked, still disbelieving but morbidly curious.

"I don't know. They didn't say. But I saw what Klaus Fischer did to Peg before she killed him. He almost strangled her to death."

"She says."

"Yeah, she says. But I guess it all makes sense. I saw bruises on her neck."

"Well, Eliza, why didn't you tell me any of this? Why haven't you gone to the police?"

Eliza started choking up, sobbing the same way I had been downstairs. Finally she looked up at me. "I don't know," she blubbered. "I said I would keep the secret, and they are both...they're both so nice to me. And what if the police didn't believe me that this little old lady and the disabled guy next door buried a man in his own backyard?"

Admittedly, it didn't sound reasonable at all.

"But why are you telling me now?"

"I can't hold it in anymore. Every time I'm at home, I think about Peg and that dead man, and I just know something bad is going to happen. Maybe to me."

I stood up and walked over to Eliza, now bawling openly. Something about this whole situation made me start crying too, and I hugged her tightly. We cried together for a long while, until finally I thought we were all out of tears.

"I'm leaving," I finally said, breaking away.

"What?" Eliza said, still sniffling.

"I'm leaving. I've saved up a lot of money from my Amazon work and my other jobs, and I'm running away."

"You're not serious, right? I mean, you're fifteen years old. Where are you going to go?"

"I'm not sure yet, but I can't stay here. I'll find a room in San Francisco. Or take a bus to Sacramento or L.A. I don't know. I'll figure it out."

I started looking around the room, thinking about what I would need to pack. It would have to be light. Even getting to San Francisco, which was only thirty miles away, was going to be difficult. I had cash, but I didn't want to burn through the kind of money that an Uber would cost.

I found my biggest backpack and started filling it. Some clothes, my laptop, chargers, earbuds. You know, the essentials. I'd have to figure out some of the necessities as I went, and there was always thrifting if I needed more clothes.

"What am I going to do if you're not here?" Eliza asked.

"I dunno. Maybe you can come with me," I said.

"I can't. I couldn't. I really want to, but I know I wouldn't make it," she said.

"You'll figure it all out, and you can text me anytime." I wondered how long it would be before Mother found out I was gone, whether she would try to find me, and how long it would be before she canceled my cell phone plan.

Eliza sniffed. "I guess so. I just don't know what I'm going to do now."

I started to cry again a little. "Neither do I, but whatever happens, it's going to be better than this."

"I wish there was something I could do to help you," Eliza said through a mist of tears.

"Same here," I said.

"Maybe...maybe..." she stammered. "Do you think it would help if you took my bike?"

CHAPTER EIGHTY-THREE
Eisenstein

T HE STATION WAS now filled to bursting with police, federal agents, prosecutors, politicians, and other people I couldn't readily identify, having flown or driven in from all across the country. Today's meeting had one agenda item on it: What were we going to do about Peg Jurgensen?

"Does anyone seriously think this woman killed all these people?" asked a suited FBI agent. "I've been working homicides for twenty years and can count on one hand how many involved a woman as the killer. And serial killers? None, ever."

"Yeah, this woman seems totally harmless," another FBI suit said, looking at an 8x10 photograph in her file. Some picture of her on a cruise ship from years ago wearing a big straw hat and sunglasses. "The idea that she had something to do with these killings is ludicrous."

"And yet we have a yard full of bodies, all buried, and no other suspects," said one of the more senior agents in the room.

"She's guilty as hell!" yelled someone from a corner.

Never mind waiting for all the facts to arrive before arriving at a conclusion.

"A widow, right?" someone else asked. "Have we looked into the death of the husband?"

Mutterings for a moment, slowly fading to silence.

"She has to be an accomplice," said a man from the Forensic Science Institute, whom I'd heard had collected more than five hundred samples to test for DNA. "If not to Fischer, then to someone else."

"The fact that the kitchen was meticulously cleaned—and really none of the rest of the house—is especially suspicious," one of our local officers said. "I have to think this was all carefully planned."

Grunts of protest erupted from one corner.

Agent Davis, the ranking officer in the room, held his hand up to quiet everyone down. He addressed all of us. "We can try to hash this out for another week, but we keep going in circles because we just don't have enough evidence yet. I know forensics will continue gathering DNA and prints, and I'm aware that we already have at least half a dozen unique individuals placed inside the house. Some have identities and some don't, but that's a work in progress. We do know Jurgensen has been inside. We know she had some kind of a romantic relationship with Fischer. But we don't have anything tying her to a crime—yet. I'm not convinced we're going to turn up someone who's been in that house and who has a significant criminal record, making them a smoking-gun-level suspect."

Some murmurs of agreement.

"Right now, Jurgensen is all we have, and I want to continue twenty-four-hour surveillance on her house." He turned to a technician. "The wiretaps are up and running? All communications are being monitored?"

The tech nodded.

"Good." Davis took a deep breath. "In any case, I think we're at the point where we need to bring her in. We don't have enough to charge her, I know, but we do have enough to interview her. We hold her for twenty-four hours and then make a decision. She seems like the type of person who will eventually crack under the pressure and the weight of guilt if she's not telling us something, whether she's an accomplice or not. And I want to find out exactly what happened to Mr. Jurgensen, too. This woman may not be a killer in the end, but I'm reasonably sure she knows something that can help us close this investigation."

"Sounds like a plan," said Agent Harlow, his number two.

"So we're all on the same page?" Davis said to the group. "I don't want any of this information leaving this room. Especially not to the press. When we bring her in, she needs to be off guard and unprepared. I want her confused and panicked."

Davis paused and looked around, then rested his eyes on me.

"Eisenstein, I'd like you and your team to pick her up tomorrow morning, Eight a.m. sharp."

CHAPTER EIGHTY-FOUR

Alex

THE RUSTLING NOISES emerging from the backyard could only mean one thing. Sure enough, in a moment there was a persistent and aggressive rapping on the sliding glass door, and I could make out the figure of Peg, tapping away. I rose from the couch and hurried to the door as best as I could. She slid in quickly, and I shut the door behind her.

"I thought we talked about this," I said. "They're watching every house on the street. You coming here is incredibly foolish and puts us both in jeopardy."

"They're not watching the backyard," she said, rolling her eyes at me.

Peg looked exhausted, almost crazed, with deep black circles around her eyes. Based on her unkempt hair, she appeared not to have showered in at least two or three days. I wondered if she had been brushing her teeth. She dressed in sweats and carried a bulky purse, which she must have tossed over the fence before climbing over herself.

"You need to take care of yourself," I said. "You're falling apart."

"I have fallen apart," she replied, standing just a few steps inside the door. "I am working on putting things back together now." She looked like a homeless person, but her demeanor seemed oddly calm.

"Good. Do you want to sit down?"

"No, I'll stand," she said. "I need to work out some of this energy, I think."

"You mind if I sit, then?" I asked.

She shook her head.

"What is it you think I can do for you?" I continued.

"Have you talked to the police?" she asked.

"No," I said. "But it's really only a matter of time before they all but break down the door to talk to me."

"Well, that won't be good. What will you tell them?"

"Nothing, I've told you that since the beginning."

"Yeah, and I don't believe you," she said.

I was taken aback, forcing myself to sit up a little. "Why do you think that? I've done everything I said I would."

"I just don't trust you. I can see it in your eyes."

"You need a nap. Maybe you should go home, back the way you came."

Peg just stood there, staring me down. There was something in her eyes I hadn't seen before. Maybe it was the same thing Klaus Fischer saw that night, though Peg had said it was the night the lights went out, hadn't she? I couldn't recall. In those eyes there was something dark, something menacing, something you might describe as dead, as if she were looking straight through me like I was nothing more than a pane of glass.

"Look, you did me a favor a while back, then I did you

one," I said, trying to snap her back into reality and get something in the way of a coherent response from her. "But there are limits to how far I'm going to go in return. I consider us even. We're not partners in what you did, but we're even."

She shrugged a bit.

"But I have no interest in talking to the police," I said. "I'm sure I've made that clear."

Peg simply continued to stare at me.

"But if you're going to keep acting crazy, maybe I need to rethink that position," I joked, trying to lighten the mood.

It was a bad miscalculation. Instead of breaking the tension, Peg narrowed her eyes. "I *knew* you were planning something," she said. "You're going to turn me in, aren't you." It was an accusation, not a question.

"Oh, Jesus, get a grip. I'm just kidding around." Her sense of humor must have died with Klaus Fischer. "Are you sure you don't want to sit down?"

She shook her head, saying nothing.

"Listen," I said earnestly. "The reason I am avoiding the police has very little to do with you. I have a past of my own that I am not eager to have the authorities dredge up."

"I'm listening," she said.

I settled in to tell her the tale, the best I could. "When I was a teenager, I was bullied a lot. Like, really bullied by the school's football hero. You know, all-American guy, only he was really a monster. So...I killed him. I put poison in his soda every day until eventually he died. The community shut down, but they eventually blamed the school for it, not me. I never got caught, but I had to live with what I did, and it was probably worse than if I had been busted."

Peg didn't look like she knew whether to believe me or not. "Is that why you're so sick?" she asked.

"Basically," I said. "I tried to kill myself, but it didn't take."

She shook her head piteously.

"Why is it that I can always remember the bad things, but all the good stuff has faded into a haze?" I asked aloud. I didn't expect a response, not from her. "Anyway, I'm telling you this so you can see that you don't need to worry about me. I have just as much to lose as you do."

Peg stood silent for a moment but finally responded. "I may not need to worry about you, but I do need to worry about *me*. I'm not ready to give up on life the way you seem to have."

I nodded but remained confused. "OK, so what does that mean? You're going to tell the truth? Go on the run?"

"No," she said. "I'm handing you over to the police."

I wasn't sure I heard her right. Turn *me* in? "What?" I asked.

"I'm giving you to the cops. They clearly want someone to blame, an accomplice for Klaus, and you're as good as anyone on that front."

"Are you insane? Look at me," I said, gesturing up and down my frail body. "You think anyone will believe I killed any of those people and buried them? It's preposterous."

"Well, I'm sure you know as well as I do that there's no way we got all the DNA, all the footprints, all the little fibers out of that house and yard. They're over there with microscopes and hazmat suits right now, grabbing every scrap of evidence they can find. Eventually, they're going to figure out you were there, and that'll be all it takes, and they'll forget all about me. Especially with what you just told me."

This was going poorly, but her plan was full of holes.

"My being at that house once is meaningless," I said. "None of that is going to tie me to any murder."

"Maybe not," she said, "which is why I'm leaving you with this."

Peg reached into her big bag, rummaged around, and finally produced a cell phone.

"What's that?"

"Klaus's phone. I've kept it all this time."

"You did not," I said, aghast. "Are you insane?"

"No, and now we can find out if it still works."

I could see her hand headed for the power button. I noticed she was wearing latex gloves.

"Don't do that. You're going to fuck both of us, badly."

She shrugged. I saw light erupt from the screen. It was powering up.

"Turn it off!" I screamed at her, rising to my feet. "You're out of your mind!"

Peg looked at me with a twisted grin. "No, I'm perfectly in control," she snarled.

I heaved myself up off the couch and took a step toward her, and she threw the phone in my direction. It missed me, on purpose I guess, and landed in the corner of the couch, directly where I had just been sitting. I followed its flight with my eyes, then took a step back, collapsing back into the couch to grab for the phone. It was still booting up. Maybe I could get it before it tried to ping the cellular network. Never mind the fingerprints, I was desperate and would have to clean things up later. I managed to get it in hand, then fumbled with the controls, forgetting everything else around me for a moment.

I felt very little when the pillow abruptly covered my face. I don't think I even dropped the phone at first. It was just such a surprise, the lights going out as the owl-embroidered throw pillow that had been beside me was now fully smashed into my face, held in tight from behind. Peg must have walked around to the back of the couch while I was distracted by the phone, and now her plan was...what? Make this look like a suicide, driven by guilt? I didn't have time to think much about it. I tried to grab for the pillow to push it away from my face, but Peg knew as well as I that it was futile. I was simply too weak and didn't have any kind of leverage to help me. I tried to roll to one side, but she had me pinned, and I was already running out of air, getting weaker by the second.

I all but gave up, resigning myself to an imminent death. Surely, she didn't think this through. Would there be a suicide note? There would be forensic efforts undertaken in my house; what else would she leave behind in addition to the phone? How was she going to get away with any of this? But before I could think too deeply about any of that, I felt my mind starting to fade. I focused on my breathing—or the lack of it. I wasn't getting any air, and my lungs—already weak to start with—felt tighter and tighter. In a matter of seconds, they were absolutely burning. I felt the phone slip out of my hand and fall to the floor. I could hear it make a chime, then another, then another.

The pillow made everything dark, of course, but somehow I could still feel the light fading away, what was left of my vision narrowing into a tunnel. I was fading, and at some point, I just gave in. What was there to fight for, anyway? The last thirty years had been a charade, a waste of borrowed time, pointless. Frankly, I should have predicted that something like this would happen. Ultimately, I blamed myself. I should never have let the psycho in the door.

What would they do with my body? An autopsy, sure, but then what? Would there be a funeral? Who would be there? Why? *Ah, who cares?*

As I faded to black, a final notion popped into my head that took me quite by surprise. School had just returned to session after the Christmas break, and Eliza would probably need math tutoring again soon.

I was going to miss the girl.

CHAPTER EIGHTY-FIVE

Eliza

I HADN'T WALKED home from school in months. I figured eventually I'd have to explain to my parents what had happened to my bike, but so far they hadn't noticed it was gone. The sky was gray, and it was beginning to rain. Just barely, but a sign of something more to come.

The parking lot of news vans along the street leading to the cul-de-sac was beginning to dwindle, though there were still about a dozen hanging around, hoping to get a scoop of some kind—maybe the announcement of this accomplice that everyone was talking about. It seemed inevitable that Peg would eventually be arrested, and maybe Alex too.

The officer at the police blockade recognized me immediately as I approached the wooden barricades. He waved me through without saying a word. I continued along, trudging up the hill toward home.

At the top of the hill, I could see just a bit of the Charles house. Completely dark, a large piece of plywood covering the hole they'd cut in the wall next to the front door in order to move Mrs. Charles out of the place. That had been quite a spectacle. I guess she was in the hospital now. No one had mentioned what had happened to Mr. Charles. Was he sitting by her side? Or was he in some kind of trouble?

I put it out of my mind as I pushed my way through the door and into the house. Much to my surprise, Mom and Dad were sitting in the living room, opposite one another.

"Hi, honey," Mom said.

"You're not at work?" I asked my dad. This was really unusual, as he would do just about anything to escape the scene at the cul-de-sac these days. I couldn't blame him for that.

"I'm taking the day off," he said. "We wanted to talk to you when you got home."

"OK," I said, "but I have homework."

"This is important, hon," said Mom. *Hon.* This wasn't good. Mom kept talking. "You know how tough it's been around here lately, right?"

I nodded.

"And you know that's taken a toll on your dad and me," she continued.

I said nothing.

"We, well…" Mom started to get teary-eyed and clammed up.

Dad jumped in. "We think it's best for us to spend some time apart. Just for a while."

Oh shit. Not what I had expected to hear at all. Now I was starting to clam up a little. I knew they were fighting a lot, but was it really this bad? "Are you getting a divorce?" I asked. Suddenly, I began to feel sad, but I wasn't sure why. I mean, I barely spent any time with these people. Half the time I couldn't stand them. What was wrong with me?

"No," Dad said. "But I'm going to live in the City for a while, at least until things get a little less crazy around here. You can come see me on weekends, and we can hang out and do fun tourist things—you know, like we used to."

"You're not going to see Mom at all?" I asked.

"Not right now. We're just going to take a little break."

"How am I going to get to San Francisco?" I asked. "Are you going to make me take the bus?"

Mom finally regained her composure. "We'll work that out soon," she said through sniffles. "You can go visit next weekend."

"I have tutoring with Alex on the weekend," I said. "Math is going to be even harder this semester, and I'll need help."

"Oh, of course," Mom said. "We want to keep as much stability for you as possible."

"Given the circumstances, anyway," Dad said, gesturing toward the door.

"Is this all because of Klaus Fischer?" I asked.

"We've been having some problems," he said. "But none of this stuff on the cul-de-sac has helped."

Mom piped in. "I'm hoping we can regroup soon, maybe do some family therapy or something. I read on the internet about a program nearby..." Her voice trailed off and she looked away.

I resisted rolling my eyes. Therapy. Couldn't wait. The desire to crack a joke was huge, but I didn't say anything. "I wish we never moved here at all," I said.

Both Mom and Dad nodded. But now it was all too late.

Even if we wanted to move out now, who in their right mind would buy this house? I didn't have any idea how they were going to afford an apartment in the City on top of the mortgage here, but I wasn't about to go down that road, either. Maybe Dad wasn't even going to have his own place. Was there someone else already?

"You know this is not your fault," Mom said.

"Yeah, exactly. Nothing to do with you," Dad said.

"I didn't think it had anything to do with me." I hadn't, but now of course I was wondering if it really did.

"Do you have any questions for us?" Dad asked.

"When are you moving out?"

"Tonight. Today. Soon. I'm mostly packed."

"So this is goodbye?"

"Just until Saturday."

"OK," I said. "Whatever."

I walked over and gave him a weak hug. It was the best I could muster. I still had my backpack over one shoulder, so it was extra awkward, kind of one-armed. I felt broken inside and incredibly sad. My stomach began to hurt, and I felt short of breath. I wondered if I should text Jean Claire and tell her I would be in San Francisco, but I figured she would have her hands full right now. Too busy to deal with me at the moment.

"I need to get started on my homework," I said to both of them. "Is it OK if I go ask Alex a few questions real quick? And we have to move tutoring to another day, I guess."

"Of course, honey," Mom said. "Whatever you need."

I could feel the sense of relief in the room now that The

Speech was over. I'm sure Dad was anxious to get out of here pronto. You could see it on his face: *everything will be back to normal soon enough*, he must have been thinking.

I felt a tear dripping from one eye, and I hurriedly wiped it away. "OK, I'll be back before dinner," I said to Mom. "I assume we're eating here?"

"Of course." She smiled, thinly. "You and me."

Neither of them said anything more as I exited the house. I gently closed the door and trudged across the lawn to Alex's.

There was another reason I wanted to see Alex: to give him the big news. My grades had been posted online earlier in the day. A-minus in the first semester of algebra. I hadn't even told my parents yet, and now, well, I guess they could figure it out for themselves, if they even cared.

The rain, talked about for days as a potential break in the California drought, had finally started in earnest. What was a light drizzle earlier was now a steady *thump thump thump* of drops against the pavement.

As usual, I could see that the curtains at Alex's house were drawn, and inside was dark. But he had been keeping the TV off since the investigations began, so that wasn't unusual. I rang the doorbell and waited. Soon I knew I would hear the faint shuffling sounds as Alex hauled himself off the couch and lurched down the hall to open the door. There was something about those familiar sounds that were comforting, a reminder that at least a few things are consistent in the world. I listened and heard nothing, and finally I rang again.

Come on, Alex. Get up. I need you. I tried to turn the knob, but it was locked, as usual.

Maybe he was in the bathroom. Or asleep or something. I wasn't worried, but I was getting tired of waiting. Maybe he just wasn't going to come to the door anymore because of all the police still hanging around on the street.

Ah, of course. I remembered that the answer was right there with me all along. I dropped my backpack off my shoulder and fished around inside the inner pocket. Sure enough, there it was, attached to a tiny stuffed polar bear: the key to Alex's front door.

I pushed the key into the lock. Alex was going to be so proud of me.

The End

Acknowledgments

A heartfelt thank you to the following people, all of whom were instrumental in getting this book into your hands. Stefani Warcholski and Bina Bhattacharya, who read early drafts of the manuscript and have been stalwart supporters for years. Scott Ingels, who served as my expert adviser on police procedure. Julie Sturgeon, my brilliant editor whose counsel was invaluable in fine-tuning the story. And of course my family—Susanne, Zoe, and Beckett—who are the reasons I do anything at all.

Book Club Questions for *The Cul-de-sac*

Did the use of a point of view that shifts each chapter help to build your empathy for and understanding of the characters' motivations? Which character did you relate to the most?

Do Alex's medical condition and memory problems make him less reliable as a narrator?

How does the isolating nature of the cul-de-sac work to affect the overall mood of the book?

Do you believe Peg is responsible for her husband's death? The fire at the house next door? Is Peg a hero or a villain?

What do you think Eliza finds when she opens Alex's door?

In your mind, what is Peg's next move? Is her love for Eliza genuine, or is the teenager another pawn in this game?

What do you think lies ahead for Eliza?

Were you satisfied by the book's ending or do you want the story to continue?

Author Christopher Null has more to say about that suspenseful ending for *The Cul-de-sac* on the Tule website. https://tulepublishing.com/2025/02/spoiler-author-christopher-null-talks-about-that-suspenseful-ending-for-the-cul-de-sac/

About the Author

Christopher Null is an award-winning writer who regularly contributes to Wired magazine and who muses daily about wine and spirits on the website Drinkhacker, where he serves as editor in chief. His first novel, Half Mast, was hailed by critics as "the best of contemporary American fiction." He currently lives in Austin, Texas with his wife Susanne.

Thank you for reading

The Cul-de-sac

If you enjoyed this book, you can find more from all our great authors at TulePublishing.com, or from your favorite online retailer.

TULE
PUBLISHING

Printed in Great Britain
by Amazon

58456000R00223